Books By
Misha McKenzie

Burke Witches
Aria's Law
Anna's Knight
Evan's Pride

The Magic of the Heart Series
Magic Found
Magic Hidden
Magic Lost
Magic Revealed

Single Titles
RavenStorm Witches

Evan's Pride

Burke Witches

Misha McKenzie

ICASM PRESS
SAVANNAH

This book is a work of fiction. The characters, names, events and places are fictitious and products of the author's imagination or are used fictitiously. Any similarities to actual persons, living or dead, places or events is entirely coincidental.

Published by Icasm Publishing LLC
5710 Ogeechee Rd. Suite 200 #278, Savannah, GA 31405
www.icasmpress.com

Library of Congress Cataloging-in-Publication Data

McKenzie, Misha
Evan's Pride / Misha McKenzie
    p. cm.

ISBN-13:978-1-942318-36-1 (Trade Print)
ISBN-13:978-1-942318-37-8 (Mass Market Print)
ISBN-13:978-1-942318-38-5 (eBook)
I. Title

Printed and bound in the United States of America

10 9 8 7 6 5 4 3 2 1

Burke's Prophecy

"Witches born—two light, two dark
Each possessing an element's mark
Air and Water by the brightness of day
Earth and Fire by the moon's subtle ray
These signs will one day come to bear
And evil kept caged will wake and prepare
As every year passes the bindings grow weak
While the force within strengthens and seeks
Four babies born as foretold by this seer
They'll have until their twenty-fifth year
To mature, to learn, to find their right path
For it's up to them to end its wrath
Their destined arrival is the key
Personal sacrifice will set them free
On the anniversary of their birth
Four into one defeats the devil unearthed."

1

Evan hung up his phone and leaned back in his chair. A phone call from Georgia, and a subsequent one to Joe, had given his mind a brief reprieve from the endless loop of questions it had been swimming in for the last few hours.

He wasn't scheduled to be at the station, but he'd come in because these three open murder cases were pissing him off. They had no leads and no suspects. All they did have was a cause of death.

In all three homicides, the seemingly non-related men had had their throats cut with a thin, sharp blade. They didn't have a definite ID on the weapon because the killer had always taken it with him.

So Evan was spending his day off, amidst the hum and bustle of the station house, reading through the reports and statements yet again. Irritated that nothing new had jumped out at him, he set them aside and looked over the crime scene photos, hoping to catch something he'd missed the first half-dozen times he'd studied them.

Giving his head a sturdy shake, he took in the mess of paper on his desk and knew he couldn't just sit here and stare at it anymore. He was getting exactly nowhere, and he was only becoming more frustrated.

Evan reached out for his old PD mug. A quick shot of caffeine should kick his brain back into gear so he could figure this out.

Finding his cup empty, he swore and pushed away from his desk. He rolled all the facts around in his head, trying to see them from any angle he hadn't already considered. He wove his way through the other desks in the crowded bullpen to the coffee pot that sat on a long table against the wall. Taking the carafe from the hot plate, he discovered it was empty. No one had bothered to make more when they'd taken the last of it.

Evan thought briefly about doing it himself but decided against it. For some reason, no matter who made it or how it was done, it was always as strong as diesel fuel and tasted like ass.

But now that the craving had been triggered, he wanted something better. Setting the mug down on his desk on his way back by, he picked up his phone and sunglasses. There was a little café a few blocks over on Main Street that dealt a really good cup of joe.

And getting out for a walk might be just what he needed.

Stepping into the blazing late summer sun from the air-conditioning of the precinct was a shock to the system. It pressed on Evan like a weight and had his well-washed grey t-shirt clinging to his body. The slight breeze drifting in off the water was enough to tousle his black hair, but it did nothing to temper the brutal Florida humidity.

Resigned to the incessant heat, Evan slipped his shades over his midnight-black eyes. Behind the mirrored lenses, he took in his city as he walked.

Another sunny weekend was coming to an end. He couldn't believe it was August already. That left him and his siblings only six months to figure out how to combine their four elements. His sisters had been successful in merging theirs, but he and Ethan hadn't gotten there yet.

Evan and his twin weren't on the best of terms as of late. Ethan had pulled some pretty stupid shit, and Evan still wasn't sure how he was going to get past it. They were *twins*, for fuck's sake; they were supposed to be able to tell each other anything. But Ethan had hidden so much. The worst being that he'd let Noor jack around inside his head and manipulate him.

The secret to becoming one, as the prophecy demanded, had a lot to do with trust—being able to completely give yourself over to the joining. If you held anything back, the union wouldn't work.

Evan was afraid that he and his brother wouldn't be able to reach that level of faith in each other again. And if that were the case, the entire family line was doomed. They needed to work together as a single unit to finally defeat Noor once and for all.

Lost in thought, Evan was just crossing in front of an alley when someone came barreling out and plowed right into him. He vaguely heard something clatter to the ground but dismissed it as his mind continued to process the collision.

"Whoa." His hands automatically came up to grip the arms of the stranger to steady them, at the same time their palms landed flat on his chest and clutched reflexively at the material.

Evan looked down into the most stunningly beautiful face he'd ever seen. Her wide, black-lined doe-eyes were the same color as old Kentucky bourbon. As they stared up at him, the rest of her registered on his senses.

Her hair was short and choppy, like she'd hacked at it herself. It couldn't be described as merely brown, because it carried every color of the spectrum. Though a deep, rich mahogany was at the base, it also shone with blondes and reds and even some darker hues. Her features were sharp and angular, and he got the impression it wasn't for vanity's sake. She seemed to be thin to the point of gaunt. Like she'd missed too many meals.

She was tall, probably around five nine or ten. Where his hands gripped her upper arms, she felt slender but toned, telling him the weight loss may have been recent.

Under his fingers, the leather of her brown jacket still held the warmth of the sun. She wore a plain white tee beneath that hugged her body. And what a body it was. Her breasts weren't overly large, but they also weren't too small. To his muddled mind, they were perfect. *She* was perfect.

Evan was finally able to stop the speeding and out-of-control train his thoughts were on. This woman was a total stranger; he didn't need to be ogling her and wondering what she wore underneath that cotton top. Gathering his manners again, he put his gentleman hat on.

"I'm sorry. Are you..."

The sound of his voice must have shocked her out of whatever daze she'd been in, because the rest of his question was lost as she tore free from his grasp and ran off down the street. Her booted feet slapped the ground as her long, denim-clad legs quickly put distance between them.

"Well, that was odd," Evan muttered as he automatically straightened his shirt and made sure it was still tucked in. When he glanced down, he saw the red stains that her small hands had left behind.

"Son of a bitch." Evan's brows came together and his gaze snapped up to where he'd last seen her. Had someone attacked her? Was she hurt? He hadn't seen any obvious injuries, but then again, his mind hadn't been focused on assessing her medical needs.

He made a half-turn, contemplating going after her, but his shoe connected with something lying on the ground.

Evan looked down and saw a blood-slicked knife. "What the hell?" He ripped his glasses off, and black eyes rose to scan the shadowed alleyway.

About midway in, he saw a body sprawled on the ground. He took off running and a moment later was standing over the downed man. Careful not to disturb the scene or contaminate the evidence, Evan crouched and got a good look. What he saw stopped his heart and ripped a curse from his lips.

"Fuck!"

Evan pulled out his phone to make the call back to the station to report the crime. At the same time, he reached out and carefully checked for a pulse.

"Yeah, this is Detective Burke. I've got a dead body." He relayed his location. "Male. Caucasian. Mid- to late-twenties. COD is apparent. His throat's been cut."

He also gave them a description of the woman, leaving out his personal observations, and told them where he'd last seen her heading.

Rising to his feet again, Evan walked back out to the mouth of the alley. He squatted down and studied the murder weapon with a practiced eye. Overall length looked to be around seven inches. The blade itself was three-and-a-half to four inches and maybe two inches wide.

It was currently covered in what he assumed to be the victim's blood, and Evan could just make out good, usable prints on the wooden handle as the sun glinted off of it. With any luck she'd be in the system, and then they'd have her.

Evan lifted his gaze and stared off in the direction his suspect had gone and cursed for letting the killer slip right through his fingers.

2

The body had already been taken to the morgue, all evidence had been collected and recorded, and still Evan stood planted where he'd held a murderer in his grasp. He knew he had work that needed to be done back at the station, yet here he was. Scanning the streets for any sign of her.

Movement out of the corner of his eye drew his attention. He turned his head to see Seth approaching on foot. Evan had sent him a short text about the new murder and requested he meet him at the precinct. Since he'd never made it back there, Seth had obviously come looking for him. Evan slid his hands into the front pockets of his jeans and waited for his partner to join him.

"Ran into the tech guys; they said you were still here." Seth glanced around the scene. "Wanna fill me in?"

"We've got a fourth. Found him in there." Evan indicated with his head into the alley behind them. "Slit throat, just like the others. The perp was still here when I happened upon them. If I'd been ten minutes earlier, I could have stopped it." Evan shook his head in disgust. "I had her, man. I had her in my hands, and I let her slip away."

"Wait. *Her?* You're saying a woman did this?" Surprise registered on Seth's face and in his dark brown eyes. "And you think she did all of them?"

Evan, along with every other cop on the job, knew female

serial killers existed. They were rare—only about one in six—but in the last fifty years, thirty-eight had been recorded in the U.S. alone. Though definitely less common, it wasn't entirely unheard of.

"Yeah, I do."

"Are you sure?" Seth glanced down the alley to the large stain on the concrete. "What's to say she didn't stumble across this guy? Maybe she was running to get help?"

Evan shook his head, running his fingers through his hair.

"How can you be so certain?" Seth challenged, obviously not completely convinced yet.

"If she had innocently come across this scene like you're suggesting, why didn't she ask me for help? Most concerned citizens call the police or shout to high heaven for someone else to. She did none of that," Evan argued, confident in his beliefs. "An innocent person, one with nothing to hide, would have stuck around to make sure someone was coming. She didn't—she *ran*. From a body with a wound that matches three others exactly. She just had the bad luck to plow into me as she was trying to get away."

Evan went on before Seth could offer up any more questions. "This victim's blood was, literally, all over her hands." He looked down at the borrowed shirt he wore since his had been taken into evidence. "She had possession of the murder weapon, for Christ's sake, a key piece of evidence that, up to this point, has been removed from every scene. She was intending to take it with her this time too, but bumping into me made her drop it. I'll bet my badge that when the blade of that knife is compared to all the other wounds, it's going to be a match, complete with traces from her previous kills."

"It's hard to reconcile that a woman could kill so savagely. From all the studies I've seen, they're more apt to use poison or drugs. But I guess we'll see what Forensics has to say."

He paused a moment and Evan felt his scrutiny. "Now,

you want to tell me what has you staring off into the distance instead of being back at the station delving into this new information?"

No matter how hard he tried, Evan just couldn't understand his reaction to meeting the girl with the whiskey-colored eyes. The shame and revulsion at his own male weakness soured his mouth at the same time his cock twitched in remembrance of her. She was wanted in connection to four murders, and damn it if he still couldn't push her out of his mind.

To cover anything the perceptive Seth might read in his face, Evan slid his sunglasses on.

"Nothing," he denied. "I'm just fucking pissed that I let her get away."

"Okay." There was skepticism in the way Seth drew out the word, but he didn't elaborate any further.

Evan turned and walked away. "Let's go find her."

By the time they got back to the station, the fingerprints had been lifted cleanly off the knife hilt and a run through their database was already in progress. It was never like it appeared in the movies or on TV; coming back with a match within minutes was unheard of. There were millions of samples that it would need to be compared to, and that took time.

While the computer was doing its thing, Evan and Seth sat down to identify this new victim and dig deeper into these four men's lives. This woman had to have intersected with each one of them at some point. Where a good majority of men who killed chose their victims at random, most women preyed on people they knew. And the leading motive was financial gain. So in addition to becoming intimately involved with these guys' histories, Evan would look into those who might benefit from their deaths.

Evan grabbed the file on the first victim, a retired middle-school teacher in his late seventies. He'd worked for the public school system in Florida for forty-plus years and had never married.

It seemed his life was his job. Evan made a note to check his employment records to see if anything there jumped out at him. He jotted down a few more things to look into and reached for the next.

The second was a fifty-year-old party store owner—married, three kids, and one grandkid. The store had been in his family for three generations and his only son, the eldest of the three, was being groomed to take it over from him.

As far as Evan could find, no one had had any beef with him. The place had never even been robbed. As a matter of fact, the owner was known for helping those who were less fortunate. Any and all perishables that would ordinarily be thrown out at the end of the night were given to the destitute in the area.

Victim three worked for a local company that sold off-road motorcycles and sport bikes. He'd been in his early thirties. Associates who were interviewed said he was a nice guy. Loved his job and spent the weekends taking road trips on his own motorcycle and camping out with a close group of friends. A group which included a girl he'd recently started dating.

From Evan's one encounter with the killer, he estimated her to be in her mid-twenties. That would match up nicely with this vic. Now that he knew he was looking for a woman, Evan would take another look at the girlfriend. Hard.

They didn't have much on the fourth and latest victim yet. According to his ID, he was also in his mid-twenties, but the address listed had been a dead end. Uniforms had checked the location and found the owner of the residence who described their vic as a nomad. He'd crashed there temporarily some time ago but had since moved on. A free spirit who'd lived life the way he wanted. He earned whatever cash he had by performing on the streets.

Evan couldn't comprehend that mentality. How could someone go through life and not want to make a difference?

To just float with nothing to show for their time here? Evan was exactly the opposite. He loved being a cop and took the job seriously, knowing he made the world a better place, one perp at a time.

It also gave him the control he'd so desperately needed in a life that was ruled by fate.

Thanks to a prophecy foretold centuries ago, his and his siblings' destinies had been determined. As the Four, it would be up to them to take on an evil bastard bent on the destruction of their entire family line.

With that knowledge propelling them forward, their parents had done everything possible to prepare them for the battle that lay ahead. Evan, his twin brother Ethan, and their sisters Aria and Anna—who were also identical twins—had trained since they were old enough to understand.

With so much of his life seemingly on autopilot, Evan had searched for something that would be solely his. He'd found that in the police academy and had signed up right out of high school. He'd put on the uniform and hadn't looked back.

As a detective now, he'd made it a point of pride to keep his magical world separate from his cop life. He never took shortcuts at work by using his Burke ancestry, and relied exclusively on good instincts, research, attention to detail, and always doing things by the book. The satisfaction it gave him to close cases by his wits alone was matched by nothing he'd done as a witch so far.

Evan cleared his thoughts and put his considerable intellect back to work on the puzzle in front of him—finding a link between these men and identifying their killer.

It wasn't going to be an easy task. Each victim, through the professions they'd chosen, had had hundreds, if not thousands, of people in and out of their lives. Finding this one woman among all of them was going to take some significant man-hours.

But Evan vowed he wouldn't give up until he found her. Despite his reaction to her, he wouldn't let that stop him from slamming the door on her cage.

~~~

It wasn't until the next day that they learned the fingerprints hadn't resulted in any matches. That was a setback, but when the analysis of the knife came back, they got some good news. It was just as Evan had predicted. It showed trace evidence from each of the three previous victims. When it was dismantled, flecks of dried blood were found under the hilt.

Bleach had also been detected, so an attempt had been made to clean it. But not well enough.

She should have taken better care not to link herself to all four murders. Did she think she'd never be caught? Or did she just not care? Pretty cold-blooded, Evan thought, and instantly a picture of large, whiskey-colored eyes flashed into his mind.

Evan shook his head to dispel the vision and swore under his breath. To push it further away, he scrubbed his hands over his face and eyes.

"Problem?" Seth turned away from his computer screen to face his partner.

Evan forced a yawn. "No, just didn't get much sleep. Spent half the night racking my brain for how these four guys crossed paths with our perp."

"Did you come up with anything?"

"Yeah. Too many possibilities." Evan was only slightly lying. He *had* spent part of the night trying to find that connection. Just not as much as he'd alluded to. The rest of the time he'd fought to pretend she didn't exist. But just as they had a few moments ago, thoughts and images popped unbidden into his mind too often for comfort.

He didn't know what the hell his problem was. He'd seen
~~~

good-looking women before. Hell, he'd had his fair share of them over the years. At six foot four, shaggy black hair, and mysterious black eyes, Evan never had trouble getting, or forgetting, a woman.

The fact that this one was different pissed him off. Not only because of how his body had responded, but because she was a stone-cold killer, and the very last person who should ever occupy his mind.

"All right." Seth swiveled around in his chair to face Evan fully. "What gives? You've been acting weird ever since yesterday. Did something else happen in that alley that you're not telling me?"

"No, it went down just like I said." The rest, Evan would have to ignore. He looked at his watch and then stood. "Martinez should be in by now. I want to get the sketch of this woman done so we can get it distributed."

"Yeah, okay."

Evan could feel Seth's gaze following him out of the room but he kept walking.

Bryn Martinez was indeed at her desk, and for the next hour, Evan described the woman they were hunting in as much detail as he could remember. They'd started out on the computer with a composite program, but Evan could never quite get her face right. Bryn suggested going old school and doing it by hand.

When they were done and she flipped the picture around, he was stunned at how life-like the pencil sketch was.

He didn't let himself linger over it and told her to get it out to all patrols. He was just about to leave when she called him back. "Hey, Burke, let me make a quick copy for your file."

"Oh, yeah, thanks." He took it from her but didn't look at it. When he got back to his desk, he slid it over to Seth.

Seth picked it up and studied it. "So this is her?"

"Yup." Evan sat down and tried to act like the image on that paper wasn't haunting him. "Hopefully with everyone looking for her now, she won't have any place to hide."

"This is pretty detailed." Seth raised his eyes to meet Evan's.

Evan made an affirmative sound and busied himself by clicking the email icon on his computer. "I got a pretty good look at her when she ran into me." He found one that, thankfully, needed his immediate attention. He'd read through about half of it when Seth asked him a question.

"You said she has brown hair?"

"Yeah," he responded off-hand, truly preoccupied now by what he was reading. "But it's not really just brown. It also looks blonde or red, depending on which way the light is hitting it."

Slight pause. "Eyes are brown too?"

He hit the button to reply and began typing. "More aged bourbon than chocolate."

"Tall?"

"Hmm? Oh. Yeah. Very near five ten."

"Build?"

Evan sent off his answer and looked across at Seth. His partner had a peculiar expression on his face.

He thought back over his answers and realized his mistake. In his attempt to distract himself, he'd given too much away. With all of his focus on hiding his reaction to her, he hadn't noticed when the filter between his brain and his mouth had stopped working.

To maybe salvage his dignity and put Seth off the scent of what was best left alone, Evan answered his last question with a flippant edge.

"Too thin in my opinion but still decent, I guess." Evan looked at his partner and grinned. "That is, if you go for long-legged and dangerous. I, myself, prefer them a little less... murderous."

Evan went back to his emails and ignored Seth's pointed stare. Eventually Seth gave up and set the drawing aside to resume his own work.

They pushed through the rest of the day and it was now well after end of shift. Seth left to go home to Aria, but Evan remained. Since he couldn't get this case out of his head, he figured he may as well just stay and work it. It wasn't like he had anyone at home waiting for him. And, hopefully, something would break soon.

He got his wish about an hour later when a patrol car out on rounds spotted her coming out of a convenience store. His heart kicked hard in his chest. But that was soon tempered with the news that they'd lost her.

Unable to sit back and do nothing, Evan asked for all the pertinent details. He was on his way out the door before he could talk himself out of it.

A brief thought crossed his mind to call his partner, but he decided against it. Going out there was probably going to be a waste of time. Smart money would put her miles away by now. She'd obviously seen the patrol car and knew they were looking for her. She'd want to be as far from Daytona as physically possible now that she'd been tagged.

Even with that in mind, Evan jumped into his car and tore out of the parking lot.

He easily found the area where the cruiser had last seen her. It was a rundown part of town with lots of abandoned houses and buildings.

As he drove slowly through the darkened streets, he kept an eye out for the high-end sport bike she'd been reportedly driving. A machine like that would have a lot more speed and maneuverability than a heavy cop car. It was no wonder she'd outrun them.

Admittedly, Evan had been a little surprised to learn that she'd been on a bike. But as he thought about it, it made sense. She would have the power and handling of a fine-tuned engine, plus the ability to hide out easier.

Roll that sucker right into a house or shed, and no one would be the wiser it was there.

He had to question if that's how the salesman had come to be on her radar. Had he sold her the bike? Evan made a mental note to run the names of anyone who'd purchased a similar motorcycle from him in the last six months. No, he decided; better to make it a full year.

Evan prowled the streets for hours looking for any sign of her. At four a.m., with a new workday only a few hours away, Evan had to suspend the search. He needed at least a couple hours' sleep and a hot shower before his shift started again.

That had been the plan anyway, until he heard the faint purr of a powerful engine somewhere in the quiet night. Rolling the rest of his windows down, he tried to figure out which direction it was coming from.

Reaching the next intersection, he stopped and listened. It seemed to be growing louder to the right. He'd just made the turn when, up ahead in the distance, he saw a single headlight pull onto the road and head in his direction.

He couldn't be sure if it was actually her, but just as a precaution he hit the button to lift the car windows. The tint on the glass would hinder her ID'ing him before he could get a good glimpse of her.

When the rider drew near, Evan knew instantly it was his suspect. Despite wearing a full-faced helmet, her shape and form were imprinted on his mind and body.

He didn't take his eyes off of her until he lost sight out the side window. Switching his gaze to the rearview mirror, he tracked her movements there. He watched as she turned left at the end of the street. Evan quickly circled the block so that he would emerge on the next street and could fall in behind her. He made sure to leave enough space between them to avoid spooking her.

That bike she was on could outrun almost anything on the

roads. The chances of her evading him were likely if she spotted him. He'd have to wait until she stopped and was away from it to approach her.

When that happened though, he'd better have a damned good plan in place. As much as he wanted otherwise, he couldn't just scoop her up, haul her back to Daytona, and throw her in a cell. Without having a positive ID or a match on the prints, no warrant for her arrest would be issued.

Even though Evan knew in his bones she was guilty, there was nothing he could do about it right now. So unless she sped, had a taillight out, or did something else unrelated to get arrested for, his hands were tied. And yet, he kept the high-powered motorcycle in sight as they headed west across the state.

3

A little over two hours later, she pulled into a small, out-of-the-way restaurant called Tammy's. According to the map on Evan's phone, they were in Dade City—a small-ish town about an hour north of Tampa.

Why had she come here? Was there another victim over here, or did she just think she could hide out on the opposite coast?

Keeping her in sight, he slowed and maneuvered his car into the parking lot of a neighboring business. He hung back and watched as she dismounted her bike and took her helmet off. After setting it on the seat, she lifted her arms and ran her fingers through her short, multi-colored hair.

Evan's mind took that moment to jump ship and wonder about its texture. Swearing, he shut it down and went back to observing her with a detective's eye.

Once her bike was secured, she strode inside. He waited to make sure she wasn't coming right back out. When he knew she was staying put for a while, he set his vehicle in motion again. Choosing a spot on the end of the building, well out of sight of the windows, he got out and walked back to the trunk.

Opening it wide, he rummaged inside for a minute. He'd learned a long time ago to carry everything he might need. He took out a camera with a long lens. Easing around the side of his car, Evan clicked off about a dozen shots of her bike to add to the file. He made sure to get clear shots of the make, model, and plate number.

Setting the camera aside, he caught a glimpse of another, smaller case. Opening that one, he looked down at the tiny tracking device. Barely noticeable unless you knew what you were looking for, it would stick to anything it was pressed against.

Not strictly legal without a warrant, but maybe he could make use of it. Tucking it into his pocket, he started for the door.

Pulling it open, he took in the small space in one swift glance. The kitchen area took up the whole left rear quarter of the room, a line of six tables was arranged along the wall on the right, and four more were laid out in the front left corner.

She'd had her choice of tables as only a few were occupied, and had chosen one near the front. She sat with her back against the wall, facing the rest of the room.

When she heard the door open, she looked up from the menu she'd been studying. Instant recognition lit her brown eyes, and then it dimmed to wariness. She had to be wondering what the hell he was doing here. The last time they'd seen each other, she'd been running from the scene of a murder.

He saw the quick debate that went on in her head about whether or not to make a run for it. Evan quirked a full black brow at her as if to ask what her decision would be.

When she laid the menu down in front of her with a resigned sigh, Evan knew he had her. As he started across the room to her table, he weighed the best way to play this.

As he saw it, he had two options. Go for the jugular and tell her who he was, at which point she'd likely clam up and he'd get nowhere. She had no obligation to cooperate or even talk to him, and without a warrant, he'd be unable to detain her. When she ran—and she *would*—he probably wouldn't luck into finding her again.

Which left his only other option. Use the fact that she didn't know his profession and try to get her talking. If he could gain enough of her trust, maybe she'd confide in him and let something slip. Incriminate herself.

Remembering the crime scene photos, he felt the bile rise in his throat. It wouldn't be easy to hide his aversion to what she'd done. Or the steely determination to see her brought to justice. But Evan needed her to talk. Anonymity was on his side. In this part of the state, no one would recognize him and blow his cover. He swallowed everything else back and focused on the task at hand.

The next question was what approach to take with her. Considering their first meeting and what she'd left behind, he didn't think the 'hey, fancy meeting you here' flirty good guy would work. He might be better off appealing to her harder edges.

With a rough plan in mind, Evan came to stop at the edge of her table.

"You following me, Ace?" She bit the words out, trying to disguise her shock at seeing him again.

He pulled out the chair across from her and sat, but the waitress stepped up to them before he could answer.

"Hi, I'm Kayci. Janice will actually be your server this morning, but what can I get you started with?"

Evan reluctantly took his gaze away from the woman eyeing him suspiciously to acknowledge the question. He took in everything about her while still keeping his prey in sight out of the corner of his eye, lest she try something.

Kayci was petite with long, dark brown hair that she wore pulled back from her strikingly pretty face.

"Just coffee, please."

"Cream or sugar?"

"No, thank you." When his quarry held silent, he turned his coal-black eyes back to her.

She held his stare defiantly for a moment before relenting.

"Same for me."

As Kayci moved off, Evan returned his gaze to the woman across from him. He reluctantly acknowledged that she could still stop his breath, but he bore down and ignored the unsettling and unwanted effect she had on him.

He had a job to do, and nothing could get in the way of that. Forcing his mind away from her wiles and back to the fugitive she was, Evan set his plan into motion.

"You and I have some unfinished business." His tone was easy and confident.

"Really." She tilted her head wryly at him. "And you figure that, how?"

"You owe me a shirt, for one." Evan sat back and laced his fingers over his stomach. He let his mouth quirk just a bit. "The last time we met, you left me with some…hard-to-explain stains."

In an arrogant move, his target copied his posture, spiked full of bad attitude and contempt. "You followed me all this way just to demand a new shirt?"

"What can I say? You intrigue me." He sent her a small grin.

She ignored it. "How did you even find me?"

"I keep my ears open. I'd heard you'd been spotted and, after our last meeting, I decided I needed to find you."

"You don't say."

"You left quite a mess in your wake. And if I'm not mistaken, it wasn't your first."

"It would seem that way, wouldn't it?" Neither her expression nor her words gave anything away, and he wasn't sure how to take her comment.

"Did you have something against those men?"

"What business is that of yours?"

Evan shrugged. "Just being cautious. Wouldn't want to do something that would add me to the list."

Her gaze slid over his body briefly, lingering on his tall frame and broad shoulders. "I'd think you can take care of yourself. But a sure way to stay alive would be to get the hell out of here and never look back."

"What fun is there in doing that?"

Another woman, Janice probably, approached the table. She set their drinks down and asked if they were ready to order. Since his perp hadn't given him anything concrete yet, he decided ordering would give him the time he needed to press her.

After he'd finished listing what he wanted, he looked across the table. She wore a surprised but bemused look on her face.

He chuckled. "Takes a lot of fuel to run this body."

She stared at him for another beat and then ordered her own, considerably smaller, breakfast.

As Janice went to put the ticket in, Evan turned back to his companion. "Since we're being all friendly and having a meal together, we should at least know each other's names. I'm Evan Burke."

"And I don't recall asking you to join me." She picked up her coffee cup and took a long sip, watching him over the rim, daring him to respond.

The longer he held her gaze, the harder Evan's heart thumped, and the hotter the blood in his veins ran. Like the aged whiskey he used to snitch from his father's liquor stash, her brown eyes were rich and smooth and filled with fire.

Disgusted with himself yet again, Evan did his best to hide his frustration. Where the hell was the anger he should be feeling at what she'd done? Where was the need to seek justice for those men? He was an officer of the law for fuck's sake, and she was a murderer. He shouldn't be content to sit here and banter with her. He would have to guard himself better against letting her get to him.

Pasting what he hoped was a calm expression on his face, he pushed her. "Come on. What'll it hurt?"

"You'd be surprised," she answered as she finally set her mug on the table. She studied him carefully and then, evidently finding what she needed, gave him his first clue. "Kyra. Kyra Pride."

Finally, a name. "Pride. That's an unusual last name."

"You don't like it? I'm crushed." She placed her palm on her chest as if holding her broken heart. The look in her eyes was anything but pained. "And to think I picked it out myself."

He made a mental note to mention that to Seth when he called to fill him in on what he was doing. "Why choose that?"

A cocky grin settled over her face. Her compelling eyes scorched a trail over his body before lifting again to meet his gaze. "Doesn't everyone desire a little...Pride?"

Evan caught the insinuation easily and felt the muscles in his stomach tense. He wondered if she knew the effect she had on him. The answer was obvious. *Of course she does.* It's probably how she'd snared all the men she'd killed.

He knew she'd be expecting some kind of response, so he let his lips slip into a secretive grin.

"*Pride*...can be a dangerous thing. Too much can get you into trouble. Not enough, and you miss out on too much."

Janice returned with their food at that point and both of them held silent as she set the plates in front of them.

"Let me know if I can get you anything else." She smiled and walked away.

They both dug in and Evan waited a few bites before picking the conversation up again.

"Okay, spill it." He needed more background on her. "There has to be a better story behind choosing that name than innuendos and sly remarks."

"Why all the questions?" She forked up a bite of fluffy scrambled eggs.

"I'm a curious guy."

"Well, I'm a cautious girl who doesn't believe in coincidence."

She wiped her mouth and pushed her plate away. "So tell me the real reason you're here and what you want."

Evan had an unexpected twinge of guilt for having cost her another meal. "I don't want anything."

"Oh, really? And you thinking you saw me kill a guy has nothing to do with you being here now?"

"Actually, I never said it didn't. In fact, it has everything to do with me being here." Evan had to think fast. "I can help you."

Everything about her went still. "Did he send you?"

Was that fear he heard?

Whatever it was, it had Evan's full attention. Who was she talking about? Partner? Boss? Lover? She didn't sound too pleased at the prospect. "No one sent me. Who is *he*?"

Kyra relaxed. "Never mind."

This was interesting. Did she have someone she answered to?

"Look." Evan set his fork aside and leaned forward. "Once I saw what was in that alley, I didn't stick around much longer than you did. The last thing either of us needs is for the cops to tie that to us. I've got some connections, and I did a little digging before I left town. They had no idea I was there, but they have your prints on that knife you dropped. And it sounds like they've also connected it to three other homicides in the area."

"Nothing I didn't already know."

"Well, what you may not know is that they also have your name." Or they would as soon as he called Seth.

That apparently shocked her. "How?"

"My source wouldn't tell me that. He has to be careful what he lets slip. But my point is, Daytona is too hot for you now. You can't move around freely without being spotted. I can get you some new papers and get you out of the country."

"Why would you do that?" He could read her distrust easily.

"Why would you help me?"

"That day you ran into me...Something about you grabbed hold of me and won't let go." Evan didn't have to make it up because it was the honest truth. He hated that it was, but he used it now. "I can't get you out of my head."

"Well, I'm sorry for your luck, Ace." Kyra shook her head. "But this isn't going to happen. You need to go."

"Why?"

"That's not your concern. You just have to leave."

"And what are you going to do? Hide out over here? That's not a good idea either. They'll find you."

"I have something I need to do here."

Was she on the hunt again?

So far, she hadn't given up anything he could use in his case against her. He needed more. "What's so important that you'd risk being caught?"

"You wouldn't believe me, even if I told you."

"Try me."

"Maybe next time, Ace." Kyra rose and threw down enough money to cover her barely-touched food and coffee.

By the time Evan did the same, she was almost to the door. He jumped up, and in a few long strides, had caught up with her. He reached out and grabbed hold of her arm to stop her.

She swung around, eyes flashing with heat. "Back off, asshole."

Kayci, Janice, and the few other patrons watched with open-mouthed awe. "Sorry," he called. "We'll take this outside."

Without releasing his grip, Evan got her out the door. Once there, she jerked her arm free.

"Don't touch me again. I don't appreciate being manhandled and hauled around."

"You *will* be hauled around, right to prison for murder if the cops track you down."

"I didn't kill anyone," she said through gritted teeth before storming off to her bike.

"Really." He crossed his arms over his chest. "So your fingerprints on the knife is just a coincidence. And my seeing you only moments after, with that guy's blood literally all over your hands, was all just a big misunderstanding."

"Yes, to both." She picked up her helmet and swung a leg over the seat. "But I don't expect you, or anyone else, to believe that. People, cops especially, only hear what they want to hear. And you, Ace—you're no different. You made up your mind about me the moment you met me."

"So I shouldn't have assumed you killed that man as you were running from the scene?"

"Like I said, there's nothing I can say that's going to change your judgment of me."

"You don't have a very high opinion of people, do you?"

"Why should I? They've screwed me over since I was a kid. Now," she gave him a snarky grin, "I like to return the favor whenever I can."

Kyra pulled the helmet over her head and secured the chin strap. She raised the visor and then hit the button that had her bike revving.

Evan laid his hand on hers where it gripped the throttle. The instant their flesh connected, he felt a sharp jolt to his system. Framed by the black plastic of the helmet, Evan saw her pupils expand as if she'd felt something too.

He had to take a moment to fight it back. "Let me help you." It was slightly disconcerting that those words held a ring of truth in them.

"You can't." Kyra pulled her hand from beneath his and snapped her visor down. She walked her motorcycle backward a few yards and, with a stomp on the shifter, sped out of the parking lot.

Pulling out his phone, Evan pulled up the GPS for the tracker he'd affixed to her jacket when he'd grabbed her.

Confirming her signal and location were being monitored he relaxed, knowing he didn't have to be right on her ass. Since he had a moment, he called his partner to give him an update.

It was still early so Evan wasn't surprised by the sleepy gruffness of Seth's voice.

"Lawson."

"I found her."

The next words were fully alert. "What? Evan? Tell me where—I'll meet you."

"We're not in Daytona." Evan explained the events of the previous night.

"Why the hell didn't you call me?" Seth's voice was clipped.

"Chances were, it wouldn't amount to anything." Evan rubbed the back of his neck because he knew how weak that sounded. But he'd made the decision to do this on his own, so now he had to play it out. "When it did, I had to move fast and I couldn't wait. She was running. I had to follow her."

"You still should have called. I would have hauled ass to meet you anywhere you said. Evan, man," he could hear the frustration and concern in Seth's tone, "your head hasn't been screwed on right since you first saw this chick. For all you knew, she could have been leading your ass into a trap. And you would have walked blindly into it."

The fact that Seth was right made him bristle. "I know what the hell I'm doing."

"I sincerely hope so." Seth was silent for a moment before he spoke again. "So what's the plan? Are you bringing her in?"

"I can't. We don't have a warrant, and she didn't give me enough information to justify asking for it. But I did get one thing. I need you to run a background on her. She said her name is Kyra Pride, but she admitted she'd picked that last name herself. So if she's in the system, it may be under a different name."

"Perfect. And while I'm sitting on my ass here, what are you going to be doing?"

"I'm working her on this end."

"What do you mean working her?"

"She doesn't know I'm a cop. I'll use that to try to get close to her."

Another pause told Evan that Seth didn't think much of his plan. But, thankfully, he didn't argue.

"Okay. While you're doing that, get something with her prints on it and get it to me. I'll run a comparison to the ones lifted from the knife. If they match, I'll put in for a warrant and you can bring her in."

At Seth's suggestion, Evan turned and glanced back through the front window of the diner just in time to see Kayci already clearing the table. As he watched, she grasped Kyra's coffee mug and dropped it into the bin with the rest of the dirty dishes. Making the prints on it unusable.

Evan grimaced at the opportunity lost. He really needed to keep his head in the game. But to Seth he said, "I'll get them to you as soon as I can. I gotta go. I'll keep you posted."

He disconnected the call and again pulled up the GPS app. Once he had a general direction, he set off after his prey.

~~~

As Kyra sped away, she couldn't settle her racing heart or her jittering stomach. No matter how fast she rode, the encounter at the restaurant stayed with her. When she'd first seen him enter the diner, she'd known exactly who he was.

The tall lean frame, the long black hair that looked so silky in texture. It hadn't mattered that the first time she'd seen him he'd been wearing sunglasses. She would have recognized him anywhere. From just the way heat and need pooled low in her belly.

Slamming into that rock-hard chest in that alley had been a
~~~

shock, but it was more her awareness of him that had rendered her immobile and senseless.

It had only been the smooth sound of his sexy voice that had snapped her out of her dazed stupor. Self-preservation had kicked in and she'd run. As humiliating as it was to admit, the fact that she'd fled and hidden had been more to escape her physical response to him than because he could identify her to the police.

And now here she was, running from him again. It was enough to piss her off. And that was an emotion she could better deal with. Grasping onto that anger with both hands, she twisted the throttle with a decisive snap. With the wind buffeting her heated body, she tried once again to outrun the effect he had on her.

4

The longer he followed her, the more convinced he became that she was hunting. He needed to stop her before she added a fifth to her kill sheet. Evan had kept a good distance between them, but that was ending. Now. He'd have to be close enough to be there when she struck.

When the blinking dot on the map stopped moving, Evan was sure she'd found her next victim. Leaving his car a block away, he crept nearer on foot and tried to find a vantage point where he could keep an eye on her. There was no way of knowing who she'd chosen, so watching her was his only option. When she attacked, he'd be there to take her down.

By the flashing beacon on his phone, he knew she was about twenty yards ahead of him. Scanning the area, he caught sight of her on a park bench. She'd added a sweatshirt under her leather jacket and had pulled the hood up around her face, concealing it within. And to further disguise her appearance, she'd donned dark sunglasses.

She looked to be concentrating on the phone in her hand but Evan would bet, behind those tinted lenses, her eyes were taking in everything around her. Looking for some poor, unsuspecting sap.

Evan never took his gaze off of her. As soon as she made a move, he'd have her.

They'd been in position for about half an hour when there

was a loud crash on the street that bordered the park.

Instinct and training distracted him, and in the time it took him to lift his focus, ascertain it was only a fender bender, and return his attention to the bench, Kyra was gone. And there was a man lying on the sidewalk nearby.

"Fuck!" How had she pulled that off so fast? His eyes had left her for only seconds.

After consulting the app to make sure it was still tracking her, he put in an anonymous call to report the murder. He'd have to call Seth so he could coordinate with the Dade City police. But he'd do that later.

Inching forward, Evan joined in with the other people trying to get a look at the body. It was just as he'd guessed. There was a gaping wound at the throat that was now pooling underneath him.

He slowly backed away and returned to his car. Checking her whereabouts again, he saw that the dot was moving quickly, but not so fast as to indicate that she was on her bike. She had to be running on foot.

He kept pace with her easily, but there didn't seem to be a reason for what she was doing. Evan assumed her motorcycle was somewhere close to the park, but the direction she was heading took her farther and farther away from the scene.

And why was she even running with a bike like hers? He doubted anyone had seen what she'd done. Who would be chasing her other than him? She should have just walked calmly to where she'd parked and taken off.

Her behavior didn't make any sense.

Suddenly the blip stopped just ahead of him, causing him to slam on his brakes to avoid being seen. He caught sight of her immediately. She was standing on the sidewalk, her gaze jumping and jerking in every direction.

What the hell is she doing? It was almost as if she were looking for someone. But who?

Kyra plowed her hands through her hair and gripped handfuls. Evan could clearly read the curses that flew from her lips as, dropping her hands, she turned back towards the park and started walking.

By the time he got turned around and made it back to where she'd parked her bike, she was throwing her leg over the saddle. Seated, she lifted the helmet to her head at the same time he pulled up next to her.

Kyra glanced to the side and saw it was him. A string of angry profanities erupted as she rose, dismounted, and stormed up to the driver's side. Quite unexpectedly, she slammed her helmet down on the hood.

"Hey!" Evan shouted at her. "What the hell?"

"*What the hell?*" Hers was louder and said with more disgust. "You need to leave me the hell alone. I don't want or need anyone's help!" Kyra put one hand on the roof and leaned down into his window. "Listen up, Ace. I take care of myself, and I prefer it that way. So back the fuck off."

She returned to her bike, jumped on, and tore out.

Evan exited his car and watched her drive away. Once she was out of sight, he calmly went to the trunk and opened it. Rummaging through his supplies, he found a fingerprint collection kit.

Ten minutes later, he'd pulled a clean, usable set of Kyra's prints from the roof of his car. Sitting back in his seat, he scrolled through his phone until he found the camera app.

Being a detective with such a large police force definitely had its perks. The department equipped them with some decent gadgetry, making his job a lot easier with less time invested. The resolution of his camera phone rivaled that of pricier stand-alone digital versions and made forwarding the fingerprints fast and seamless. At the click of a button, Seth had a quality copy of prints to compare back to the ones they already had from the knife found at the previous crime scene.

He put the hard copy in a plastic bag and stored it away to be added into evidence when he returned to the office.

Once the confirmation showed it had been delivered, Evan called Seth to break the news of the fifth murder and tell him to check his messages for the prints.

With nothing to do but wait, Evan resumed tracking Kyra. He'd let her think she'd lost him until word came in that he could pick her up. Then he'd swoop in and haul her ass back to Daytona.

~~~

Two hours later, he had the email and words he'd been waiting for.

Bring her in.

Evan had been keeping tabs on where she went, staying close so when the warrant came through, he would be right there.

When he pulled up, she was using the seat of her motorcycle as a base for the map she had laid out. The parking lot she was in housed a small building that, by the looks of it, had been abandoned for years. She was parked on the shaded side of the structure, out of sight to most on the road.

Kyra glanced up, startled when she heard a vehicle approach. Suspicion changed to annoyance as she saw who it was.

She folded the map and stowed it away as she waited for him to exit his car. "Hard of hearing, aren't you, Ace?"

Evan approached her slowly. He slid his badge out of his pocket and held it up so she could see it.

A quick flash of fear saturated her brown eyes before she hid it and the snarky attitude came back. "Well, isn't that a kick in the ass? What can I do for you, officer?"

"You're under arrest."

"For what?"
~~~

Evan sent her an incredulous look. "Murder."

Her expressive eyes glinted with resentment. "I haven't killed anyone."

"I have five dead men that say otherwise." Evan knew his black eyes would be cold as ice. It was a practiced look he'd perfected while still in the academy for interviewing suspects. "And all evidence points to you."

"You don't have shit on me," she hissed at him.

Evan slid his hands into his pockets, confident. "I've got an eyewitness account from a pretty reliable source—me. A cop. I also have the murder weapon that *you* dropped, which was not only covered in the victim's blood, but also the three others before him, as well as *your* fingerprints. My partner compared those to the ones I lifted off the roof of my car from earlier today and...what do you know? They're a match." He pressed even closer. "I'd say that's far more than mere shit."

"And I was just stupid enough to give you the exact evidence you needed? I don't think so."

Evan shrugged, entirely unconcerned. "You hadn't counted on me. You were taking the weapon with you, just as you had in all the other cases. Bumping into me that day fucked your plan."

"*My* plan," she sneered. "So all that talk before about getting me a new identity to flee the country was just another setup?"

"Just doing my job. I thought I could get you to incriminate yourself."

"And how'd that work out for you, Ace?"

"I wasn't able to get want I wanted, but I still got what I needed. Your prints. Now I'm taking you back to Daytona to face charges."

"And why would I let you do that, knowing what it would mean for me?"

"You really don't have much of a choice. Did you think you could get away with killing all those men?

Before Evan could anticipate her next move, she shoved him hard and spun back to her bike. She was on it and had it running even as Evan was regaining his balance.

As she attempted to drive around him, Evan managed to snag her arm and pull her right out of her seat. The motorcycle went a few more feet and then dropped. She fought viciously against his hold and nearly landed a punch to his face. Thankfully, at the last second, he saw it and was able to jerk his head to the side to avoid it.

When she missed, her momentum swung her around. He used that to pin her against him—her back to his front. His arms wrapped tightly around her middle, trapping her arms against her sides. She wrestled and bucked but he only squeezed her tighter.

Evan hauled her up and, avoiding her kicking feet and butting head, started for his car. When she saw where he was taking her, she fought even harder to escape him.

He'd always been strong, and since working out with his sister's fiancé he'd gained more muscle mass, but even with his added strength, she was hard as hell to hold on to. Feeling her slipping from his grip, Evan did the only thing available to him.

He turned and plastered her up against the outside wall of the empty building. Her front was pressed into the unforgiving bricks, and her backside was in full contact with him, from chest to thighs.

Evan felt his body instantly heat and struggled to ignore it.

"Stop, damn it!" he ground out, though he didn't know if he were telling her or himself.

Either way, she paid no attention to his words and thrashed even more. He leaned more of his weight into her just to keep her from hurting herself. Or so he told himself as her alluring scent made its way into his lungs. It filled his system, jumbling his senses and tangling his thoughts.

Thankfully, before he could do something stupid like bury his face in her neck, she finally relented and her body went slack.

Evan took a breath and closed his eyes briefly in an attempt to regain his composure and calm his libido. To hide his embarrassing predicament, he angled his hips away from her.

When he felt like he was more in control, he asked her gruffly, "Are you done? Because I can do this all day."

"Ha," she bit out a laugh. "I highly doubt that."

Evan treated the loaded statement like dynamite and stayed well clear of it. Instead, he shifted enough that he could hold her with one hand and reach for his cuffs with the other.

Once they were snapped securely around her wrists, he pulled her away from the wall and recited her Miranda Rights on the way to his car. "Do you understand these rights as they've been given?"

Her eyes shot daggers his way but she gave a sharp nod. Satisfied, he loaded her in and shut the door. Rounding the hood, Evan settled into the driver's seat. He turned in his seat to look back at her.

"Comfy?"

Her glare was scathing before staring out the side window and disregarding him completely. It was just as well. Evan didn't need to have his mind on her any more than it already was.

As a result, it was a long and silent trip.

It was nearing noon when Evan pulled into the lot of the precinct. After parking, Evan brought her in and escorted her straight to an interview room. While he waited for the legal system to grind away, he'd try to get some answers out of her.

When she balked, he gave her a small push into the chair.

Unlocking the cuffs from behind her, he brought her hands forward and snapped them closed around the steel loop on the table. He gave them a quick tug to make sure they were secure and then turned and walked out.

As he approached his desk, he saw Seth sitting there all rested and fresh.

Bastard. Evan felt like he'd been dragged under a bus.

"Wow, you look like shit," Seth observed.

"Thanks." *Leave it to friends to tell it like it is.* Evan had been up all night, and now that his suspect was in custody and he had a chance to sit down, he was exhausted.

Evan scrubbed his hands over his face. "So, the prints from my car obviously matched the ones from the knife. Were you able to dig up anything else on her?"

"Oh yeah. Look what else I found." Seth handed him the file.

It turned out to be a juvenile record on one Kyra Henry. Evan's fatigue disappeared. "This is her?"

"Yup." Seth sat back in his seat. "Once you'd finally ID'ed her, I got a hit on the documents from when she changed her name. From there I researched her surname, and then all I had to do was put in a request for her history from the state."

Evan stared at his partner for a moment and then dropped his gaze to the papers in his hands. Starting from the first page, he read every single word.

There was a long list of trouble beginning from when she was eight years old. Removed from a bad home life, seven-year-old Kyra had been placed in the system. Within the year, she'd been caught stealing from her first foster home. The woman in charge had told the police that Kyra had been nothing but trouble since they'd taken her in.

Kyra had moved on from that facility to another, and another—never staying in one place very long. Wherever she went, she brought difficulty and discordance with her. Along the way, she'd graduated from simple theft to shoplifting, assault, and finally joyriding.

None of this had shown up when her prints were initially run because all of her offenses had been misdemeanors—and evidently she'd never been fingerprinted in those cases as a minor.

Evan couldn't believe there were actually court documents legally changing Kyra's name from Henry to Pride soon after she'd aged out of the system. Instead of simply taking on an alias and assuming another name—which would have been much easier—she'd taken it further and done it legitimately. He couldn't help but be a bit impressed by her initiative.

After that, she'd stayed off the radar until Evan had caught her running from the scene of the crime in the alley. Date of birth put her at twenty-five now. Since there'd been no other sign of her during the intervening years, there was no telling what she'd been doing since then to progress to murder.

Seth had also discovered the link between her and the first victim. He'd been a teacher where she'd gone to school. It wasn't a stretch to figure she'd been in his class at one time. But why wait so long to take him out? What had triggered her spree? And how did the others fit in?

Evan relayed everything he'd learned before he'd brought her in and together he and Seth came up with a plan. When they were ready, they took what they had and went to talk with her.

The evidence in this case would be more than enough to put her away, but their goal was to get a confession. Evan wanted to know why.

When they walked into Interview One, she was sitting exactly as he'd left her over an hour before. Attitude and defiance firmly in place.

Evan set her file down on the table as he and Seth took their seats across from her. He reached out and hit a button on the microphone attached to the table that would engage the voice recorder for the room. He knew the closed-circuit camera that overlooked them would also record their every move.

"This interview will be documented. You've already been

read your rights, so will you please state your name for the record?"

"No," she answered and cocked a brow at him.

"Okay," Evan countered calmly. "Let the record show that Detective Evan Burke and Detective Seth Lawson are in interview with Kyra Henry." He deliberately used her old name to prove the depth of their knowledge.

She shifted in her seat.

"Sorry," he acknowledged. "Kyra Pride, in regards to the four counts of murder currently being weighed against her, and possibly five pending the investigation of the Dade City PD."

He glanced up at her. "Do you have anything to say to that?"

"Nope."

"Well, we have a few questions." Seth's tone was sharp.

"Let's see how that goes for you, Sport," was Kyra's snide remark as she slouched back in her chair.

Evan let Seth take the lead. He'd hold off and just focus on her reactions.

"We found the connection between you and the first victim, Daniel Edwards." Seth glanced down at the file in his hands. "According to this, he was a teacher at one of the schools you attended while in foster care."

Something flashed in Kyra's eyes. Sadness? Remorse? If Evan hadn't been watching her so intently, he never would have seen it. It had only lasted a split second as Seth checked the file. When his partner's focus returned to her, the obstinate woman was in control again.

"It's only a matter of time before we link you to the other three." Evan copied her posture as she'd done to him back at the diner. The move wasn't lost on her. "Why not just save us the trouble and tell us how you knew the others?"

Kyra's gaze slowly tracked to his and she grinned at him. "Now, why would I want to do that?"

"I don't know." Evan tilted his head a little and eyed her.

"Maybe out of the goodness of your heart?"

"Oh, really." She laughed out loud. "Yeah, I don't think so."

Evan quirked a dark brow at her. "No heart, or no goodness?"

"Take your pick."

"Well, here's how it plays out for us." Seth took over again to try and keep her off balance. "Vic two—Fred Wilson owned a corner store and had a reputation for helping out those in need. Were you in need, Miss Pride? Did he help you? Or maybe he didn't and that pissed you off."

"Hmm," she hummed as if thinking about it and narrowed her eyes. "Doesn't ring a bell."

"Todd Seals, victim three." Seth sat forward. "See, this one is pretty easy. He sells bikes, and you just happen to have a bike. I'll bet if we run his sales records for the last few years, we'll find you."

"Well, you just never know, do you?"

"Last one. Dylan Gates. He's a little tougher. Lived mostly off the grid, crashed at friends' places. Liked to live free. We may not be able to tie him to you right now, but here's something we do know about him—about all of these men."

Seth's voice went cold and hard. "Every single one of them was a good, decent man who didn't deserve to die."

Kyra shrugged, but Evan noticed her shoulders were tight and stiff. "Life's a bitch."

The interview continued, but no matter what the question was or how it was asked, she gave them nothing. They hammered at her, but the next few hours turned into a study in frustration.

He looked at Seth and gave him a slight shake of his head that said 'no go.' Their case would be made on the evidence alone. It would have to be enough for him.

Standing, he went to the intercom by the door to call for a uniform to take her to a holding cell until they finished booking her in.

A few minutes later, there was a knock at the door. Evan went to open it and allowed the officer to enter and take Kyra in hand.

As they left, Evan turned and followed their progress through the door and down the hall. He hated that she tempted him in ways no one ever had. But at least she'd be gone soon, and he wouldn't have to deal with her much longer.

5

When the steel door slammed shut behind her, Kyra walked straight to the cot and lay down. She was exhausted...and scared shitless.

Not that she'd ever show that to any of *them*.

She'd had countless dealings with the cops, and talking had never gotten her anywhere. From her earliest memory, no one had ever listened to *her*. They'd all believed what they were told by the adults in her life, and not one of them had ever looked deeper to see if maybe there'd been reasons for her actions.

This fool upstairs was no different. He'd decided from day one she was a murderer, and that was that. It didn't matter that she hadn't killed any of those men. Or that she'd been set up. Hell, she even knew who was doing it. Though proving it would be a nearly impossible.

Not that she'd tell anyone anyway. Who'd believe that some weird-ass crazy-as-fuck psycho was coming into her dreams and threatening her? Calling her by a different name. Telling her that she belonged to him. That she would come crawling back to him or he'd make her regret it?

Shit, *she* hadn't even believed it.

At first.

Until men she'd known had started to die.

When she'd learned on the news that her old teacher had been found with his throat cut, she'd thought it had just been an awful act of random violence. Mr. Edwards had been the first adult in her life who had taken an interest in her and had wanted to help. But being who, and what, she was—embittered, cold, and distrustful—she'd rebuffed any attempt he'd made to befriend her.

Kyra had been thirteen at the time but to this day, she could still remember his earnest face and heartfelt efforts to get through to her. To find out he'd been killed had broken her heart.

She'd been utterly shocked when another man she'd known had died. In exactly the same manner.

Like the beefy cop had said, he'd been an old guy who owned a small store. She'd been ten and on the streets more than in any fucked-up foster home they'd put her in. Through other kids, she'd heard there was a bleeding heart that would feed those in need. She'd stopped by a few times when she'd been desperate.

The cop had it right when he'd guessed she'd bought the motorcycle from the third victim. It had been two years ago. He'd been cute and they'd kind of flirted. Not the I-want-to-get-into-your-pants kind of flirting, but just the fun, harmless type when they'd been haggling over the price of the motorcycle.

After that, she'd had no choice but to finally admit to herself that the nut-job from her dreams was somehow responsible. He'd promised to leave her with nowhere else to turn other than him.

Having always been a loner without any real circle of friends, Kyra hadn't put much stock into his threats.

Until she'd suddenly found herself being set up for the murders of the men from her past.

The big cop had been right about something else too. None of those men had deserved to lose their lives for the simple transgression of knowing her. In an effort to stop it from happening again, she'd racked her brain to come up with a list of possible targets. The three already dead had had a common thread. They had all been nice to her or tried to help her in some way.

With that in mind, she'd narrowed down her list and had come up with the next likely target. An ex-boyfriend. She hadn't seen him in years, but they'd had a good thing going until she'd felt the itch and had to move on.

Since he liked to roam it had taken her a while, but she'd finally tracked him down. She'd decided to just keep watch and see what happened. As a result, Kyra was right there when someone had come out of the shadowed alley and, with one vicious swipe, had slit his throat.

She'd purposely kept her distance to avoid explaining why she was stalking him, but in taking such precaution, it had put her too far away to help. When she saw what had been done, she'd called out, startling the attacker.

As he'd jumped and ran, he'd dropped the knife he'd used. Kyra ran after him, snatching up the blade on the fly, but he was gone.

With nothing else to do, she'd gone back to Dylan. Dropping to the ground next to him, she'd set the knife aside and reached out to try and staunch the flow of blood draining out of him.

But it was too late. He was already dead.

A noise behind her had drawn her attention. Thinking the attacker had returned, she grabbed the weapon again and spun around.

When only a stray dog materialized, it occurred to her how bad this looked. She knew Dylan had been killed in the same way as the others, and here she was, huddled over his body with blood on her hands.

Yeah, like that wasn't incriminating. Knowing she couldn't trust the cops to listen, she decided to get the hell out of there before she was discovered.

Only to barrel into some drop-dead gorgeous guy. She'd stood there like an idiot staring up at him until she found her brain again and hightailed it out of there.

And then to have it happen again across the state. She'd gone there thinking she could save Patrick, but in the blink of an eye, he was gone too. It was just her luck that the hot piece of man-flesh was a cop. And that he'd tracked her down. She still didn't know how he'd been able to pull that off.

What did it matter, though? He'd found her and locked her in this place. If she were convicted of the killings, which was starting to look like a very real possibility, she'd never see the light of day again.

And all because of some nightmarish wacko.

True to his threats, she was alone and scared and had no one else to turn to. He'd accomplished his goal. So, what now? Was a figment of her imagination supposed to come swooping in to save the day?

Kyra laughed humorlessly. *Yeah, right.* The only one she'd ever been able to rely on was herself. This situation was no different, and she'd find a way out of it too.

Her eyes drifted closed as exhaustion took hold. The next thing she knew, she was being chased by a demon from hell. Its big, black hairless body bulged with muscle. Its massive head was some weird concoction of bear and ram with large bat-like ears sprouting out of the top. Its jaws snapped together mercilessly like an obscene parody of those windup toy teeth. Spit and drool flew in every direction in its frenzy to get to her.

Kyra ran as it bore down on her, the bulky form more nimble than she would have thought. It ran like a wolf on the scent of a kill. She was losing ground fast and soon felt its hot, acrid breath on the back of her neck.

She fought to stay out of its gaping jaws, but it overtook her. Just as it was about to crunch down on her, she screamed.

~~~
~~~

Evan grabbed his phone without looking when it rang. "Yeah."

Desk Sergeant Henderson was on the other end. "Burke, you'd better get down to Holding, ASAP. Your suspect is in her cell screaming loud enough to wake the dead."

Evan rose to his feet. "I'm on my way."

Seth looked up at him. "What's going on?"

"I don't know. Henderson said Kyra's screaming."

They both took off out of the room and down the stairs. The holding cells were in the basement of the building and they reached them in just under two minutes. Evan burst through the door to be assaulted by a sound he hoped never to hear again.

It was as if she were being flayed alive. Blood-curdling screams amidst raw desperation and agony.

He swung around to Henderson who had followed them in. "Open it."

The DS fumbled with his keys but soon had the heavy steel door sliding wide. Evan was the first one through, but he wasn't sure what to do for her. He'd never seen anyone in the throes of a nightmare this nasty. Evan made a move to go to her, but Seth hooked his arm and halted him.

"Not too close," Seth warned in a low voice. "It could be a ruse."

Evan looked at his partner and pointed at Kyra. "Does it look like she's faking?"

Seth held firm. "No, but you can't be too careful."

Evan eased a little closer. Seth made another attempt to stop him, but Evan waved him off.

Still a few feet away from where she lay, Evan called out trying to wake her. "Kyra. Wake up."

The screaming only continued.

He inched closer and tried a little louder. "Kyra! Kyra Pride!"

She came out of it so suddenly no one was ready for her

reaction. She launched herself off the end of the bed. But instead of racing for the door, she stood with her back plastered in the rear corner against the bars. Her big brown eyes were wheeling around the room looking for the danger that still lingered in her mind.

"Kyra, it's okay." Evan slowly approached, his hands out in front to show her he meant no harm. "You were dreaming. You're okay now."

He saw the horror slowly fade out of her eyes and clarity fill her gaze. Lucidity turned to suspicion and fury when she saw him standing before her. "What the fuck are you doing in here? Get out! In case you haven't gotten it, I'm not talking to you!"

Evan kept his voice calm. "You were shrieking in your sleep. It sounded pretty bad."

"And it's your business *why*, Ace?" Her attitude was back in full swing. She straightened away from the support of the cell wall. Her spine stiffened and her features went rigid. "Get out."

With no other reason to stay, Evan, Seth, and DS Henderson left.

"It's surprising someone like that could have a bad dream," Henderson muttered as they walked out of the cell area. "I wouldn't think anything could faze a cold-blooded killer like her."

Evan didn't say anything. Being the closest to her, he'd been the only one to witness the stark fear in her eyes when she'd awoken. And he'd had a front row seat to how she'd cowered against the wall waiting for whatever had been in her nightmare to destroy her. He just didn't know what to think of it.

In the short time he'd known her, she been mostly tough and brash and full of bitchy snark. But at odd times, she seemed almost fragile or insecure. She'd quickly covered those moments, but Evan had still seen them.

What did it mean?

He didn't know and he couldn't let himself get pulled in. He had a case to build against her and five men to find justice for.

He and Seth worked the rest of the day making sure that everything in the file was correct and in order. There was no way she was getting off because of some fucking typo.

When he'd done all he could, they headed to Joe's gym in separate cars. Evan and his siblings were getting together tonight to work on their combined magic again. He and Ethan had yet to merge theirs. If they were going to take Noor down come the day of their twenty-fifth birthdays, they needed to figure this out.

Several failed attempts to unify the four elements had brought only frustration and disappointment. Until Jacob, his nephew who can see a person's true inner self, told them that Aria and Anna 'looked the same' inside when they wielded their power.

Anna had thought over what he'd said and decided to try working with just her identical twin one-on-one to see if that made a difference. It had, and air and water had formed into one unified entity.

They'd learned from the girls that it took a complete melding into one being—mind, soul, heart, and magic—to successfully bring their elements together.

Evan hoped that the anger he still felt towards Ethan wouldn't hinder the joining. The survival of their line depended on them being able to do this. Once he and Ethan could stand united as Aria and Anna had, they'd be one more hurdle closer to their ultimate goal.

Which was the linking of all four witches and their elements as the prophecy decreed. 'Four into one to defeat the devil unearthed.'

Evan pulled into the parking lot behind Seth. The rest of the crew were all there waiting when they walked in.

Joe was an ex-MMA fighter who, when he'd hung up his

gloves, had bought this facility. He was quite successful at training new competitors to the sport, along with the average guy who just wanted to sweat in a place where pop hits didn't pump from speakers and mirrors didn't line the walls.

Evan's sister Anna—second born in their quad group—had come to Joe's, unbeknownst to anyone in the family, to learn how to fight and defend herself.

Growing up, her empathic abilities had been more than she could handle on her own at a young age. The family had protected her through the worst of it, but even long after she'd developed the necessary mental shields to block out the chaos, they'd never stopped treating her as though she'd break. As they'd entered adulthood, she'd felt the need to prove herself.

Her reasons for coming to Joe had been two-fold—the need to exert her independence as a strong, capable woman and, with the prophecy nearing, the desire to ready herself physically as well as magically.

All four of them were in the crosshairs of a medieval lunatic because they were the only ones standing between him and freedom. If he could take out even one of them, his cage door would spring open come February, and he'd be free to wreak havoc on the Burke clan, and then on the world.

Evan, his twin brother Ethan, and their sisters were the only ones who could send him to hell for good. Five hundred years ago, their Burke ancestors had helped a woman and her children to escape a dangerous and abusive man.

That man had been Edrick Noor. In his rage over losing his possessions, he had somehow acquired great power. He became so strong that even the powerful witches of Evan's family hadn't been able to stop him. They'd only been able to imprison him until four special and gifted babies were born.

Evan and his siblings had been those babies. Two sets of identical twins—two light, two dark. Each possessing an element's mark.

The girls had come first while the sun shone bright in the sky. Delicate and tiny with pale skin, hair, and light blue eyes. Aria was air and her mark had formed on her right shoulder blade. Anna was next with water riding low on the left side of her abdomen.

He and Ethan had made their arrival only once the moon had risen. Big where the girls were small, dark where they were light—black hair, black eyes, dark olive-toned skin. Evan's earth symbol was on his right upper arm, and Ethan's fire emblazoned the left side of his chest.

They'd been taught everything their mother, and a long line of Burke witches, could teach them. Their father, a non-witch, had also been instrumental in guiding them and forming them into the kind, caring, self-assured adults they were today.

The prophecy gave them until they turned twenty-five—in roughly six months' time—to learn everything they needed. For on that day, whether they were ready or not, Noor's cage would open.

When Evan stepped into the large open space of the training facility, he spotted Anna. She, Joe, and Jacob—their six-year-old son—were working on punches and blocks. Aria and Ethan sat off to the side watching and cheering them on.

Evan marveled at how much his sister had come into her own since meeting and falling in love with Joe Conrad. He hoped that one day, after they'd finally beaten Noor, he would find someone like both of his sisters had.

An image of Kyra popped unbidden into his mind. He shook his head to clear it, determined to focus on tonight's training.

He and Seth approached the group and stood watching Jacob.

"Looking good, short-stuff," Evan praised with a grin. "You and I are gonna have to spar pretty soon. You can show me what you've got."

Jacob beamed and Evan felt his heart melt. This little boy

had come so far.

He was actually the son of a distant Burke cousin who had, by chance, married a descendant of Edrick Noor.

In his search for an army, Noor had found Jacob through his father's line. Unaware of where Jacob had gotten his abilities from, Noor decided he wanted the boy. In his bid to obtain the gifted child, he'd possessed Jacob's father.

During an attempt to protect her son, Jacob's mother was lost. After witnessing her being killed, and he too being hurt and left for dead, Jacob had shut down. Once he'd healed physically, he'd been ripped from the only world he'd known and thrust into not only foster care, but the witness protection program. Surrounded by strangers and things he didn't understand, Jacob had only receded further into himself.

By the time his path had finally crossed Anna's, he'd been mute and withdrawn, avoiding eye contact at all costs.

They'd eventually found out that Jacob had the ability to see a person's true inner self. Because of that, he'd been able to see Noor's monster inside his father. Fearful of seeing it again in someone else, he'd just refused to look anyone in the face.

It had taken Anna and Joe many weeks to pull him out of his self-induced exile. He was now growing and thriving and learning to control and wield the magic that had come to him through his Burke heritage.

As an added layer of protection, Joe was also teaching him how to defend himself from the dangers of regular men. He'd need all the safeguarding he could get, as he was still a big target on Noor's radar.

Evan's entire family was trying to give this child all the advantages he needed to remain safe and unharmed.

Jacob turned from Joe to look up at Evan. "Are you and Ethan gonna try and do what Anna and Aria did with your special magic?"

"That's the plan." Evan ruffed up Jacob's short brown hair.

He glanced over when he saw his brother walk up. "You ready?"

"Hell, yeah." Ethan sounded eager, but Evan would see just how willing his brother really was to opening himself up so completely. If this worked, Evan would be able to see and feel and experience everything Ethan was. And vice-versa.

As the others backed off to give them some space, they moved into position and faced each other.

"Use your telepathic link to start," Anna advised. "Once you're connected, just open your minds and...flow into each other."

They both took a deep, cleansing breath and called to their powers. Evan went first.

"Sand and soil, dirt and stone
Neither you nor I will stand alone
I am Earth and Earth is me
As I will, so mote it be."

Evan's mark flared and lit with deep earthy tones of yellows, oranges, and browns. When his element manifested, it instantly engulfed him in raw, primal energy. He reveled in it even as Ethan spoke the words that would bring forth his fire.

"Smoke, spark, ember, flame
You and I forever the same
I am Fire and Fire is me
As I will, so mote it be."

Evan waited for Ethan to experience and bask in the rush. It was something that never got old.

Before either would have liked, they banked the wilder edges of the forces they controlled. He and Ethan reached out and grasped hands.

He held his twin's gaze. *"Ready?"*

"Bring it."

Evan opened up and slowly felt a stirring in his mind he knew to be his twin. When he started to catch glimpses of Ethan's thoughts and feelings, he knew it was working.

But no matter how hard they tried, the joining wouldn't go beyond just that surface connection. They tried for well over an hour, but they couldn't fully merge together. Something was stopping them.

"Sorry, guys." Ethan looked at each of his siblings. There was frustration and guilt in his dark eyes. "What if I'm subconsciously blocking *everyone* from getting in? I allowed Noor to do it and look where that got me."

Anna went to him and reached up to touch the side of his face. "I really don't think that's the case. We'll figure it out, but not tonight. I think we need to call it a day. We can try again another time."

They split off shortly after that and Aria, Seth, and Ethan headed home. Evan hung back and thought he'd try to clear his head by working up a sweat.

When he came out of the locker room, the place was empty. Joe and Anna would be around somewhere, but at the moment Evan was grateful for the solitude.

He was well into his reps at the weight bench, his breath puffing out with every lift. Out of the corner of his eye, he saw Anna approach. Still hefting the heavy weights, Evan shored up the walls in his mind.

Anna wouldn't look intentionally, but he didn't want her to pick up on anything going on in his head.

"You want to talk about it?" she asked him when she stood over him.

He set the bar back into the safety hooks with a clang and sat up. Despite knowing the opposite, Evan let his simmering temper take over his mouth.

"I thought invading someone's mind without their permission

was against your precious rules." He sent her a look that matched his nasty mood and wiped the sweat off his face with the tail of his shirt.

Anna set her fists on her hips. "I didn't have to *invade* your measly little mind to know something was bothering you, you big ass. It's written all over your face. I would have expected you to be happy—you caught the killer you were after. But if you'd rather wallow in whatever it is that's crawled up your butt, far be it from me to interrupt."

She turned to stalk off, but then abruptly cut back and pointed a finger at him. "And you might want to give this a little thought. Maybe it wasn't *Ethan* that blocked your merging tonight."

She waved her hand at him dismissively before he could ask what the hell she meant by that. "Enjoy your brood, jerk." With that, Anna stomped off.

Evan ignored the twinge of guilt he felt at how he'd treated her and stood. Needing to pound on something, he moved to one of the heavy bags and pulled on his gloves.

With every hit, the shame over hurting Anna's feelings dug in deeper. No matter how hard he worked, he couldn't sweat away the remorse. It wasn't her fault he was twisted up in knots, and he knew she hadn't looked into his mind. Her caring nature had just wanted to help, and he'd jumped all over her for it. She'd been right to suggest he'd been the one to mess up the link with Ethan. He'd suspected that as well but hadn't wanted to draw any further attention to himself.

And now he had amends to make.

Evan waited until he'd showered before approaching her. As he did, she completely ignored him.

He'd evidently done more than hurt her feelings—he'd pissed her off. She'd gloved up too and was beating the hell out of a heavy bag.

He could guess at what she saw as her target. His face.

"I'm sorry," he led with. "I have something I'm trying to work through, but I shouldn't have taken it out on you."

She didn't acknowledge him; she just kept wailing away.

Being quadruplets had its advantages. Evan knew her almost as well as he knew himself, and she wasn't capable of staying mad at him for long. Anna's temper didn't spike often but when it did, it burned quick and bright and then snuffed out.

"Anna, I know you wouldn't push into anyone's head, and I'm sorry I accused you of that."

Her arms dropped to her sides and on a deep sigh, she turned to face him. Her cheeks were flushed and her breathing heaved in and out from exertion.

"I could see you were hurting." She stripped her gloves off. "I wanted to help."

"I know that too."

It struck him, as it often did at odd moments, just how small his sisters were. They both had such a presence about them, it made it easy to forget that he and Ethan towered over them by a foot and outweighed them by at least a hundred pounds.

They were smart and loyal and didn't take shit off of anyone, their younger brothers especially. Evan looked down into Anna's upturned face and marveled at how capable and confident she was.

"I'm sorry," he repeated. "This is just something I have to figure out myself."

She nodded. "I'm here if you need me. I'll listen. No judgments."

That was just like her. Evan bent and gave her a hug, whispering in her ear, "I love you, sis."

She squeezed her arms around his neck. "I love you too, dork."

Evan grinned and released her. "I'd better go so you and Joe can get home."

"They left a while ago." Anna reached up and cupped the side of his face with her small hand. It was a gesture she and Aria had learned from their mother. It was a sign of how much and how deeply they loved. "I wanted to stay and see if you needed me."

"I always will. But I've got this. Come on, I'll take you home."

6

When Evan finally got to his place, it was late. He grabbed a beer and settled in front of the TV. He hoped the ballgame he'd recorded earlier would occupy his still-muddled mind.

When his phone rang and vibrated from his pocket, it woke him. He didn't remember dozing off but he hadn't been asleep for long; he'd only missed a few innings. Sliding his hand in, he grasped the phone and pulled it out. A quick peek at the screen showed it was after midnight and the call was from the station.

"Hello?" He cleared the gruffness from his voice. "Yeah, Burke here."

His captain was on the other end. "You're needed back at the station, Detective."

"What's happened, sir?"

"Your suspect is gone."

Evan bolted upright. "What the hell do you mean, she's gone? How?"

"Security video shows that at ten forty-two p.m., an unidentified male in a DBPD uniform walked in, opened her cell, and escorted her right the fuck out."

Evan had wondered off and on if she'd had an accomplice. He'd never seen any signs of one until now though. "Any way to ID him?"

"No," Captain Reynolds told him. "He made sure to keep his face averted."

Evan's brain was already mapping out what he'd need to do to find her. "I'll call Lawson and have him meet me there. We'll get on it, sir."

He was in his car and racing back to the PD within seconds. Not wanting to cause an accident by dealing with his phone, Evan used the telepathic link with Aria.

"Ari?"

"Evan?" Her voice was sleepy. "What is it?"

"Tell Seth to meet me back at work. Our suspect escaped. Someone came right in and walked her out."

"What? How?"

"I don't know yet. Just tell Seth."

Yeah, okay. I will."

"Thanks."

Evan made it back in record time. His first stop was the security room where all the camera feeds were monitored and recorded. The men there were already going over the tapes, but Evan wanted to see for himself.

"Roll it back from when she was first locked up." He grabbed a chair and slid it up next to the operator so he could get a closer look.

A click of the mouse had the feed resetting at the exact point he'd asked. The officer who had taken her from the interview room showed her into the cell. The footage showed him locking the door and then having her turn her back and thread her hands through the bars so he could remove the cuffs.

Evan watched her move straight to the cot and lay down. She stayed there staring at the ceiling for a while and then her eyes drifted closed and she appeared to fall asleep. A few minutes passed, and just as she started to twitch and writhe, Seth walked into the room behind him.

"What do we have?"

"Nothing yet." Evan didn't take his eyes off the screen.

Kyra began to thrash around more violently and suddenly

her mouth opened and Evan knew she was screaming. For legal reasons, the video didn't have audio, but he would never forget that sound.

A short time later, he could see himself and Seth rushing into the cell. He observed again how she'd suffered from her nightmare. Then they were leaving again when she'd stood firm.

Once they were gone, Kyra sat on the bed and dropped her head into her hands. Evan could almost feel her pain until, with a jerk, she raised her head and looked directly at the camera. Any softness or vulnerability she may have displayed was quickly hidden as she remembered she was being watched.

The next few hours passed with her sitting with her back against the wall looking straight ahead.

The operator fast-forwarded until a man approached her door. They all shifted forward to get a closer look.

"Captain's right," Evan muttered. "Kept his face hidden. No way to ID."

"She's leery but not scared," Seth noted as Kyra rose off the cot to move towards the man. "Giving him attitude."

Evan pointed at the screen. "Look. He's saying something she doesn't like. She's shaking her head and backing away."

"He's unlocking the door," another officer stated. "How the hell does he have a key?"

"He's either one of ours that's on the take," Seth suggested, "or he stole it. We need to run an audit to find out who has access to the cells, and see if any of their keys are missing. Each officer should also check their uniforms and report if anything has been taken or is out of place."

"I'll go back over the footage when we're done here," the camera operator offered. "I might be able to zoom in and identify what it says on the name plate."

Evan just stared mutely and watched as the cop walked into Kyra's cell, grabbed her roughly by the arm, and tried to haul her out. She fought him until he suddenly jerked her in close and said something that led to her complete submission. He maintained a hold on her, but she followed him without resisting.

Evan never took his eyes off of her. Just before she was marched out of camera range, she looked up and right into the lens. He felt the impact of that plea all the way to the center of his being. Evan knew it was meant for him alone.

"She didn't want to go with him." Evan rubbed the back of his neck. "Whoever that was, he must've threatened her with something."

"Or," Seth countered, sending Evan a steely look, "she's working for someone, and they're not happy that she's been busted.

Evan wasn't going to argue with him. "Either way, we need to find her."

~~~

They worked, taking only short breaks, for the next two days and could find absolutely no trace of her. Given that Kyra Pride had dropped off the grid once before at eighteen, Evan figured he and Seth had pretty much no chance of finding her now unless she made a move. She and the man who'd come for her had vanished.

Evan had read her file backward and forward countless times. Would she pick up where she left off and kill more men? Would she disappear, never to be seen again? They just had no way of knowing where or when she'd surface. Or if she even would. He and Seth were pushing hard, and sleep was at the bottom of the priorities list until something broke.

When the endless cups of coffee no longer worked and the exhaustion became too much, Evan would rest his head in his hands and close his eyes. Only to have them spring open again
~~~

when he remembered the look Kyra had sent him through the camera lens when she'd been led away.

It was Seth's belief that she'd been taunting them with her escape, but Evan couldn't agree. Something deep down inside him said the opposite had been true and she'd been scared into leaving.

In his mind, he'd replayed their every encounter over and over, trying to figure out the puzzle that was Kyra Pride. But there weren't any clues to be found. Wherever she was, though, Evan had a sinking suspicion she needed him.

7

When the doors had slammed on her jail cell, Kyra had begged for a way out of that mess. Now she was trying to find a way out of the new hell she'd found herself in.

After being escorted out of lockup and pushed into a car, her *rescuer* had slapped a nasty-smelling cloth over her mouth and nose. She'd woken up sometime later to find herself tied to this metal chair. She glanced around the small empty room and guessed she was in a house somewhere. And at the moment, she was also very much alone.

Kyra knew the nutcase from her dreams was supposed to make an appearance. After the goon had threatened to kill more people if she didn't cooperate, he'd warned that the boss was expecting her.

The thought of meeting him in the real world sent a chill down Kyra's spine. Even when he was only in her mind, he gave her the creepiest feeling. It made her skin crawl. She didn't even want to think about what meeting his crazy ass in the flesh would be like.

What she needed to do was get the hell out of here before he made an appearance. Kyra fought against the bindings trapping her wrists and ankles, but they held securely in place. She wore herself out and tore up the skin on her arms, but she still wasn't going anywhere.

Shit. Now what?

Before she could come up with a better plan, she heard footsteps on the other side of the door. Kyra braced herself to meet her nightmare, but when the door opened, it was only the stooge who had brought her here.

But there was something…his eyes didn't look right. They were lifeless and empty. Kind of glazed over. Was he high or something?

Great, a pot head. Though maybe that would work in her favor and she could somehow manipulate him into letting her go. Maybe she could still get out of this after all.

"Look, buddy—" Her words were cut off as his arm whipped out and backhanded her hard across the cheek.

"You will not speak until I give you leave to. You will learn your place this time, Isabel, or suffer the consequences."

The right side of Kyra's face was pounding in pain and she could taste her own blood in her mouth. This wasn't the same man. Outwardly he looked identical, but the eyes and the way he carried himself had changed. Even the way he spoke had shifted.

The sound of the voice itself was unaltered, but the cadence of his speech was different. And his manner was almost… ancient.

She'd heard that pattern of dialogue, even that woman's name, before. In her dreams. What the hell was going on? None of this made any sense.

Not one to sit back and be bossed around, Kyra looked up into that vacant yet deranged stare. "My name isn't Isabel. I don't know why you think I'm her, but you're mistaken. My name is—"

His hand snapped out and another blow landed in the same spot on her face. Her head spun and her eyes watered, reeling from the impact.

"You do not speak!" He gripped the lower half of her face in his hand and squeezed until she thought her jaw was going to snap. While his fingers dug deep into bone and tissue, he leaned in close. "You made a grave error in judgment, wife. You ran from me. You took my sons, and you went to those abhorrent witches. But now...now you and those Burkes will be punished for taking what was mine."

He increased the pressure and then released her with a shove. Her face throbbed with every heartbeat, but Kyra held silent as her mind raced. The first thing that registered was that this guy was off-his-rocker insane. He thought she was his wife. And if the way he was acting was any indication, Isabel was lucky to have gotten away.

But what did he mean by *witches*? Did he honestly think they existed? Kyra figured that was just another indication of how totally psychotic he was. But that other name—Burke. Why did it sound so familiar?

She didn't have a chance to think about it as he continued his tirade.

"Thanks to you, my sons were lost to me these many years, but the descendants they've given me are countless. I am finding the best of them and adding them to my ranks. You, too, my feckless wife, will bow to me as you should have always done. You thought you could escape me, but I found you, you filthy whore. Just as I always will. I am stronger than any other that has ever lived. With my power and my new children, I will be unstoppable."

There was so much that Kyra wanted to say to him, but she didn't dare. Her face couldn't take a third assault. The second had rattled her brain and she was trying to stay conscious. Instead, she sat quietly and tried to look meek and subdued— not something she usually excelled at.

"You have much to atone for, my dear, the least of which is how you have shorn your hair. You know my preferences. This," he reached out and swiped at the short mahogany strands, "this disgusts me. You look like a scrawny boy. When I return, you will begin to know my displeasure."

Kyra thought she had seen it all, but what happened next was entirely foreign. The man standing in front of her morphed right before her eyes. In a blink, he was once again the man who had broken her out of jail. The glassy eyes were gone and he was his old self again.

She took a chance the crazy mean one was gone. "Dude, do you have multiple personalities or something? What the hell was that?"

"No," he sneered at her. "That was our boss and, damn, is he angry with *you*."

"Yeah, I got that loud and clear. But it doesn't explain why you seemed to change into a different person."

"He's not of this world yet, so he has to possess another in order to exist here. A group of witches, jealous of his power, wrongly imprisoned him in a magical cage for over five hundred years. When he is free, he's going to wreak havoc on them all and reward the rest of us for our loyalty."

Kyra's brows drew together in incredulity. "Do you even hear yourself right now? That bullshit isn't possible and you know it."

"That's what I thought at first too. He started by coming into my dreams, telling me I was special—of his *blood*. He told me I could be more powerful than anything I could imagine. That if I joined him, he'd repay me in ways that would rival only God himself. It's the same for all of us."

"All of you?" That didn't sound good. How many of these screwy people were there?

"At last count, we numbered close to fifty. But that's growing as Noor finds more and more worthy to join his army. Out of these, he's given a select few of us the added privilege of acting as host for him. If he's especially pleased with how we've served him, then he permits us to watch while he works."

That is so fucked up. But she set that aside and latched on to an important piece of information. "Noor?"

"The guy in charge."

Kyra absorbed that for a moment. "Why does he think I'm Isabel?"

"I don't know. But I wouldn't want to be her. Or you." He chuckled. "Good luck with that." He turned and left, leaving Kyra to work through all the nonsense she'd just heard.

She was still skeptical of the whole thing, but the part about the dreams…that prompted her to give it more thought.

Various phrases kept echoing in her mind. Not of this world? Locked in a magical cage? *Five hundred years?* It all sounded so farfetched. But somewhere deep inside, she was starting to actually believe. How could she not when she herself had just witnessed something she thought to be impossible?

If all that other stuff were true, what about the witches he was talking about? The Burkes. Did they still exist? And what were the chances she could find them? If they'd helped Isabel to get away from the crazy fuck, maybe they could help her too.

Kyra shook her head as she reminded herself of a long-held, hard-taught truth. There wasn't anyone out there who was going to help her but herself. That's all she'd ever been able to count on, and that's who she would count on now.

Suddenly, something clicked in her head. Wait a minute. Burke. Evan Burke. That pain-in-the-ass detective that chased her across the state and was bound and determined to put her away for murder. Was he a…? A *witch*?

Just the thought was ridiculous. Burke was a fairly common name. And what kind of twisted sense of humor could the universe have for a hard-as-nails, strictly-by-the-book cop to be doing hocus pocus in his garage?

There's no way it was the same family Noor had mentioned.

Kyra rolled her eyes and almost laughed at herself. And even if, by some fucked-up coincidence, it *was* the same family, Evan Burke would be the last fucking witch she'd go to.

~~~

Three days later, she was seriously rethinking that vow. Every fiber of her being hurt from the beatings Noor dished out in his daily attempts to break her. Or rather, to break Isabel. Each day may have presented a different face, but it was still Noor at the dark, evil center.

No matter how hard she'd tried, she hadn't been able to make him understand that she wasn't his errant wife. Every time she'd try to explain who she was, the punishment would only get worse. The last time, he'd called another man in and he'd stripped her upper body. Together, they'd strung her up by the arms from a hook in the ceiling, so Noor could whip lashes across her back, raging that she would stop lying and obey him.

When they were finished, she'd hung limply. Unable to stand or support herself, they'd released her hands and watched as she dropped to the floor in a heap. Noor's minion had carelessly redressed her, hauled her up, and tied her into the chair again. The raw and bleeding gashes quickly soaked through her blouse, and as time had passed and the blood dried, the shirt had become stuck in the wounds. Every time she moved, it pulled painfully.

Since then she'd tried to act contrite—be what he wanted her to be in the hopes that her full surrender would bring an end to the violent assaults. But no amount of submission ebbed the attacks, and Kyra soon realized the sick bastard was getting off on the pain he inflicted.

She had to find a way out of this. She just didn't know how. By the number of men who allowed Noor to ride them in, she had no idea how many more were out there. Did they only come when Noor needed them, or were they out there all the time? Was she in the middle of their secret hideout?
~~~

Kyra heard nothing at all outside of the room she was in, so there was no way to know. At this point, it didn't matter how many men were between her and freedom—she was just too weak to fight her way out.

She refused to give up, though. It wasn't in her to quit. She'd stay alert for another way and when it came, she'd be ready.

An opportunity finally presented itself two days later. When Noor came in, she noticed that the dude he was wearing had a smart phone clipped to his belt. Maybe if she could get her hands on it without him realizing it, she could call for help.

For this to work, however, she'd have to get him in close. With her hands bound the way they were, he would have to be all but on top of her to reach it.

A plan started to form in her mind. It wasn't a good one and it would probably hurt like hell, but she was running out of options.

She watched him as he sauntered up to where she sat.

"Have you learned your place yet, Isabel? Have you learned that no one escapes me? No one crosses me. You will submit to your husband, your master, and beg for my forgiveness."

She took a deep breath before raising her gaze to meet his. "Yeah, see," she dropped the submissive charade and let all the rage and loathing she was feeling show, "here's the thing. You're not my husband, and you're most definitely *not* my fucking master."

When the blow came, Kyra lent her weight to it. Between the two forces, she and her seat went toppling to the side. But with no way to brace for it, her head struck the hard floor and sent little dots popping and blinking in front of her eyes.

She tried to shake them off as he came to stand in front of her. Kyra was still trying to find her wits when he reared back his leg and kicked her in the stomach. The breath whooshed out of her all at once and left her light-headed.

"Insolent whore," he growled.

Suddenly, he was there. Right in her face as he knelt down to grasp the chair to heave her up. Kyra centered her sluggish mind and got her reluctant limbs to move. Finally, she was able to slip the phone out of its holster just as she was upright again. She quickly pushed the end of the cell as far as it would go into the tight space between her wrist and the metal beneath it. The rest she hid as best she could beneath her hand.

Kyra's single-minded goal was to keep her only chance at rescue hidden. Such was her concentration, she barely registered the rest of Noor's punishment. When he thought she'd been properly chastised for her disobedience, he strolled back out.

As his footsteps led away from her prison, Kyra waited for any sound of his return. As usual, once the heavy footfalls were far enough away, silence met her ear. Taking a chance, she slowly inched the phone out and into her hand.

Her head was woozy and darkness was slowly invading the edges of her vision. It reminded her of a curtain closing after the last act in a stage show. Between the battering he'd given her and being slammed into the floor, she most likely had a concussion. Since passing out was highly likely, she needed to get this done.

With her thumb she tapped the home button. When the 'slide to unlock' command came up, she prayed he hadn't enabled the passcode feature. Taking a breath, she swiped over the screen.

It opened. *Oh, thank God.* Not knowing how much time she had before someone came back or she lost consciousness, Kyra quickly found the internet app.

Her vision faded out so Kyra gave her aching head a shake to rouse it again. The sharpness returned enough that she could, with only her thumb, type in what she wanted. Since her sight was blurring, she squinted to check that she had it spelled correctly. It looked okay so she hit search.

She found the listing and touched it. When it asked if she

wanted to call that number she stabbed at yes.

With her hand trapped low, she leaned her body down as far as she could. She was still inches away from the speaker but it would have to do. The faint rings coming through seemed to go on forever before someone answered.

"Daytona Beach Police Department. How may I direct your call?"

"Evan Burke, please." Kyra kept her voice low and hoped it was loud enough to reach the operator on the other end. "It's an emergency."

"I'll connect you."

Silence met her ear and she began to second-guess her decision to call this particular man. All he wanted to do was lock her up. He hadn't even pretended to listen when she'd told him she hadn't killed any of those men.

What was she doing?

There was a faint click… "This is Burke."

Kyra said nothing as she wondered how she could have thought he'd help her. He'd probably think she was getting what she deserved.

"Hello? Is anyone there?"

The blackness dimmed more of her sight and she knew she was out of time. It was a case of the devil you knew. "You have to help me."

"Who is this?" his deep voice demanded.

"Kyra…Pride," she mumbled. Bent forward the way she was made her head throb with each beat of her pulse. And with every pound, the pain took her further under.

"Where are you?"

"Don't know…Drugged me…House, maybe?" Now that she had him on the line, she hated to lose contact with her only hope. But she had to keep the call short. If she blacked out with the phone in her hand, they'd know what she'd done.

If they killed her or moved her, she'd never be found.

"Hurting. Gonna pass out. Find me, Ace. Can't take much more."

After ending the call, she had enough sense to fumble through deleting the search and the call. Once that was done, she did one last thing before locking it again. It killed her to do it, but she bent her wrist, and slung it across the room. If the dude came back looking for it, hopefully he'd think it had just fallen off his belt when he bent to pick her ass up.

Kyra had fought off the darkness as long as she could. The phone had barely skidded to a stop when everything went dark.

8

As soon as the line went dead in his ear, Evan was in motion. He immediately placed a call to the tech department. At the first voice he heard, he started to issue orders.

"The call that just came in on my desk line. Please tell me it was it recorded."

"Yeah, all calls are."

"Send me a copy and then see if you can trace it back. It pertains to the suspect that escaped custody, so I need to know where it came from. Find out who that number is registered to and locate them. Get back to me as soon as you can."

He hung up and Seth was right there. "What the hell was that? Who was on the phone?"

"Our fugitive."

"What did she say?"

As he filled Seth in, he started checking his email for the recording of the call. He needed to hear it again. "She asked for my help. She sounded bad. I could hardly hear her, and then the call cut off."

"You've got the number; call it back," Seth suggested.

No new emails. He hit the refresh button on his inbox and waited.

"What if in doing that, it alerts whoever has her that she placed that call?" He shook his head. "Too dangerous."

Still no recording. He clicked it again and watched the

status bar at the bottom of the screen fill as it completed the task. Finally, it popped up. He opened the file and hit the play button where Seth could hear it too.

The operator's voice came through the computer speakers, followed by a weak and hushed Kyra. Evan listened to it three times before looking up at his partner.

Seth was leaning on his hands on the edge of Evan's desk. "This makes no sense. Why would she call you?"

"She wouldn't. Unless she was in serious trouble and had no other choice. Whatever she's going through right now has to be worse than the possibility of going to prison for murder."

Evan thought about what he'd heard in her voice. "She doesn't sound good. Her words were muffled, like her mouth was stuffed with cotton. She said she's hurt. And if she's calling me, it means that it wasn't a partner that took her out of here."

Seth rose to stand his full six feet in height. "Yeah, okay, I'll give you that. But who the hell has her then?"

"I don't know. Disgruntled boss, vigilante, take your pick. But the game just changed on us. Now, not only is she a wanted criminal, but she's also a victim." Evan leaned back in his chair and scrubbed his hands over his tired eyes.

What Evan made sure *not* to show was how the sound of her voice had affected him. Hearing the distress and fear she was suffering had caused him physical pain. He was fighting the sudden compulsion to fuck the rules and use his Burke magic to find and free her.

Just the fact that Evan considered it set him back. The one thing he prided himself on was keeping his legacy as a witch separate from his work as a cop. And yet here he was, contemplating breaking that very rule for a criminal and *murderer*. A woman detrimental to his career and ethics.

Why did she have this power over him? What was it about her that both tempted and mystified him? And why couldn't he get her out of his mind? How could he still want her despite everything she'd done?

"Evan." He heard disquiet in Seth's voice. "I know you've had a hard time with this one. If you want to step back, I can take over."

"I wish I could, man." Evan debated opening up to his closest friend, but before he could pursue that train of thought, the phone on his desk rang.

"Burke."

"You're not going to believe this, but the GPS is active on that phone. I used the same tracking system as the 911 call center. I've got a location."

"Give it to me." Evan wrote fast, ripped the sheet from the pad, and handed it across the desk. "Got it, thanks." He looked over at Seth as he hung up. His partner was already pulling the address up on the computer. Evan hated to wait even one more second, but they needed to know what they were walking into.

"It's a house," Seth confirmed. "Middle-class suburb." He glanced up at Evan. "There's going to be a lot of innocents in a neighborhood like this. How do you want to handle it?"

Evan ran plans through his mind and decided on the simplest one. "I have an idea." He scanned the room searching for what he needed. He found it on the same table as the coffee pot. "Grab that pizza box and let's go."

It only took about ten minutes to reach the address where the phone was last positioned. They drove by the first time to scope it out. Evan saw that all the windows were shuttered by blinds with no view of the interior.

After turning around, Evan parked about three houses down. He reached for the empty box in the back seat. "I'll try to get a visual inside—find out how many are in there and what the setup is."

"Watch yourself."

Evan nodded, unfolded his large frame from the car, and

approached the house. He walked confidently up the walk and rang the bell.

The door was yanked open with an impatient, "Yeah, what?"

Evan took his measure in a heartbeat: mid-thirties, five-nine, about one sixty, blond and brown. Worn jeans, t-shirt, tennis shoes. Assorted tats both arms. No weapons in sight, but cocky ass-hat was written all over him.

"What the hell do you want?" the ass-hat demanded.

Evan plastered a harried smile on his face. "Large, loaded. That'll be fifteen twenty-seven." He tried to see past him and into the house, but the doorway was blocked by his body.

"What? No one got pizza here."

"You sure?" Evan pulled a gas receipt out of his pocket and pretended to study it. "It says 3453 Willow Court. That's this place, right?"

"Yeah it is, but I'm the only one here, and I didn't order no fucking pizza."

"Do you mind if I come in and call the boss? My cell died on the way, and I'll get shit-canned if I mess up another delivery."

Evan made a move to enter, but his path was barred when Ass-hat stepped further into the opening.

"You can't come in. You'll just have to take it back."

Evan had to back up or get hit with the door that slammed shut in his face. He made a show of grumbling as he returned to his car in case he was being watched.

He tossed the empty box behind him. "I couldn't see in, but the occupant admitted to being there by himself."

"Any sign of the woman?"

"No. But this is where the GPS signal is coming from. I say we move in now."

Seth nodded. "What's your plan?"

Evan smiled. "I think the pizza man needs to try one more time to deliver his pie. While I've got him distracted at the front, you go in the back. Watch yourself though, just in case he was lying."

He gave Seth a minute to skirt around the house before he strode up to the door again. The large square box rested in one hand while the other, hidden underneath, held his 9mm.

Evan gave the door two good kicks and then yelled, "Hey, man. Screw the boss. It's your lucky day. I'm gonna let you have this for free."

As soon as the door opened, Evan shoved his foot over the threshold. At the same time, he pitched the prop to the ground and took up his gun in a two-handed grip, pointing it right in the ass-hat's face.

"Back up, nice and easy, and keep those hands right where I can see them." Evan advanced into the house slowly, pushing the other guy to retreat whether he wanted to or not.

"What's this about?"

With one hand, Evan pulled his badge out and introduced himself. "We have reason to believe that someone is being held here against their will."

"It's only me, I swear."

Just then Seth emerged from the hall.

"Is she here?" Evan held his breath as he waited for Seth's reply.

"She is. But she's been worked over pretty bad. I called an ambulance."

Kyra's condition must be severe for Seth to have called it in already. Was this the fucker that had hurt her? He returned his attention to the douchebag in front of him. Evan's voice was low and deadly.

"Turn around and drop to your knees. Put your hands on your head."

"You don't know what you're dealing with here, man." All pretenses were gone. He smirked now with secretive delight, even as he did what Evan directed.

"Is that so?" Evan holstered his weapon and pulled the

suspect's arms down one at a time to snap the cuffs on. "Well, why don't you enlighten me then?"

"He won't take kindly to you taking what's his."

"Oh yeah? And who is he? Your boss?" Evan hauled him to his feet. "Give me his number and we'll just call him. I'd like to have a little chat."

"He'll come for her," the thug promised.

"Let's see him try," Evan muttered. He turned to Seth. "Watch him."

Evan started in the direction Seth had come from but stopped when his partner called his name.

"You sure you want to go in there?"

Evan didn't feel as if he had a choice. He had to go to her. With a quick nod, he stalked off down the hall.

He thought he was prepared. But the sight of her slumped in the chair, every visible inch of her beaten and battered, caused a cold fury to settle over him. The way she breathed— so shallowly and gingerly—told him the rest of her had taken a fair share of punishment too. The longer he looked and took in the extent of her injuries, the colder his rage ran. Until the ground shook beneath his feet.

The unexpected rumble diverted his attention to his barely restrained power. Never in all his life had he *ever* lost control like that. Evan looked incredulously from Kyra to his hands, slowly balling them into fists as he took a deep breath to calm his rioting emotions. To know it had happened over *this* woman…Evan's mind spun.

He mentally took hold of his magic and locked it down. As he slowly approached Kyra, he assumed she was unconscious. But as he squatted down beside her to cut away the bindings, her eyes just barely blinked open.

"Hey, Ace." Her voice was barely above a whisper and filled with such agony. He recognized the muffled speech and now knew the cause of it. Her whole face was swollen and bruised.

"Come to take me to jail?"

This close, he could easily see the crisscrossed blood pattern that had saturated and dried on the back of her shirt, indicating she'd been whipped. Repeatedly. The material wasn't damaged which meant they'd lashed her bare skin. Now the fabric was essentially glued to her torn flesh.

Evan swallowed down the bile that tried to rise in his throat. "I think you'll need to stop off at the hospital for a little while before I put you back in that cell."

"Yeah." She tried to laugh but gasped. When she had her breath back, she went on. "You see how well that worked out last time."

"You were the one who walked out with him."

"He didn't really leave me much choice."

Sirens closed in on the house, and soon it was filled with first responders and more cops. As Seth took care of getting the male suspect transported to the PD, Evan stuck close to Kyra hoping to ask her more questions. But the medics only dismissed him in their attempts to ready her for transport to the hospital.

Until Kyra was settled in and checked over by the doctors, there was someone Evan *could* get answers from. As he and Seth drove back to the station, he gripped the steering wheel in crazed anticipation. He was anxious to get their suspect into interrogation and find out who was behind this brutal torture. And why.

But by the time they'd reached their desks, they got word that he'd lawyered up. They could try to grill him but with his lawyer present, Evan doubted they'd get anything useful.

As he sat in frustrated silence, his mind turned to the only other person who knew the truth—Kyra. If she could ID this guy as the one who'd beaten her, they'd have him nailed up tight.

"We need to find out what the hell went on." Evan's gaze

swung to his partner. "Since this guy isn't going to talk, I'm going to see what Kyra has to say."

"Want me to come with you?" Seth offered.

"No. I've got this."

When Evan walked into the hospital ER a short time later, he was directed to the curtained-off cubicle where they were still working on her. The doctor came out just as he approached.

"How is she?"

He listened as the ER attendant listed off her numerous injuries. There were so many and some were pretty severe. Evan had to fight not to flinch as each one was described.

"Physically, she'll make a full recovery," the doctor went on to say. "Mentally, only time will tell. She's suffered a traumatic experience, and everyone handles that differently."

"I need to speak with her. We need to find out if she knows who did this."

"Keep it brief," he warned with a hard eye at Evan. "She needs rest now, not an interrogation."

"You have my word." Evan nodded as the doctor hurried off to his next patient.

Pulling back the privacy panel, he saw her.

She was on her side facing away from him. The nurse bandaging her long slender back turned his direction with a raised eyebrow. Evan held up his badge and she nodded, waving him in.

From what he could see, it was a mass of raised red welts and open wounds. Where the skin had been sliced open, it was oozing fresh blood. He thought of what she must have gone through and cringed.

Clearing his throat, he addressed the nurse. "Can I speak with her?"

"She's conscious, but she's been given some heavy-duty pain killers. I'm not sure how lucid or clear-headed she'll be."

Evan nodded and walked around the foot of the bed. The

eye that wasn't swollen shut was closed and there were tears leaking out of the corner. The skin of her cheek was a dark mottled purple. He could clearly make out where knuckles had struck her face.

On the opposite side were smaller round bruises. Evan took those to be from fingers where someone had gripped her face too tightly.

His gaze traveled down her shoulder and arm to her side. The gown she was wearing had slipped forward to reveal the edge of a large and marbled contusion to the ribs. Evan hated to think about what else had been done to her.

When she shifted under the nurse's touch, the cuff on her wrist rattled against the bed rail. Because she was still a murder suspect, she'd had to be secured.

"Kyra?"

Her lashes fluttered and opened to reveal one rich whiskey eye. It was dulled by pain and the drugs in her system, but it focused in on him.

"Ace?"

"Yeah. Can you talk to me? We need to know what happened to you."

"Came for me." Her words were slurred behind puffy lips. "Said he'd come. Didn't believe."

"The man we found in the house with you. Is that the man who hurt you?"

She made some kind of humming sound in her throat, but Evan couldn't tell if it were a yes or a no.

He needed to keep her on track. "Kyra, who hurt you?"

"Different—Always him."

"What does that mean? Was there more than one man?"

"Yeah. Came every day. Thinks I'm her. Wanted to hurt her. Hurt me." Her voice was fading as the drugs tried to drag her out of pain's reach.

He didn't know what to think. First she said there were

multiple men, but then she switched to there being only one. Evan wasn't sure he'd get any reliable information from her in this condition, but he tried one more time.

He leaned down close. "Kyra. Look at me." Evan waited for her gaze to connect with his. "Who hurt you? Who came every day?"

"Crazy...fuck." The words were said slowly and dragged out.

"Who is that?"

"No..." On a sigh, she was out.

No? Was she refusing to answer, or was she trying to say something else?

Evan watched for a few moments but she was under deep. He'd get no more out of her right now.

He switched his attention to the nurse who was cleaning up the supplies she'd used on Kyra. "How long do you think she'll be sleeping?"

"Doctors had to give her a pretty hefty dose of meds to get her blouse off. It'll probably be a couple of hours before she's awake again."

"Thank you." Evan remembered what the guy in the house had said about his boss coming for Kyra again. "I'm posting a guard on her. No one other than her medical team and me or my partner will have access to her."

"I'll make a note of that in her chart." She turned and walked out.

He gazed at Kyra again before stepping outside the curtain to make his calls. Within the hour, there was a uniform standing outside her cubicle. His orders were to follow her to a room once she'd been transferred.

All he wanted was to go back to her, but Evan knew he needed to put some distance between them. Every time he was close to her, he could feel his attraction to her growing. He was fighting the pull with everything he had, but no amount of resistance made any difference.

Despite the fact that she was responsible for the deaths of five men, Evan still wanted her with every breath in his body. If he didn't do something soon, he'd end up compromising a career that was the focus of his whole life.

Struggling with this on his own suddenly brought his brother to mind. Noor had been tormenting Ethan with his lost love, Honor, for months. He'd suffered through it by himself and had hurt the people who loved him by not trusting them to help. Shame swamped him. He was doing the very thing that had caused the rift between him and his brother in the first place.

Firming his resolve, he decided to take Anna up on her offer. As he left the hospital, he used the telepathic link he shared with his quad-mates to connect with his sister.

"Anna?"

"Come to the house, Evan. Joe and Jacob are out for a while. I'll be waiting for you."

Some of the weight in his chest lessened just knowing she would listen without judgment. And true to her word, when he pulled into the driveway of the house she shared with Joe and Jacob, she was standing in the open doorway.

"Come on in, hon."

When he stepped in, she closed the door behind him. Evan stopped, turned, and collected her up into his arms. He lifted her right off her feet and hugged her tight.

He set her back down and she looked up at him, studying him. "It's about time. This is tearing you up."

All he could do was nod.

Anna took his hand and guided him to the couch. Together they sat. "Tell me."

Evan laid it all out. He kept nothing to himself. Starting with their first meeting, he took her through everything he'd seen and felt and learned. He explained what and who Kyra was and how his attraction to her was blurring his ethical boundaries. Evan bared his soul to his sister, hoping it would lead him to some clarity.

When he was done, Anna remained quiet for a moment.

"And she told you she didn't kill those men? You obviously don't believe her."

Evan shook his head. "Just about every criminal ever caught maintains his innocence, even in the face of overwhelming evidence."

"And it's overwhelming in her case?"

"It is. I witnessed her at the scene of two murders myself. She had the knife that killed four of the five victims in her possession. Her prints were all over it. Can't get much more slam-dunk than that."

"What did she say when you presented it to her like that?"

"That it was all just a coincidence."

"Could it be?"

"Anything is possible, I suppose," he admitted. "But it just doesn't seem likely. To make matters worse, every time I question her, she gives me snarky comments and ambiguous answers. Not playing it straight with me just makes her look that much more guilty."

"Can you blame her? From what you've told me of her past, I can see why she wouldn't be willing to open herself up. Especially to a cop."

Evan straightened in surprise. "What the hell does that mean?"

"Well, it seems to me that the child in those juvenile reports was thrown under the bus over and over again. By the very adults who were meant to protect her. I'm going to take a wild guess and say there were never any statements taken from her about any of the incidents."

That set Evan back. He mentally flipped through each incident and couldn't recall having seen a single instance where she'd been questioned. He'd read through those files countless times. How had he not noticed that nowhere in all those pages was an actual statement from a young Kyra Henry?

"In the end," Anna went on, "it doesn't matter what I think. You have to dig down and find the basis of the conflict that's weighing on you. Your cop side sees her as a serial murderer. End of story. But I think somewhere deep inside, you're not one-hundred percent sure of that. You are an outstanding detective with incredible instincts, Evan. You might want to ask yourself why you're actively ignoring them."

Anna held his gaze. "I know you don't like to let your Burke legacy into your police work, and I completely understand that. We all have our ways of dealing with what fate handed to us. But you know as well as I do that when the magical world decides something is going to happen, it usually does."

That's what bit Evan in the ass every time. The loss of control. Magic had jerked him around since before he'd even been born. Police work was the only thing he had that *he* could dictate.

"Kyra was put in your path for a reason. You need to figure out what it is."

"It doesn't matter. She's a stone-cold killer, Anna."

Anna cocked an eyebrow and sat back, folding her arms over her chest, her ice-blue eyes boring into him. "Is she?"

Evan left shortly afterward. It hadn't been a long conversation with Anna, but it had been a thought-provoking one. As he drove home, he mulled over the questions she'd posed.

Was Kyra actually guilty of those murders? Or was he only interpreting the evidence in a way that backed up his assumptions? Had he done exactly what Kyra had accused him of? Judging her to be guilty without looking at any other possibilities? Was that how people had always treated her throughout her life?

Why *did* he want her put away so badly? Or so quickly? Was it a case of out of sight, out of mind? Was he worried if she remained within reach, he'd be tempted too far? Evan thought back to his initial reaction to her when she'd plowed into him on the sidewalk.

He could remember his exact thoughts. *She was perfect.*

Had he known something right then? Had he sensed that she would be important to him in some way? That their chance meeting had been preordained, so like the rest of his existence? Was he rejecting the idea of a relationship with her solely on the basis that she may have been chosen for him?

Was he really that much of a control freak? That he would condemn a potentially innocent woman in order to stand his own moral high ground against the powers that be? Or was he just that much of a coward?

Before he delved too much further into this, he needed to find out one way or another if she'd killed those men.

Making a U-turn, Evan headed back to the office.

9

Kyra woke a few times in the night but fell back to sleep almost immediately. Whatever they'd given her for the pain had knocked her out. So deeply that even dreams hadn't haunted her. She thought she remembered the cop coming to ask her questions, but she'd been so out of it, she didn't know if it was a memory or just her imagination.

When she opened her eyes this time, the sun was shining brightly into the room, telling her it was morning. Kyra felt a wave of relief at not being in Noor's clutches any longer. Until she felt the binding on her right wrist and remembered she'd only traded one kind of hell for another. But at least in prison she wouldn't be beaten bloody every day.

Or at least, she *hoped* not.

She wondered how long she'd have before they took her back to jail. Would she be safe from Noor this time? He'd be coming for her—she knew that. He'd promised as much. It was only a matter of when.

During her sleep, she'd rolled onto her back and now she was quite uncomfortable. Her wounds didn't appreciate being mashed into a hard mattress. Trying to shift to find a more forgiving position wasn't easy, and Kyra gasped as fire spread through her.

"Don't try to move."

The deep voice startled her and had her head jerking to the

side. The sight that greeted her was a shock. Evan Burke sat forward in the chair next to her bed. He was positioned opposite the door and in front of the window.

Kyra let her head fall back and closed her eyes. "What are you doing here, Ace?"

"I came to ask you some questions."

Blocking out the sight of him had been a mistake. It allowed her hearing to pick up every nuance of his deep, silky-smooth voice. The low timbre of it rolled right through her and settled somewhere deep and secret. Her stomach fluttered with a familiar reaction. It was one she'd been fighting off for weeks. Opening her eyes again, she glued them to the ceiling.

"Ask and then leave."

"Are you in pain? Do you want me to get the nurse?"

The gashes from the whipping were screaming at her, and she'd love nothing more than pain meds right now, but she'd never admit that to him.

"I'm fine."

The creak of the chair was the only warning she had before his tall frame appeared towering over her.

"You're not fine. Let me at least help you roll to your side."

Much to her amazement, his large hands reached across her body. One gripped her left shoulder and the other came to rest on her hip. Where he touched her, it warmed and tingled and caused her breath to catch.

Mistaking her reaction, Evan gentled his touch. "Did I hurt you?"

She didn't answer, she couldn't.

"We'll go slow. Let me do all of the work."

Kyra eyed him suspiciously. "Why are you doing this?"

"I'd want someone to do it for me if I were in your situation."

He watched her for a moment. Those hooded dark eyes gave nothing away. "You ready? Here we go."

As the weight of her body shifted from her back to her right side, a moan slipped past her tightly clamped lips.

"Just breathe." He soothed her by rubbing his hand back and forth over the arch of her hip bone. "Give it a minute."

He held her in place until the wave passed and she could breathe again. Which wasn't easy as his touch still set off her nerve endings.

Evan further surprised her by plumping the pillow more firmly under her head before resuming his seat. Sitting on the front edge, he braced his elbows on his knees.

As she lay facing him, she studied him. He was tall and sexy as hell. He had bottomless black eyes and a body that made her mouth water. But something was subtly different about him.

"You're looking a little flush," he interrupted her thoughts. "Are you sure you don't need something? I can call the nurse in here."

She ignored his concern. "What do you want, Ace?"

"I told you. I have some questions."

"For what purpose? You already think you know all the answers."

He didn't comment on her barb. He just waited in silence.

"Fine." She breathed out an exasperated sigh. "What do you want to know?"

"A great many things," he said cryptically. "But first…when you were eight…why did you steal from your foster mother?"

That was the very last thing Kyra had expected to come out of his mouth. It made her vaguely unnerved that he was asking her about it now. Why would he do that? What was he hoping to gain?

"That's ancient history. Move on."

Those dark-as-night eyes held her pinned. "Humor me. Please."

Kyra inhaled cautiously so as not to set off the pain again. "Not that it matters, but I was hungry."

"Enough to steal?"

Just those three words told Kyra he had never had to do without. People who had never been hungry like that didn't know. They didn't understand the desperation that would make you do things you normally wouldn't.

She'd gotten good at fending for herself early on. For as long as she could remember, she'd had to take care of herself. Kyra, at age five, had been more of an adult in that household than either of her parents. The people who had given her life had been more interested in where their next fix or bottle was coming from than whether or not their daughter had been fed or cared for.

The state had come in when she was seven and had her taken away. She hadn't really cared that she'd likely never see her mom or dad again. Little Kyra had only hoped that she wouldn't have to fight so hard anymore.

But that hadn't been the case. No matter where she'd gone, she'd still had to struggle to survive.

"After two days with no food, you bet your ass."

"Why hadn't you eaten in so long?"

Kyra watched him closely, but she couldn't gauge anything at all from him. His face was expressionless and the tone of his voice was low and even. Neither told her what he was thinking.

She ignored the butterflies in her stomach and continued her story. "I think that particular time I hadn't made my bed just the way she liked. My foster mother. Withholding food was her punishment of choice."

His shoulders rose and fell as he inhaled deeply and released it. His gaze fell to the floor between his feet.

"Doesn't quite match the official report, does it?" Kyra was surprised by how much his believing her mattered. She'd stopped caring what people thought of her a long time ago. So why did his opinion mean so much to her?

Kyra needed to take control of this conversation and steer it away from topics better left alone. "Look, Ace—"

His black eyes lifted and connected with hers again. They weren't so neutral now. There was something glittering in them...she just didn't know how to interpret it. Anger? If that was it, was he angry with her? Did he think she was lying?

"The assault. The joyriding. What happened there?"

"I don't know why you're dragging all of this back to the surface. It really has nothing to do with what's going on right now."

"I think it does. Will you please tell me?"

Whatever. It wasn't like him knowing was going to change anything.

"Some men think that because they provide a roof over your head and food on your plate, that they're entitled to certain privileges. When a girl objects, fights back, and say...breaks their nose...they don't take too kindly to it."

That drew a response. A cold hardness froze the blackness of his eyes. "Your foster father assaulted you?"

She couldn't let his reaction on her behalf affect her. She wasn't that girl anymore, and she didn't need anyone to protect her. Kyra pushed it all away. "Fathers, brothers, uncles, cousins—take your pick. As far as the joyriding, I ran away a lot. I was hitchhiking and the douchebag that picked me up tried to get handsy. I shoved him out of his own car and took off. As soon as I was far enough away, I ditched the car. He had to call his wife to come pick him up. When she asked him what happened, he told her I stole his car to cover his own ass. They called the police."

His temper still simmered but Evan's attention never wavered from her. "The man in the alley."

Kyra heaved out a sigh. "And we've come full circle. All right, since I owe you for getting me out of that house, I'll give it to you straight. As you know, I knew him. He was an ex-boyfriend. After I'd worked out what connected the men who were being killed, I tried to figure out who would be next. I foolishly thought I could stop it from happening again. Though I hadn't seen him in years, I tracked Dylan down and was watching him. Except I was too far away, and someone got to him before I could act."

Evan remained silent and just listened. He had to be comparing what he'd seen the day they'd met with her account of the incident. Kyra wondered what he was thinking as she went on. "I shouted and must have startled the attacker because he dropped the knife. I chased after him and as I ran by, I picked it up. I don't really know what I would have done if I'd caught him, but it didn't matter because I lost him. I returned to Dylan and tried to stop the blood. I put pressure on his neck but it didn't do any good. Once I realized he was gone, I knew how it would look, no matter what I said. I was getting out of there when you got in my way."

She accepted the grief she felt for a friend's passing but slipped her don't-give-a-shit mask back into place. "Well, there you have it. The whole sordid story. Still want to throw me in jail, officer?" Kyra added with a flippant quirk of her brow.

"I want to help you."

Those simple words struck fear into her soul. She shouldn't care what happened to this nosy cop, but for some reason, she did. And if Noor found out about him, he'd become the next target. She'd already lost everyone who mattered.

And Kyra refused to be the cause of anyone else's death.

"Well, you know what, Ace? I don't need or want your help." She turned away from him as much as she could. "I answered your questions, so now you can go."

She heard the chair groan again and knew he was standing. When he approached, Kyra braced herself and looked defiantly up at him.

The intensity of his focus as he just stared at her felt like it was boring holes into her. It made her twitchy but she held herself still.

"Just go. Don't you have other criminals to pursue?" She held up her shackled wrist. "It's not like I'm going anywhere."

He held silent another beat before speaking. "That's the connection, isn't it? All of those men helped you in some way."

She needed him to leave. "I don't know what you're talking about. I don't need anyone's help."

"I'm fairly familiar with the barriers people use to keep others at bay, Kyra. I understand the need to protect yourself. But hear this...I *know* there's more to you than the snarky pain-in-the-ass I've met up until now. I'm beginning to see what you've got hidden underneath all that."

Kyra didn't want him to see her. She was quickly learning that he saw way too much. "Sorry, Ace. There really isn't. What you see is what you get. Snark and all."

When he turned to walk around the foot of her bed, she thought he was going. She told herself she only had to maintain the facade a few seconds longer. Except that he stopped just beyond her feet.

"We'll talk again, Kyra."

"No, Ace, we won't. I'm done. Throw me in a cell and forget about me."

He studied her in silence for a moment longer before his mind seemed to settle. "Something tells me I'll never be able to do that." Evan turned and stalked out of the room.

Once he was gone, Kyra took several calming breaths. With her free hand, she gently ran her fingers back through her short hair.

"Just forget him," she muttered to herself. "You don't need that man—witch or not. It's not worth the cost you'll have to pay. You'll get out of this on your own." She just wished she knew how to do that. Because right now, her future looked seriously fucked.

He must have said something to the nurse on his way out, because she came in carrying a little paper cup with two pills in it. After Kyra gladly swallowed them, she dozed off and on throughout the rest of the morning and into the afternoon. When she heard the door open, she turned her head to see the doctor walking in who was overseeing her care.

As he neared the bed though, she knew she was in trouble. His eyes were glassy and vague.

"Shit." Ignoring the pain, Kyra pushed herself up in the bed to a sitting position and scooted as far away as she could. She pulled on the cuff securing her to the bed but it held firm.

"You'll never escape me, Isabel. The sooner you learn that, the sooner we can move past this behavior. Haven't you realized yet? I'm all there is for you."

Noor sauntered right up to the bed. Confident and crazy. "What, no yelling? No hysterics?"

"Never been much of a screamer." Kyra took a second to flick a glance past him to the door.

"Oh, there's no one out there, my dear," he informed her gleefully. "They've all been called away by another matter." His lips pulled back in a self-satisfied sneer. "Your ward included."

"Well, aren't you just a smart sack of wacko." Kyra's mind raced for a way out. She jerked on the cuffs again. Being chained to the bed was really going to limit her options. If she were going to have any chance of escape, she needed it removed.

Or…maybe it was a blessing in disguise. He probably hadn't taken into account that she'd be restrained when he came for her. There was no way he could take her out of here without someone noticing.

"As I see it, you're shit out of luck." She held up her right arm. "Unless, of course, you'd planned on taking me *and the bed* out of here."

He gave her hand a cursory glance and shrugged. "Not a problem. I'll just break your hand."

Yeah, okay. Kyra hadn't considered that option. As he reached for her, some bright, happy God decided to take pity on her because the door behind Noor suddenly opened. And in stepped Evan, followed closely by another man the size of a bulldozer. His partner. She couldn't remember his name, but she was glad as hell to see them both.

When they saw her huddled up at the head of her hospital bed, Evan gave the doctor a guarded look. "What the hell is going on here?"

At the unexpected intrusion, Noor swung around.

Before Kyra could issue a warning that this wasn't who they thought it was, the big guy took a giant stride forward and swung a massive fist. He cold-cocked the doctor, dropping him like a stone.

She eyed the two new arrivals. It seemed kind of strange that they would come in and just knock a guy out that way. Could they have known who it really was? With Evan, if he were part of that same Burke family that had run up against Noor before, it would make sense. But what about his partner? Could he know too? His actions would imply that he might.

Kyra watched him carefully. "Do you always go around punching people like that, Sport?"

He looked rather surprised at her inquiry. "That, uh, wasn't..."

So, he did know. "The doctor—yeah, I know." She nodded to the downed man. "Is Noor still in there?"

"Um..." The partner looked slightly perplexed as he looked between her and Evan. Like he wasn't quite sure how to answer her. "No, probably not. Knocking out the meatsuit is the quickest way we've found to make him vacate. He can't control an unconscious mind."

"Good to know." Kyra filed that away. And then it struck her what he'd said and she grinned. "Meatsuit?"

"Can we chit-chat later?" Evan interrupted testily. "What I'd like to know is how did *you* know about Noor?"

"I've had the misfortune of meeting up with him before."

Kyra circled a pointed finger around her face. "I wasn't looking forward to being a guest of his again so," she gave him a big thumbs-up, "good job on the timing."

"He's who had you escorted out of the jail?" Evan glanced at his partner and back at her. "What the hell does he want with you?"

"He mistakenly seems to think I'm his wife."

"Isabel?" Evan seemed genuinely surprised.

"Does he have another?" Kyra snapped. Her back was letting her know it hadn't appreciated the quick scramble earlier, and her head was threatening to pound.

Groaning from the floor interrupted any further discussion. The big guy turned back to the doctor and helped him to come around and slowly stand.

"What happened?" He rubbed his head.

The partner took control of that situation and led the doctor from the room while Evan came to stand close to her bed. "Explain this to me. Please."

"Let me ask you something first." She gingerly scooted back down her bed. Finding the controls, she raised it to an upright position. Evan automatically reached behind her, pulled her pillow down, and bunched it under her head. "Your last name is Burke, right?"

"Yes."

"Would that make you...?" Kyra felt kind of stupid for asking, but she needed to know. The words rushed out. "Are you a witch?"

He looked like he'd been struck. Then those full dark brows dipped together in wariness. "Why would you ask me that?"

"I answered your questions. The least you could do is answer mine."

Evan stared at her so hard she could almost see the wheels turning in his head as he tried to figure out what to tell her. Eventually, he gave her a quick nod.

"Prove it."

The command was met with a stony glare, and his response was pushed past clenched teeth. "I'm not your goddamned trained monkey."

"Come on. One little nose-twitch." Kyra tried to wriggle her own in demonstration.

Evan visibly tried to gather his temper. He grasped the side rail so tightly his knuckles went white. "What the hell is going on here, Kyra?"

She gave in. "Fine. I wanted to know if what Noor had said about your family was true." Her head was truly pounding now, so she rested it back on the pillow and closed her eyes. "A few weeks ago, I started having these dreams. This nutso shows up calling me Isabel, telling me that I'm his wife and I'll pay for thinking I could get away from him. He said he was going to make it so I had nowhere else to turn but to him."

Kyra heard a rustle of sound and opened her eyes. Finished with the doctor, the big guy had come over to stand next to Evan. She continued. "That's when the murders started. A sliced throat is one thing; two could be a coincidence, but three? I couldn't ignore it anymore. Somehow, my dream had come to life. And the rest you know."

Kyra caught and held Evan's gaze. "Your family helped his wife, right? They helped Isabel to escape him? Well, now *I* need your help."

10

Evan's mind was reeling at this new twist.

He'd been slowly, on his own, coming around to face the fact that Kyra may not have murdered those men. After his talk with Anna, he'd gone back and studied all the evidence again with non-jaded eyes. Then he'd come to Kyra this morning and really listened to what she'd had to say. Once he'd taken a few hours to process the new information, he discovered there were just a few more details he needed in order to make up his mind. The most important being if she had any idea who was behind it all.

To do that he'd wanted, needed, to see her again.

Knowing it was time to come clean with his partner, Evan had asked Seth to join him. On the way to the hospital, he'd explained what had been going on in his head.

"I knew there was something about this woman that messed you up. Right from the start. I didn't realize it had gotten so bad. What are you going to do?" Seth had paused. "Well, I guess there's really nothing *to* do. She'll be sent to prison soon enough, and you won't have to worry about it."

"That's the thing," Evan had sent him a quick glance. "I'm beginning to think she didn't do it."

Seth had turned sideways in his seat to fully look at him. "As you've said from the beginning, everything points to her. Our case is solid. Do you have any proof there was another perp...

or is this just what you *want* to have happen so you can justify caring about her?"

Evan had understood Seth's cynicism. But that didn't mean it hadn't pissed him off. His partner, and friend, should have known him better than that.

"I don't care if the Fates themselves offer her up to me on a silver platter. If she's guilty, that's it. My job is too important to me to sacrifice it like that." Evan silently prayed that was true. "But I'm truly starting to think she was set up."

"How? Why?"

"I'm not sure yet. I talked to Anna last night. She called me out for blocking the merge with Ethan the other day. I was trying to hide what this is doing to me. I ended up telling her everything. She posed some challenging questions and made me look at this case in a different way. And then I talked to Kyra. I asked her about a few of the incidents in her file. Once she got past her wariness, she told me about the more horrific side of the foster care program."

"She could have been playing you, trying to gain your sympathy."

"Yeah," Evan gave a half laugh, "I don't think so. You've met her. She doesn't give two fucks about anyone's pity. Least of all mine. That attitude of hers is a defense mechanism. She's been fucked over by everyone she's ever known. Except for the men who were killed. And *that's* why they were targeted in the first place."

"Say you're right. Who would set her up for multiple murders?"

"I don't know. That's one of the things I wanted to talk to her about today."

They'd spent the rest of the drive deep in thought and when they'd walked in and realized Noor was there, Evan had the answer to the question he'd been going to ask. Everything that hadn't added up about this case suddenly clicked into place.

This was the crazy fuck she'd referred to. Her switching from multiple men to only one who had hurt her made more sense now. And Evan remembered, just before she'd slipped into sleep, she'd been about to tell him something. '*No.*' She'd been about to say Noor.

As that knowledge had taken root, Evan almost wished Noor were still here. He was owed plenty for the acts of violence he'd committed already, but for what he'd done to Kyra—the setup and brutal nature of her injuries—Evan really wanted a shot at him.

But his chance would have to wait for another time. Evan had plenty in the here and now to work through.

"Did Noor give you any indication why he thinks you're his wife, or is he just falling farther off the rails?"

"I'm assuming I must look like her, but I don't know for sure. He did tell me he's not happy with my haircut." Kyra shook her head. "What *I* want to know is how the hell he even knew about me. From what I've been able to gather, he can't come into this world unless he has a host, right? So how could he have seen me to know whether or not I resemble her?"

"You must have a link to him," Seth offered, which drew both of their attention. "We already know he's looking for descendants." He nodded to Kyra. "If she looks like Isabel, maybe it's because she's one of them, and the reason Noor found her in the first place."

"So, you're saying we're *related*? That's a comforting thought." Kyra paused and then a look of disgust struck her face. "Whoa. Hold up a minute. That makes him...what? My however-many times great-grandfather? And he wants..." She made a sound as if she were dry-heaving. "That is just so sick."

Evan caught her shudder of revulsion.

"If it's any consolation," Seth offered, "you're not the only one related to him."

Her focus returned to Seth. "You too?" She paused a moment.

"So, you and I are…cousins?"

"If you really are one of his descendants," Seth qualified, "then yes, but probably only in a very distant sort of way. You'd have to track your ancestry back to know for sure."

"Yeah, that's not going to happen. If there's any of my family left, which I doubt, I don't think they'd care too much about the past. The ones I knew only seemed to care about what benefitted them in any given moment."

Slowly, bit by bit, Evan was piecing more of her past together. And it all told him she hadn't had an easy life.

Kyra rattling the cuff on her wrist brought him out of his thoughts.

"Since we all seem to agree I didn't kill anyone, how do we get me out of this mess?"

"We can't." Evan hated the way she seemed to deflate at that. "Not right away, anyhow. We can't just drop the charges against you without proof you didn't do it. Finding the real killer would prove that, but uncovering who that was is going to take some time, and we can't very well say Noor did it."

"So what do I do in the meantime?" Kyra was frustrated and Evan couldn't blame her. "I'm a sitting duck like this. You know he'll be back."

Evan did know. Noor was relentless when he wanted something or someone. His new nephew, Jacob, was one such example. As soon as he discovered that Jacob had power, he'd become obsessed with adding him to his ranks. He wanted to groom Jacob to be his heir, to have him stand at his side and help him destroy anything good.

To date, he'd made several attempts to kidnap the six-year-old. But Anna and the rest of the Burkes had protected him and thwarted any further abduction efforts.

Even before that, Noor had set his sights on Aria. After five hundred years alone in a cage, he was able to send his consciousness out into the human realm. His first contact had been with Aria, and upon seeing her had decided to claim her for himself. He'd started in with his torturous games and had killed Seth in her dreams, even going so far as to try to rape her, twice. First, within her own mind, and then again in the real world by possessing the body of another man.

And now there was Kyra Pride. What the hell was he going to do about her? As Noor's newest fixation, she'd need to be protected. And as with anything that pertained to Noor, the family would need to be brought up to speed.

Evan looked into those potent whiskey eyes and vowed, "I won't let anything happen to you."

She held his gaze and something happened between them. He felt a part of himself deep down inside settle. Like a missing piece had been fit into its slot. He wasn't sure how he felt about that.

Seth spoke into the silence and broke the connection. "How do we find out which of Noor's men was sent to do the deed?"

Evan thought on that for a moment before addressing Kyra. "You've been up close and personal for two of the killings. Did you get a good enough look at who did it to identify them?"

It seemed as if whatever had taken place between them had affected her also. She took a second before answering. "Yeah. It was the same guy both times."

Evan remembered something she'd told him. "You said that different men had come and gone at the house you were kept at. Were any of those the one we're looking for?"

"He could have been there, but he wasn't one that came into the room where I was."

"I think we should put the house under surveillance." Evan turned to his partner. "Just in case someone shows up there. We can tail them, see where they go. Maybe they'll lead us right to the one we want."

"And what do I do until then?" Kyra asked again. "As you said, I'm still a wanted criminal. You throw me in a cell, and

Noor will just send another goon for me. I would really prefer not to fall back into his clutches again."

"You won't," Evan promised. "We'll think of something."

"The family is going to need to know about all this," Seth advised.

"I was thinking the same thing." Evan nodded. "We'll call a meeting."

Kyra's rich brown eyes narrowed. "If you're planning on talking about me and my life at this little get-together, I'd better damned well be there."

"You know that's not possible," Evan argued. "If we don't find the real killer by the time you're released from here, you'll be headed back to the PD."

The way she gingerly shifted to lean forward, her mid-section must still be painful. "Well then, Ace, you'd better get them all here before that happens. No one makes decisions about my life but me."

"She's a part of this now, Evan."

He didn't like that Seth was right. But if he were going to protect her, he'd need the full weight of his family.

Evan nodded and opened the connection to his siblings. *"Hey guys. We have a new problem."* He relayed the details of where to meet, and the responses started flooding in.

"We'll drop Jacob at Mom and Dad's and be there soon," Anna relayed.

"I'm in my studio," Aria said. *"I'll grab a ride in with Anna and Joe."*

Ethan was the last to confirm. *"I'm on my way."*

Evan turned to Seth. "They're all on their way. Anna and Joe will pick Aria up and bring her."

"Good. I'm glad she's not driving in alone."

"Hold up there, Ace. What do you mean they're all on their way? Who is? And how would they even know to come?"

"You said to bring my family here. So I called them."

Evan smirked and deliberately wiggled his nose at her. "Telepathically."

"You're shitting me." Kyra's eyes went wide. "You can do that?"

She wasn't quite so blasé about him being a witch as she pretended. "And more."

~~~

Kyra was still trying to wrap her mind around his 'and more' comment. Just what the hell was he capable of? She'd never met anyone who claimed to be a witch, real or otherwise. She wanted to ask more, but he chose right then to step out and consult with the hospital staff. Seth stayed behind, either to keep her company or to guard over her—she wasn't sure which.

She watched him carefully as he moved to lean against the wall. He pulled out his phone and idly busied himself with something on it.

Finding out they had a mutual enemy seemed to have altered their attitudes towards her, but Kyra was still leery. Trust was a hard-won concept for her. She didn't do it easily or often. She'd been burned so many times she'd learned to protect herself at all costs.

Except when it came to Evan. For some reason, she'd come to believe in him despite her best efforts to the contrary. Even when he'd been hunting her down believing she'd committed heinous crimes. She should have hated him, but he'd been able to sneak past all of her defenses. Why else would she have called him—a *cop*—for help?

And now he was bringing in his family. Kyra didn't know these people. Didn't want to know them. She'd give them a chance, for him, but if they didn't prove themselves to her, she'd be gone.

Seth's head came up and his attention focused on the door.
~~~

Kyra braced herself for whatever was about to come through it. She wasn't sure what she expected, but it wasn't the two identical women who breezed in.

Both were petite with long silvery-blonde hair. One wore it straight down her back while the other had hers pulled up into a messy knot on the top of her head. Their features were delicate and...refined was the only word that came to mind. What stood out most though were their eyes. They were such a pale blue they appeared almost translucent. She'd never seen anything like them before.

The rest of them were just as striking as their facial features. They looked to top out at only five foot, or maybe a little more. Fair porcelain skin glowed flawlessly.

She could really hate these two just on principle alone.

The one with her hair pulled up was dressed in faded jeans and a light summer-weight sleeveless blouse. She smiled softly and split off to go to Seth as he pushed away from the wall. She wrapped her dainty arm around his waist and leaned into his side. He gazed down into her upturned face, and Kyra could actually feel the love flowing between them.

Watching them, she realized she felt oddly jealous of their connection. She'd never had anyone look at her in just that way and figured she never would.

Uncomfortable with her reaction to the embrace, she turned her head away just as the door to her room swung inward again. A handsome mix-raced man entered, and just behind him was Evan...No. Wait, that wasn't...

"Who the hell are *you*?"

11

Everyone in the room went still. They slowly traded surprised glances, but before anyone could speak, Evan strode in.

He instantly picked up on the unease. Kyra watched as his eyes tracked to each person. "What's going on?"

The other blonde, who was now standing with the dark-skinned man, turned to Evan. She gave him a strange, message-laden look. "She knew Ethan wasn't you."

Evan's black eyes held pale blue ones briefly before sliding back to Kyra. The rest followed until every eye was on her.

What the hell? Kyra paused a beat, her guarded nature kicking in. "You want to explain why everyone is looking at me as if I've grown two heads, Ace?"

"They were just...uh...taken aback for a minute. Not many outside the family can tell any of the twins apart."

Kyra sensed that wasn't quite all there was to it. Their reactions seemed a little too intense for such a simple matter.

Yes, Evan and his brother looked very similar, as twins do. But why would it surprise them that she'd known Ethan wasn't Evan? It wasn't really that hard to spot their differences. Not like the women, Kyra thought. She knew she'd have a hell of a time telling them apart the next time she saw them and their clothes and hair were different.

Something more was there, but no one gave the impression they were ready to enlighten her. Kyra was about to press it further but Evan diverted the conversation.

"I guess I'd better take care of the introductions." He nodded towards the other tall man. "As you now know, this is my twin brother, Ethan. These are our sisters." He looked at the one standing with Seth. "Aria. And the other is Anna. That guy with her is Joe, her fiancé."

Kyra greeted each of them. It fascinated her that not only was Evan a twin, but so were his sisters.

"So your mom had two sets of identical twins, huh? That is so wild. That had to be interesting growing up."

"It's a little more than that." Evan came the rest of the way into the room and moved to stand beside her bed. "We're quadruplets."

That honestly shocked her. "No way. What are the chances of that?"

"Pretty good, it turns out," he glanced around at his family, "when there's a prophecy that foretells of our birth."

"A prophecy?" Kyra didn't know what to say to that. Her world had been blown so far out of its natural orbit in recent weeks, her only solution had been to hold on tight and hope for the best.

And now here was another element she couldn't even hope to understand. A prophecy? Was he serious? Kyra was trying to wrap her head around that and come up with some coherent questions when someone else was speaking.

"We can discuss family history at another time. Can we get to why you brought us all here?" Jeans, messy bun. That was Aria. "I'm assuming it must involve Noor, as do most of our problems nowadays."

Evan stayed close to Kyra as he laid out the entire clusterfuck. When he was finished, four heads swiveled around to stare at her.

His sisters, Joe, and Ethan each wore the same stunned expression. Aria was the first to recover.

"I've been on the receiving end of Noor's fixation and his temper. It's not a fun or healthy place to be."

"Yeah, you've got that right." Kyra touched her still-swollen and painful cheek.

Aria stepped out from under Seth's arm and approached the bed. She elbowed her brother aside.

"I don't have much in the way of healing, but I can help some." She held out her hand. "May I?"

Healing? Kyra didn't know what to say to that. She darted a glance up at Evan and he gave her a small nod.

"Uh, sure, I guess." Kyra watched Aria closely as she came nearer. She was more than a little skeptical about whatever was coming next. She'd asked Evan if he were a witch and he'd confirmed it, but she had yet to see any sign of that. Evidently, she was about to get one from his sister.

"We'll *all* help." Anna's message was clear, and Evan and his twin joined the women. They took up positions around the bed, two on either side. Aria and Anna each grasped one of Kyra's shoulders while the guys laid a hand on her thighs.

Where Evan's rested, Kyra felt the warmth of him more intensely than the others. She peeked up at him and met his eyes as they were glued to hers. The heat in them set off flutters in her stomach.

"It's not a healing so much as a transfer of energy," Aria explained, drawing Kyra's attention back. "I'll get things going, and then they'll kind of boost it. This will help your body to repair itself faster. Cut your recovery time."

If it took some of the pain away, Kyra would consider this experiment a success. "Sounds good. Let's do it."

There wasn't an overwhelming relief from the pain so much as a dulling of the sharpest edges. Whatever these four were doing made it feel as though a week had gone by. She was still sore, but the worst of her discomfort was gone.

As all but Evan moved back, she shifted around to test it out and discovered she could sink back into the mattress without suffering. "Wow, thanks."

Grateful as she was, this little family meeting had been called because of her. She wanted out from under these murder charges. She wanted to be free again. Kyra thought it was time to get that plan in motion.

Looking around, she noticed that Joe and Seth had repositioned themselves. They were now standing in front of the door, she assumed acting as sentries. Well, at least she wouldn't have to worry about anyone interrupting them. She got right to the point.

"So what's Noor's story, anyway? I was able to pick up a bits and pieces from his rants, but I'm guessing there's a lot more to it. And not just the twisted version he spewed at me of how your family unjustly imprisoned him."

"Unjus..." Aria scoffed and shook her head. The mass of hair perched on her head wobbled.

"Hey. I'm only repeating what he told me. The tale he's selling to his goons is that he was ambushed and unfairly jailed because he dared to demand his loved ones be returned to him."

"If our ancestors hadn't put him in that cage," Aria went on, clearly upset by Noor's fabrication, "he would have destroyed our entire line. When Isabel left him, he went nuts. He disappeared for several years and when he returned, he had power. A lot of it. We're not sure where it came from yet, but we believe he went through some kind of dark ritual to get it. We're still trying to track that down."

"That sounds menacing." Other than his ability to possess people, Kyra hadn't seen any evidence of power on Noor's part, but just the thought of what he *might* be capable of gave her a really bad vibe.

"Menacing doesn't even describe the half of it." Anna picked up the thread. "It took all the magic our family had to fight him and, in the end, the best they could do was lock him away."

"And that's where the prophecy comes in." Evan recited the ancient words to her.

Kyra studied each of the quads. Two light, two dark. Yup, check, nailed that one. Air, water, earth, fire—elemental magic. What did that even mean? This whole situation was so much more than she could grasp.

But she would, because what other choice did she have? If putting her life in the hands of these four was the only way out, she'd make damned sure she could count on them.

"And how old are all of you now?"

"Twenty-four," Ethan told her. "D-day is the twenty-eighth of February."

"And according to the rules, you can't end him before that. He's free to wreak havoc for the next six months and no one can stop him?"

"Not quite free," Aria corrected. "He's limited to what he can affect in this world. His manifestations can only be seen by us and those with a blood-link. The general public has no idea he's out there. He does get stronger as the time counts down, but then, so do we. Every time he uses his power, it drains him and he has to go into a dormant stage to recover. The bigger the display, the longer it takes to recharge."

Anna glanced across at Aria. "The last time we met there was a huge fight, and Aria and I actually ejected him from the person he was possessing. He slunk away, defeated, and we thought he was still down. We didn't realize he'd targeted you and had been making your life a living hell."

Kyra thought back over her time as his captive. "He didn't seem to lose energy as he was pounding on me."

Aria winced. "Unfortunately, the possessions don't take that much out of him anymore. If you can take out the host, though, Noor will have no choice but to vacate."

"Yeah. I got a demonstration of that earlier." Kyra fought to assimilate everything she was learning and make sense of it in her mind. "Okay, so after we clear my name, all we have to do is make it until the end of February, and you guys will take him out for good."

Ethan's gaze flicked to Evan. That minimal little action told Kyra it wasn't quite that simple. "Please tell me you know how to stop him."

"We're working on it." Ethan's words didn't reassure her at all.

"Well, damn, Skippy. Don't you think that's something you need to figure out?"

Evan sent her a look that said to ease off. "We know what we have to do. And we *will* be ready when the time comes."

Kyra gave him a narrow-eyed frown in return but heeded his warning and changed the subject.

"So, since killing him is off the table, how do we get him off my ass?"

"We can't." Anna's flat statement was so *not* what she wanted to hear. And acted as the proverbial straw.

"Great, you got any other good news you want to share, Glenda?" Kyra switched her attention back to Evan. "That's two strikes. So far, Ace, the mighty Burke clan hasn't shown much to inspire my confidence. I think I'm better off on my own before that third one nails me right in the face. Next time I get a hangnail or something equally nontoxic, I'll call."

"Yeah," he argued, "and we all know how well handling it on your own went for you."

"Hey. I," she pointed to herself, "was fine until you threw me in that cell. That's the only reason Noor was able to get his hands on me. If not for *you*," Kyra stabbed her finger at Evan, "I wouldn't have been kidnapped, beaten, and whipped to shreds by a sadistic fuck that *your* family pissed off in the first place."

"So...what?" Evan was seething, and it was easy to see he was barely holding onto his temper. His voice was hard as stone and just as cold. "You're just going to vanish and let more men, more people you care for, *die*?"

Kyra shrugged carelessly, even though she wasn't feeling that way. "I doubt there's any more on his list. Most aren't willing to help anyone, let alone me." She sighed in dismissal. "Just leave, and take your crew with you. I'll get out of this on my own and be gone. You won't have to worry about it anymore."

What she wouldn't say was that there might still be few on that list, but she refused to let them die because of her. She would get to them first and save them. All she had to do was find them and hope she wasn't too late again.

Kyra's planning was interrupted when the room seemed to shake around them. Earthquake? But that couldn't be right. This was Florida, not California. They didn't have those here.

"Evan!" The command in Seth's voice snapped out sharp and stern, startling her attention back to the crowded room.

When no one said anything, she scanned the faces around her. They all regarded Evan with a kind of shocked alarm. *What the hell had she missed?* She slid her gaze to his and he was staring down at her. Something flashed in his coal-black eyes.

"That's twice now you've caused me to lose control. Who the hell *are* you?"

Kyra held his glare with one of her own. "I'm no one you need to concern yourself with, Ace." The way he was watching her was making her uncomfortable. She let her head drop onto the pillow and closed her eyes, blocking out him, his family, and the hope she'd had that they could actually get her out of this.

She should have known better.

Kyra waited and listened and at first, all she heard was silence. Then the rustle of clothing and the shuffle of feet told her they were taking her at her word and leaving. She refused to let them know how hurt and disappointed she was. She'd taken a chance and put her faith in someone besides herself, and it had gotten her exactly nowhere, as usual.

Now all she had to do was hold it together until they were gone.

When all sound faded away, Kyra waited another few moments. As she did, moisture gathered behind her eyelids and burned. She would not cry. It never did any good anyway. Taking a deep breath, Kyra pushed all but the anger away. That was the safest emotion to deal with right now.

Lashes still wet with unshed tears, she opened her eyes. And found Evan standing next to her bed.

Kyra prayed he wouldn't notice as she slipped her bitch-face back on. "What are you still doing here? I told you to leave."

"I know. But you and I have a few things to hash out. One of those being your complete lack of faith in me. I said I wouldn't let anything happen to you, and I meant every word I said, Kyra."

He sat down on the edge of the bed. She could feel the heat of him through the blanket over her legs. That and his closeness caused her stomach to quiver. When he picked her hand up in his, her breath caught in her lungs.

As Evan studied it, his thumb rubbed back and forth over the top. He seemed lost in thought.

The bottomless pools of his eyes slowly lifted to find hers. "I know you have no reason to trust me. Hell, twenty-four hours ago, I was convinced you were a serial killer and wanted nothing more than to see you rot in prison for the rest of your life. A lot has changed in the last day. For both of us."

He inhaled and let it out. "But some things haven't. Like how I know you're just as aware of me as I am of you. I can feel how your pulse is pounding through your veins right now. And how your hand trembles in mine. I can hear the way your breathing has shortened. I know, for whatever reason the fates have deemed, you and I have a…connection."

His other hand came up to slide around the side of her neck. He gripped the back of her head in his firm grasp and slowly eased her forward.

"I fought it." His gaze never wavered from her face. "It didn't do any good."

Kyra was caught and helpless. Her focus dropped and locked onto his mouth as it drew nearer and nearer to her own. When his tongue came out to glide over his lips, her heart tripped over itself.

"Evan," she could only whisper.

He stopped with just a hairsbreadth separating them. "Do you know that's the first time you've ever said my name?"

She did know. It was a way to keep people at a distance. "We shouldn't..."

"Fuck shouldn't."

More pressure on the back of her neck drew her the rest of the way in. Evan's mouth captured hers in a kiss so freaking hot it burned through whatever resistance she'd had. He skipped right over the getting-to-know-you stage and went right for the I-want-to-fuck-you-blind section of the program.

His tongue plundered—there was no other word for it—every inch of her mouth. Soon after, Kyra lost all ability to think. She could only feel and react.

She didn't know when or how it had happened, but her hand had found its way to his chest and fisted in the material there. The body beneath was solid steel. He may be tall and lean, but what she felt under her palm was athletic and ripped.

As her brain short-circuited, she completely forgot that her other arm was bound to the bed rail. When she tried to bring it up to join the first, it was jerked to a stop. The obscene sound of the cuff rattling brought them both out of their haze of want and need.

The stark reminder of her situation chilled Kyra's blood. The hand on his chest, that only moments before had been pulling him closer, now pushed him away.

It took her a second to find her voice. "There is no magical connection between us. That's simple biology, Ace. Lust. It means less than nothing." Kyra forced herself to believe what she was saying. "I don't need you, and I don't need your help. Just go."

With an exasperated sigh, Evan rose. He slid his hands into his pockets. "You'll have to trust someone someday, Kyra. Swallow a little of that pride you hold so tightly to and let me in."

She sneered up at him. "And why should that someone be you?"

He shook his head. "It doesn't have to be. But I'm your best shot at getting out of this alive. Who else will know how to fight the kind of evil that's stalking you? Think about that."

Evan walked a few paces towards the door before swinging back around. "Take a chance, Kyra. You might be surprised. I promise I'll have answers when I get back."

When the door shut behind him, Kyra let out the breath she'd been holding. As she exhaled, she also swore. "Fuck. Fuck. Fuck. No goddamned way am I staying here one more minute." She searched frantically for something to pick the cuffs with. She'd never had the need to open handcuffs before, but she'd finessed a few other locks in her time.

The bed tray table was over next to the window. Lying on top was a bundle of papers. Holding them together was a paper clip. *Bingo!*

Wasting no time, Kyra rolled out of bed on the side she was locked to. Thanks to the freaky four, she could make the move without a twinge. Sliding the metal as far down the rail as it would go, Kyra judged the distance to the legs of the cart.

Just out of reach. Extending her shackled arm as far as she could, Kyra stretched out her long leg behind her and hooked the upright support. Being five foot nine had its advantages.

Grinning, she pulled it close. Once she had the clip in hand, she carefully returned the table to its previous position.

She immediately bent to the task of gaining her freedom.

It took her a little longer than she thought it would. And each second it hadn't opened, she'd expected Evan to come striding back through the door to catch her.

But he didn't, and she finally heard the click that released the inner mechanism. Rubbing her wrist, she scanned the room. First she needed some clothes. She couldn't very well walk out of here in this stupid gown with the back flapping open. Kyra searched every cupboard and cubby but found nothing.

Shit.

Okay. No problem. She'd just find something once she was out. There had to be some scrubs or something lying around. Now, how to get past the guard? Noor had caused a diversion. Could she do the same?

Probably not. Evan would have warned him against falling for the same ruse again. Maybe she could knock him out. Kyra started to look for something sturdy enough but stopped.

Son of a bitch. She knew she didn't have it in her to hurt an innocent man like that. It wasn't his fault he'd been charged with guarding her.

And, truthfully, what exactly were her chances if she *did* get out of here? Despite what she'd said earlier, probably not good. She had no doubt she could stay a step ahead of Noor, but Evan was another matter. He'd probably just use his witchy powers to follow her anywhere she went. That had to be how he'd tracked her before.

Resigned to what she needed to do, Kyra settled in to wait. She didn't bother to reattach the restraint; she wanted Evan to know she'd had the opportunity to leave but had instead decided to stay.

She was casually flipping through the TV channels a few hours later when he walked back through the door. He eyed her freed hand but said nothing.

Kyra hit the power button and set the remote aside. "I stayed. So, what's your plan?"

12

Since learning the whole story, Evan had thought long and hard about what he was going to do next.

Kyra couldn't go back to jail. As she'd said, Noor would be coming for her again. It was only a matter of time. And Evan wouldn't put it past the megalomaniac to send his men in, guns blazing, just for the hell of it. Evan refused to risk any of his brothers-in-blue being harmed, so he'd just have to take that chance out of the equation altogether.

The most likely option would be to let her disappear. She could do it—she'd done it before—but just the thought of it nearly stopped his heart. He knew himself well enough to know he couldn't live with that possibility. He'd never rest knowing she was out there on her own against Noor and all his minions.

As it was, the last couple of hours had been a study in self-control. He'd had to stop himself from calling the guard at least half a dozen times. Not knowing if she'd still be there when he returned had tormented him.

He'd been relieved to see her here, but the message her unbound wrist had sent wasn't lost on him. She could have gone easily at any time.

He took it as a positive sign that she hadn't.

She watched him closely, waiting for his answer. Evan thought again about what he'd be giving up if he went ahead with the plan he'd devised. But as he saw it, there was no other alternative, and the available window of time was narrowing quickly.

"In about an hour," Evan kept his voice from carrying any further than her, "the guard on your door is going to be called away briefly. You'll need to use that time to get yourself out of the hospital and south two blocks. Think you can do that?"

"Yes. But what am I supposed to do after that? I have no clothes and no transportation."

"I'll have a car there to take you to a secure location. And as far as clothes, just tell me what you need."

She itemized everything out, right down to the bra and panties. Which she added with a smirk.

"Oh, I wish I could see you wandering the women's department rifling through all the undergarments," she chuckled.

Evan was more than happy to wipe the grin off her face by conjuring everything she'd listed in the blink of an eye. Including the unmentionables. He couldn't resist getting his own dig in though, and made them a matching set—in red lace.

She sat forward abruptly as she stared at the clothes that had suddenly appeared on the foot of her bed.

"Holy shit, Ace." Wide whiskey eyes bounced up to his. "That's so freaking cool, it almost makes up for you picking out fuck-me wear." She winked at him. "You trying to tell me something?"

Evan was helpless to stop the mental picture of her in the rose-colored bra and panties and nothing else. He sent a silent thanks that his olive skin hid the flush that wanted to inch its way up his neck.

He clenched his jaw and tried to banish the image. "Just be ready. You won't have a lot of time."

"Mr. Law and Order is breaking me out?" Amazement lit the rich cadence of her voice.

That's exactly what he was doing. And if they couldn't find the real killer and clear Kyra's name before anyone found out what he'd done, Evan would lose his job and probably face criminal charges. His superiors wouldn't look kindly on the fact that one of their own had aided and abetted their prime suspect's escape from custody.

"One hour." Evan held up one finger just to make sure she understood.

When she nodded, he turned and left. Upon exiting, Evan gave a quick nod to the officer posted there and then headed for the elevator. The plan was for him to get back to the station. That way he'd be at his desk working when word came in that she'd escaped again.

When she'd thrown them out earlier, they'd all met up at the family home to discuss their options. His parents, his mom especially, had taken up for Kyra as soon as she'd found out what Noor had done to her and why.

They all agreed they needed to help her despite her protests. Each had offered to be the one to set up her getaway, but Evan knew it had to be him. He had the most to lose, but deep down, he knew it had to be done this way.

The plan was worked out and examined from every angle to make sure it went smoothly. With a script that Evan and Seth had written, Joe would make the call that pulled Bishop away from his post. Anna and Aria would be in the car waiting to transport her to Knight's Place where she would hide out in the apartment upstairs.

The only unknown was Kyra herself. Given what Evan knew of her history, he was sure she was capable of escaping to the rendezvous point. But would she? Or would she just walk the other way, never to be seen again?

While Evan pretended to work, he kept glancing at his watch. When the appointed hour came and went, Evan started to get worried. Would she make it out? Would she be caught?

Another hour passed, and still he hadn't heard from either of his sisters. Evan was ready to go find out for himself, but

Anna's voice finally floated into his mind.

"We've got her."

He looked over at Seth and gave a tight nod to let him know all was good.

"What the hell took so long?" he snapped at her. *"She should have been there over an hour ago."*

"I don't know." He heard the rigidity in her voice and knew she hadn't appreciated getting jumped on. *"You'll have to take that up with her when you see her."*

Evan took a breath. *"I'm sorry."*

"She's safe now. We'll see you later."

"Thanks."

Evan and Seth played their roles perfectly when they were notified of Kyra's absence. If they were lucky, no one would ever know they could be implicated in her disappearance. They worked until nothing else could be done. Only then did they pack it in and leave.

They rode together to Knight's Place and pulled into the parking lot ten minutes later. It was late so there were no other cars. They often used the gym after hours to practice and hone their magic, so them coming now wasn't all that unusual.

Evan didn't stop at the open-matted area this time, though. He stalked right through and up the staircase at the back of the room. Everyone was waiting for them there.

He swung his gaze over to Kyra where she sat on the couch. "Any problems?"

"No. The car was right where you said it would be." She slowly uncrossed her legs and then crossed them the other way. "Although you neglected to tell me who'd be waiting for me."

Evan wasn't stupid. Her body language and tone let him know she wasn't pleased. He turned to Anna and the others. "Can we have a minute?"

They nodded and filed back downstairs, closing the door behind them. Evan went to sit next to Kyra on the couch. He turned sideways with one leg folded underneath him. He drew breath to explain why it had gone the way it did, but the words stalled in his throat when those gorgeous, intoxicating eyes met his.

He fought through the sudden need to pull her against him and ravish her. His palm itched to feel the ripe mounds of her breasts. His mouth salivated at the thought of tasting the pebbled nipples.

Evan struggled to shut it down. The more he was around her, the harder it was getting to battle these feelings back. He would, though, because this wasn't the time or the place.

Would it ever be?

Steering away from that slippery slope, Evan started again. "We'll find the guy who killed your friends. We're all vested in helping you. We came up with a possible—"

"Hold up." She stopped him with a palm in the air. "I've told you once already—if a conversation concerns me, I'd damned well better be a part of it. And now you and the rest of your freak-fest family are deciding how to handle me and my problems? I don't think so."

"God, would you just listen for a damned minute?" Evan fisted the hand that was lying along the back of the sofa in frustration. "No one is telling you how to live your life or what to do with it. It's just that we know firsthand what Noor with an obsession looks like."

He kept going even though she'd opened her mouth to argue. "First it was Aria. He tormented her dreams, telling her what he'd do to her in vivid detail. In a particularly memorable one, he tried to rape her and then killed Seth right in front of her."

Her eyes widened but she stayed silent.

"As far as we can judge, around that time he started being able to connect with those of his line. Through Seth, we learned he was building an army of like-minded people. Men who have no problem hurting, or even killing innocents.

"One such innocent was the mother of a six-year-old little boy. The connection to him, to Jacob, came down through the male side of his family. Through this link, Noor discovered he had power. Magic. Well, that just made him all the more valuable. To get to him, Noor possessed Jacob's father. His intent was to just walk in and take the child away. But when his mother intervened and fought to protect him, Noor struck and killed her. Jacob witnessed it all."

He stopped to take a calming breath and was surprised when her hand slowly settled over his in an offer of comfort. He turned his hand in hers and entwined their fingers.

"Jacob was hurt too, and left for dead. When he was found alive, he was whisked away by the authorities. Through the mysterious wonders of the universe, he eventually found his way to my sister, and then to Joe. They're making a life together. They're his parents now—or will be as soon as the adoption is finalized. But that hasn't stopped Noor from trying to take him away from us, and with every attempt he makes, we beat him down.

"Back at the hospital, you asked how we were going to get Noor off your ass. You got upset when Anna told you we couldn't. She only said that out of personal experience. We know that once he gets targeted on something or someone, he won't be diverted. Him thinking you're Isabel will keep him focused on you, and there's nothing we can do about that."

He squeezed her hand. "But that's not to say we're just going to give up and let him have you. Fighting him is our destiny. And just what we'll do. We didn't know he'd be able to stir up this much trouble this quickly, but we'll do whatever it takes to minimize the damage he causes until we can put him down for good."

Kyra didn't say anything for a long time. Evan wasn't sure what she was thinking, but her hand remained clasped in his. He took that as a good sign she wouldn't run screaming from the room.

Finally, she looked him right in the eye. "Alright. We'll do it your way. For now."

Evan released a breath he hadn't known he was holding. "We'll help you. We'll get you your life back. I promise."

She pulled her hand from his and stood. "Go ahead and call in the troops. Let's get this started."

Knowing his family was waiting down in the gym, Evan sent them a quick all-clear message. Within seconds, they heard feet on the steps.

Kyra heard it too, and looked over at him. "Telepathy?"

Evan grinned at her and nodded as the door opened.

"Family meeting calls for food," Joe announced as he entered. "I ordered Mexican while we were waiting. Should be here shortly."

"Aww, Mom would be so proud," Ethan poked at Joe.

"I'll show you proud when I knock you on your ass the next time we're in the ring, smartass," Joe jabbed back with a smirk.

Evan was still chuckling when he brought them back to the reason they were there. "Get settled. We've got a lot to cover."

As they moved to find seats, Kyra stepped up. "I'd like to say something first." She paused until all eyes were focused on her.

"I know I wasn't very gracious when you all came to the hospital earlier, and I'm sorry. I've been on my own for a long time and, as a rule, I don't play well with others. I'll try to work on that, because I know you truly want to help, and I'll accept all I can get." Kyra slid her hands into the front pocket of her jeans. "With that said, please don't take it too personally when I say or do something that pisses you off. It's bound to happen—it's just the way I am."

"That is so true," Evan intoned dryly. "And it usually begins as soon as she opens her mouth."

Kyra shot him a dirty look, but it was also laced with humor. "Oh, it's all on purpose with you, Ace. You're just too easy."

"Good to know," he said on a half-laugh. He resumed his seat on the couch and patted the seat next to him for Kyra to sit. "Now, let's figure out how to find Noor's assassin and bring him in."

Before they could get into it too deeply, Joe's cell buzzed indicating the food had arrived. They took the next few minutes to fill their plates.

Evan kept a subtle eye on Kyra. He didn't like that she only took one small taco. She really needed to eat more. As was usual, Joe had ordered more than enough, so Evan snatched a couple more. He'd see if he could get her to take those too.

Once they'd returned to their seats, they resumed the conversation around bites of corn, flour, beef, beans, and cheese.

"It's going to take something pretty concrete to shift the focus away from Kyra," Seth warned. "We've got a lot working against us. Her prints are on the knife, and she was found with one of the victims' blood still on her hands. Short of the real killer confessing, that kind of evidence is going to be hard to disprove."

"Give me five minutes with him. He'll confess," Kyra muttered.

Evan understood the sentiment, but they had to be careful and do this by the book. "We're going to be walking a very fine line here. Nothing can be done that might give him a way to slip out of the charges."

"I understand that." Kyra huffed out a breath. "But he's killed five people who were kind of important to me. Has he left anything of himself at any of the scenes?"

"Not that we've seen." He gave that some thought and looked over at Seth. "I think that's where we need to start."

"Where?" Seth asked.

"At the beginning," Evan said simply. "Revisit each crime scene. Study them with new eyes. Our suspect is on the run." He flicked a glance at Kyra. "We can say we're retracing her steps, looking for any new evidence that'll point us to finding her. It'll all be true for the most part, other than we'll be trying to prove someone else had been there too."

Evan turned to Kyra. "He had to have made a mistake somewhere. We'll find it."

As they refined the plan, Evan did end up getting her to eat one additional taco and was satisfied with that. Once the dinner debris was cleaned up, the others left, leaving only Evan and Kyra.

"Seth and I will begin first thing in the morning. We'll take each scene and search it top to bottom."

"And what about me?" Kyra gave the counter one last wipe. "What am I going to be doing? I want a part in this too, Ace. I deserve that." She tossed the towel down.

"And you'll get it." Evan came to stand on the other side of the peninsula. "But for right now, you need to stay off the radar. If you're seen, it blows this whole plan."

"So I just, what?" She flung a hand out to encompass the room. "Rattle around here? For how long? And what's to stop Noor from showing up here?"

"We have this place warded so tight, no one is getting in without our notice. We had some close calls here with Jacob. We, and especially Anna, wouldn't let him be here every day if it weren't. And as far as being here alone at night, you won't be. Until we get this mess cleared up, I'll be bunking here." Evan tried to ignore the thrill that gave him. "I'm hoping this situation won't extend too long, but in the meantime, this is the safest place for you. You just have to keep your head down."

"You're staying." Kyra stabbed the countertop with her fingernail. "Here."

"Don't worry. I'll take the couch." Her tone was so cynical it bugged him. "The bedroom is right over there." He indicated the five-foot half-walls in the far corner of the open space that made up the apartment. "The bathroom is just through that door. Joe said there're new toiletries stocked in there."

The bathroom was the only concession to privacy the previous owner had given. It was the only actual room in the whole place.

Kyra moved around the counter to wander over to the sleeping area.

Evan remembered she'd come with only the clothes on her back. "Do you need me to get you anything? Sweats? Pajamas?"

"No, I'm good," was her distracted answer.

He wasn't. *What the hell did she plan on sleeping in?* Best not to think about it.

"Okay. Well, you take the bathroom first then."

When the door closed behind her, Evan walked over and slumped onto the couch. He ran his hands over his face.

What was I thinking that I could stay here with her?

Evan figured he wouldn't be getting much sleep knowing she was only a few feet away—sleeping in only God knew what. Maybe when it was his turn in the bathroom, he should take a little time to clean the pipes.

He was still debating when the door opened again. Kyra didn't spare him a glance as she went behind the short wall. She dropped out of sight as she sat down on the bed.

Taking his chance, Evan made for the bathroom.

Cranking on the shower, he left it more on the cold side. Which did absolutely nothing for the raging hard-on he was sporting. Whoever said cold showers deflated things was fucking stupid. It did absolutely nothing to help him.

Toweling dry, Evan again thought about taking the edge off, but decided it was fitting punishment for the position he'd put himself in.

God, he'd never wanted a woman so badly. Even when he'd thought she was a killer, he'd wanted her with every beat of his pulse. He wondered what would have happened if he hadn't learned she was innocent. Would he have risked it all to have her?

That wasn't an answer he wanted to look at too closely. He was pretty much risking it all already.

Conjuring a pair of sweats, Evan pulled them on and left the safety of the closed door. She'd turned the lights off, but there was just enough glow from the moon through the window to see the lump that was Kyra curled up under the blankets. He prayed she was sleeping already so she wouldn't notice the tent his dick had made of the front of his pants.

On silent feet, Evan crossed to the couch and lay down on his back. With one leg bent at the knee, the other planted on the floor, he closed his eyes and threw his arm over his face. And wished desperately for sleep.

13

Kyra lay without making a sound. She was fiercely trying to ignore the need urging her to go to Evan. He was right there. Just across the room, all warm and clean, and she was sure he smelled freaking incredible.

She'd followed the sounds of his shower. How the flow of water had changed as he stepped into and out of the steamy spray as he washed and rinsed that long, lean body. Kyra had forced herself to stay in bed so she couldn't sneak in and watch. The temptation of knowing he was in there wet and naked had been almost too much to resist.

That kiss he'd given her at the hospital had been like nothing she'd ever experienced. No one had ever affected her as he did—from that very first moment in the alley. Whenever he was near, her body heated and tingled in all the most interesting places.

And he wanted her too. Even if he hadn't basically admitted it, she'd seen it smoldering in his eyes too many times to count.

So, what the hell were they doing? Why was he over there and she lying here? Both needy and wanting.

Why should she miss out? Her future was on pretty shaky ground at the moment. If this plan of theirs didn't work out, she could either spend the rest of her days in prison, or in a prison of a different kind as the captive of a psycho. Why shouldn't she have herself one hell of a last bang with a hot, sexy guy?

Criminals on death row got a final meal of their choosing. Why shouldn't she have a farewell lay? One, if she played her cards right, she'd remember for a very long time.

Mind made up, she threw the covers aside and climbed out of bed. The red number Evan had given her was all that she wore. A quick adjustment to the bra had the cups pushing her breasts up into plump mounds. Her straight B looked more like a full C.

With moonlight to guide her way, she started towards him.

As she drew near, she wondered if he was asleep. A little shiver ran up her spine as she thought about how she could wake him up. But when she caught sight of him over the back of the couch, his coal-black eyes were staring up at her.

His left arm was folded under the back of his head. The right rested on the smooth expanse of his bare, muscled abs. Just below it was the shadowed indentation of his navel. And lower still was that happy trail of hair leading into the band of his sweats. One that barely covered the bulge that gave away just how awake he was.

Neither said a word as Kyra rounded the end of the couch to stand at his side. His gaze raked over her body, from her short cap of brown hair, down her neck, over her shoulders, past the curve of her tits, across the plane of her stomach, and landed at the juncture between her thighs. Every place his focus touched burned as he scorched a blistering trail over her.

Those deep, dark eyes lingered there a breathless instant before traveling down her long legs to her feet and unadorned toes.

When they returned to settle on her face, Kyra was burning up. With need pushing her forward, she threw her leg over him and settled astride his hips. He growled low in his chest as his hands came to rest on the tops of her legs.

Effortlessly, his upper body rose to a seated position. His palms slid up her back, moving gingerly over the still-healing wounds. Both hands came up to thread into her short locks as his fingers fisted and pulled her closer. His mouth took hers in a ravenous frenzy, his tongue breaching her lips in a brutal claim of victory. The urgency of his kiss spurred her desire, letting her know how much he too had dreamed of this moment.

His mouth gentled and finally released hers, as she felt his fingers curl over her shoulders to hold her firmly but tenderly. Captured, she could only gasp as he ran his tongue over the pillowed mounds above the crimson lace.

Kyra's eyes closed and her head fell back. Of their own accord, her hands found their way into the long hair at the back of his neck and twisted in the silky strands. His lips swept over her heated flesh, licking and nipping as he went before stopping briefly to unhook her bra. He pulled it free and let it drop, already forgotten.

With no further barrier hindering him, Evan concentrated on her aching nipples. He took one into his mouth and devoured it for endless minutes, his tongue swirling and teeth tugging until Kyra's control was nearing the breaking point.

She was panting and restless when he finally freed her. Her hips ground down into his, looking for any relief from the sweet torture. But none was to be found as he gave the other puckered nub the same lascivious treatment.

Kyra's entire body was on fire, leaving every ache, every bruise, unnoticed. A fine layer of moisture coated her skin, and all of her nerve endings were alive and buzzing. Like she'd grabbed onto a living lightning bolt.

Her core throbbed and wept, begging him for more. She wanted him inside of her. She had to have him now or she'd go mad.

Giving up her grip on his hair, Kyra slid her fingers around the curve of his shoulder and down through the spattering of hair lightly dusting his chest. His abs rippled as her nails lightly scratched a path to what she really wanted. Finding the tented waistband of his pants, she slipped her hand inside and...*wowzers*.

When she wrapped him in her tight grasp, her fingers barely reached around him. The searing heat of his massive shaft made her insides clench in anticipation. Reveling in his shape and size, she worked her hand up and down the length of him, squeezing hard to prompt him to move things further.

Evan left her breast to suck air deep into his lungs. His head came up and he stared straight into her eyes before taking her lips in another blazing kiss. His hands took hold of the side of her face and held her so his talented tongue could sweep through her mouth and drive her insane.

She was about to lose control and she wasn't alone. He hummed into her mouth, his hands moving to her hips to pull her down harder against him as he thrust against her wanting core.

They were both desperate for air when he relinquished his possession of her mouth. He never took his gaze from her as he slowly lowered back down. His hands went to the elastic band at his waist and Kyra knew it was time.

She lifted up onto her knees so he could raise his hips and push his pants out of the way, freeing his throbbing rock-hard cock.

Kyra was about to shift to remove her panties, when suddenly they disappeared. She'd think about how he did that later. Right now she was just glad they were gone.

He took himself in hand and guided his shaft to the entrance of her slippery center. Kyra settled down over the head and let it slide in, just a little. The fullness was delicious and she bit her lip, feeling her body expand to accommodate his thickness.

Evan's hands went back to her hips, but he didn't force her down onto him. He let her set the pace. It cost him, though, as Kyra discovered when she leaned forward to brace her palms on his chest. His heart pounded heavily there and sweat made his skin slick.

She rotated her pelvis and took more of him in. Inch by glorious inch. Kyra thought she'd die of pleasure before he was fully seated inside of her. She'd been on the cusp of an orgasm for what seemed like forever, and now the sensation of him filling her to bursting nearly pushed her over the edge.

Craving the pull on her inner muscles, Kyra lifted up before dropping again to take even more of him. She loved that every time he slipped further into her heat, he moaned and stiffened, trying to control his own need. She knew the slow, measured pace must be torturous for him; she was only barely holding on herself.

She wouldn't be able to take much more; she was so close. She needed it hard and fast. Rising to sit upright, Kyra lifted and fell straight down. Burying him to the hilt.

"Fuck!" The oath was ripped from his lips as his fingers pressed into the skin and muscle of her legs.

Kyra set a pounding pace, riding him ruthlessly and racing for an orgasm she knew would be blinding.

Beneath her, Evan's hips pistoned to meet hers, matching her rhythm exactly. Overwhelmed by the force of what was happening between them, Kyra cried out as she finally shattered and began to convulse.

Evidently she *was* a screamer.

Evan was right there with her as he thrust hard and swore.

Collapsing onto his chest, Kyra had nothing left. Hearts galloping, breaths sawing in and out, they lay together, the sweat from their bodies clinging to the other. He was still nestled inside of her and she didn't mind. She didn't normally do this without making the guy suit up, but she was on the pill. Pregnancy wouldn't be an issue...

Shit. Shit. Shit.

Kyra tensed as it dawned on her. She'd been arrested, thrown in jail, kidnapped, and held captive for days. She couldn't even remember the last time she'd taken her pill. Well over a week at least, since they were stowed in her bike—wherever that was—along with all of her belongings.

What the hell was she going to do if...?

"Are you regretting it so soon?" He'd clearly mistaken the reason for her sudden alarm.

Kyra forced herself to calm down as she started counting back the days, relaxing as the math indicated she should be fine. She settled more fully against him, now confident she wouldn't get pregnant. But she'd damned-well get back on birth control before this happened again.

"No regrets here. How about you?"

"Feeling better than I have in days."

They lay quietly for a time and the next thing Kyra knew, Evan was waking her. She opened her eyes to see the morning sun brightening the sky. She'd found a comfortable spot stretched out beside him, tucked between his solid body and the back of the couch. They were covered in a light blanket.

She eased her head back to look up at him. "Um, morning."

"I hated to wake you, but I need to get into work."

"Yeah, okay."

There was no graceful way of getting out of the position she was in. Kyra put her hand in the middle of Evan's chest and levered herself upright. Sliding her leg up and over his thighs, she pushed off the back of the couch.

But before her other foot could touch the floor, Evan stopped her momentum by grasping her waist. She looked down at him and saw clearly the intent in his gaze. He had a little morning romp in mind.

To torment them both, Kyra did a slow hip wiggle. "Mmm. Nothing I'd like better. But last night can't happen again. I'm usually on the pill, but with everything that's happened, I've missed quite a few. We probably should have used a condom, but I didn't realize it until after."

That had him sobering. "I didn't give it any thought either. I should have protected you better." He paused, watching her. "Do you think…?"

Kyra shook her head. "No. It should be fine." To distract him, she did another hip shimmy. "It's really a shame to waste this, though."

Back in the game, Evan flashed a grin at her and held out his hand. Six foil-wrapped packs appeared in his palm.

Kyra laughed. "Overachiever, huh? How long before you have to be at work?"

He reached up and pulled her face down to his. "Long enough."

By the time Evan left, they'd used two of the six. One there on the sofa and another one in the shower.

And now here she sat with nothing to do but pace around. Evan and his partner were out there risking their jobs to help her. She hated that she was stuck here hiding. She wanted, needed, to be contributing in some way.

Evan had asked her to stay put, but did he really think she would? She'd never been an idle person. Kyra was thinking about finding her way out of the gym when the door to the apartment slowly opened. At first she didn't see anyone, but then a small brown-haired head peeked around the edge.

Big coffee-brown eyes scanned the room and stopped when they landed on her where she stood near the bed. He sent a quick look back over his shoulder and then scuttled into the room and closed the door.

This must be Jacob. Kyra wondered what he was doing here. Did Anna know where he was? Probably not, considering the way he'd snuck in with a covert look behind him.

Kyra started across the room. "Jacob, right? I don't think you're supposed to be up here."

She could see the nerves in him but he stood tall—well, as tall as he could for a six-year-old—and faced her.

"I heard Anna and Joe talking about you. How Noor hurt you and made it so that Uncle Evan and Uncle Seth thought you'd done bad things."

Kyra sat down on the couch and then leaned forward to brace her elbows on her knees. "I really don't think they'd like it that you listened in on their conversation."

"He killed my mom."

Hearing those words come out of such a small child hurt Kyra's heart. "I know, kiddo. I'm sorry."

"I couldn't protect her. I didn't know my magic then. But I'm learning it now and I can protect you from him."

Her eyes burned with tears, but she blinked them away. "That would be a pretty big job for you. I think your uncles and the rest of your family have it covered."

"I have good control over my walls now, but if I look, I can see if he hides inside of someone. I'll know if he's coming. I can warn you."

Evan had said this little guy had abilities, but he hadn't said exactly what. This must be it.

"Well, that's a nifty power to have." Kyra hated to hurt his feelings by telling him no. But he needed to stay as far away from this as possible. He didn't need to be on Noor's hit list any more than he already was. Maybe she could come up with some kind of compromise that would make him feel included even while he wasn't.

"I'll tell you what, Big Jake. If you happen to see him anywhere, you tell your family right away. How's that?" Kyra figured that was probably something they would have told him to do anyway.

He seemed to puff up a little at that and nodded.

Kyra bit the inside of her cheek to stop the smile that wanted to spread across her face. "You'd better get back downstairs before someone realizes you're missing."

"I'll keep watch." He turned and was gone.

She sat there shaking her head, grinning.

14

Evan stood looking over what had been their first crime scene. Daniel Edwards had lost his life in this very spot. He didn't know what they were looking for, but he hoped they'd know it when they found it.

So far there was nothing here. It had been weeks since his body had been discovered. Weather, people, and life had taken their toll on what had been left. Still they scoured the scene and talked to anyone in the area who might have seen something.

A few hours later with nothing new, they moved on to where Fred Wilson, the shop owner, had died.

Again, no new clues.

Third on the list was Todd Seals, the salesman who had sold Kyra her bike. He'd been attacked and killed on a stretch of road known as The Loop. It was a beautiful scenic route and a lot of bikers often made the ride.

Todd Seals had, and on that day, his body had been found just off the side of the road. His motorcycle had been parked nearby on the shoulder.

Evan and Seth stood and looked over the site hoping to find something. Anything that would prove someone else had done it. They split up and hit it hard. Evan was in the tall grass pushing it aside as he walked, looking for any small piece of evidence that had been missed.

Seth's shout alerted him to the fact that he'd found

something. Evan headed for the tree-line where his partner had been searching.

"Whatcha' got?"

"Maybe what we're looking for." Seth pointed to the trail camera someone had strapped high in a tree.

"What the hell? Was that there when Seals was killed?" Evan didn't want to get his hopes up, but he couldn't ignore the significance. "Why wasn't it seen before?"

"It could be as simple as no one looked up." Seth shrugged. "It's pretty high. Who would expect evidence to be up there?"

Evan stared at the brown box. "Who do you think installed it?"

"My guess would be FWC. They probably wanted to track the animals in this area," Seth theorized. "Whether it was up there on the day Seals was killed? We'll have to take a look and find out."

They immediately got on the phone with the Florida Wildlife Commission. And were told that, yes, the camera had been mounted on the date in question. Evan requested permission to view the footage and was assured that it would be immediately forwarded to his email.

As badly as he wanted to examine that file, Evan knew they needed to finish searching the site. Just because they had this video didn't mean they had the proof they needed.

After scouring every possible inch for the next hour, nothing else turned up. Confident they'd found everything the scene had to offer, he and Seth jumped in the car and headed back to the station.

As soon as his ass hit his desk chair, Evan was pulling up his email.

The file was in his inbox.

Seth rolled his chair close to Evan's so they could both watch. Evan downloaded the file, double-clicked to open it, and hit the play button.

Since the incident happened in the afternoon, Evan scrolled the feed ahead until about half an hour before time of death indicated the murder likely took place. They'd watch in real-time from here. As the counter indicator moved closer and closer to TOD, Evan began to think there would be nothing to see.

But then a motorcycle rolled into the edge of the frame. A man clearly dismounts and rounds to the back of his bike. He lifts the visor but doesn't take the full-faced helmet off, the angle of the shot making identification impossible. Next he squats down next to the rear wheel and proceeds to fiddle with something. It's unclear what he is doing.

Suddenly, they see his head jerk up as he looks off in the direction he'd come from. He stands and waves his arms, as if trying to flag down someone. Evan glanced over at Seth as another rider pulls over and parks in front of the first bike. They can be seen talking. The second rider takes his half helmet off and they ID Todd Seals.

He makes a gesture to the rear of the disabled bike and the other guy nods. As Seals bends to see what the problem is, the assailant is seen sliding a knife free from his boot. He reaches around the other man, and with one quick motion, slits his throat.

Evan hit the pause button. He couldn't take his eyes off the scene in front of him. "I'd hoped we'd find something." He kept his voice low so it wouldn't carry past his partner sitting beside him. "But I honestly didn't think we'd find anything nearly this good." He turned and met Seth's eyes. "This is enough to clear her."

Seth nodded. "Time to make sure it plays out the way we need it to."

Evan nodded and, after making a couple of phone calls, made a copy of the video. He also saved it to a USB drive. With the device in hand, he crossed to his captain's office and knocked on the open doorframe.

"Yeah." He looked up from a stack of paperwork. "Burke. How's it coming on finding our fugitive?"

"That's what I wanted to talk to you about, sir. We've run across new evidence."

"Explain." He rested his arms on the desktop and leaned forward, giving Evan his full attention.

"Our search was at a standstill, so Lawson and I decided to start back at the beginning—see if there was anything we missed at any of the crime scenes. Something or someone that would give us a clue as to where she may have gone."

"Makes sense."

Evan glanced down at the thumb-drive in his hand and then passed it to his boss.

Captain Reynolds gave it the once-over. "What's this?"

"In re-visiting the third scene, we found a trail-cam," Evan told him. "It remained undiscovered until today, likely because it was situated so high up in a tree. We obtained the footage from FWC and, upon reviewing the video, it clearly showcases the murder of Todd Seals as it happens."

"By the look on your face, I'm guessing there's more."

Evan gave a quick nod. "It's not Kyra Pride, sir."

Brows dipped together and eyes went cold. "What the hell do you mean, it's not Pride? Then who the hell is it?"

"We don't know, sir. An unidentified male."

Captain Reynold plugged the USB into his own computer and watched as the murder took place.

"Partner?" he asked without looking up.

"Possibly," Evan admitted, having already decided what to say. "They could have been working together, even though she wasn't at this particular scene. I put a call into the ME to double-check his findings on each case to see if there was any way she could have had a hand in any of the murders. He stands behind his ruling that all the wounds are identical, meaning that all the victims were killed by the same hand." Evan slid his hands into his pockets. "As much as it pains me to be wrong, sir, there's no way Kyra Pride could have committed any of these homicides."

This is where he laid the groundwork that would clear Kyra's name. "Given the new evidence and everything we know about what's happened, I'm developing a new theory on this case, sir."

"And that is?" Flat eyes turned to Evan.

"I believe she's being set up." Sticking as close to the truth as possible was imperative. "Someone is stalking her, taking out men who have a connection to her, and leaving us with only one suspect to pursue. Pride. Sir, I believe the person behind her abduction from this jail is the same person that's responsible for the killings. I could never understand why she called asking for *my* help, when she's the prime suspect in five murder investigations. It never made sense to me, sir. Until this new evidence came to light."

Reynolds thought through all the possibilities and angles. He'd been a street cop for a several years before being promoted to Command. He still had plenty of street-smarts and hadn't lost any of his instincts.

"I'm not ready to rule her out completely," Reynolds finally said. "She could still have a part in this we're not seeing. Continue your search. Bring her in. And if it's like you say and she's innocent, we still need to find out what she knows. In the meantime, shift your primary focus to finding the new suspect from that video."

Evan knew a dismissal when he heard it. "Yes, sir."

He kept his face schooled all the way back to his desk. Seth was waiting to hear what the captain had decided.

"We make this new evidence our top priority. But Reynolds wants us to continue the pursuit of Kyra Pride. She's either involved in some way or she knows something. Whichever it is, we need to find her."

Seth released a breath. "Right." He nodded. "Okay. Let's get busy."

Evan wanted to break the news to Kyra himself, so he just sent Anna a quick message to pass on that they were making progress. After that, he and Seth got to work hunting down the real perp.

They'd done all they could for the day and shut it down. As a result, it wasn't too long after end of shift when Evan was pulling into Knight's Place. As was usual for this time of day, there were still quite a few cars in the lot. Walking in, he wanted to rush right upstairs, but the need to keep things normal meant he couldn't. He'd have to wait until people cleared out. Instead he headed to the locker room.

He was about halfway there when Anna appeared above him on the landing. "Evan, I need you up here for a minute?"

"Yeah, sure." Evan changed direction and jogged up the steps. As soon as the door shut behind him, Kyra was there.

"Well?"

The attitude she wore as comfortably as an old pair of jeans was firmly back in place. But Evan thought he saw a touch of guarded hopefulness deep in her eyes. She'd not had many people she could count on throughout her life, and Evan vowed, right then and there, to be exactly that for her.

With that in mind, he told her about the camera, what they'd discovered on it, and his new orders.

"Holy shit." Kyra plopped down on the couch in apparent shock. "You really did it."

Evan sat on the coffee table in front of her. He took her hands in his. "I told you we'd get you out of this. Our goal now is to get you 'found' so you can come in and give your statement. The video didn't give us a clear view of this guy, so we *need* your description to move forward."

Anna had hung back but now she came to sit next to Kyra. "Are you sure that's safe for her?"

"As far as the DBPD is concerned, she's no longer the prime suspect. She's still wanted for questioning, but that's only to get on record what she knows." He shifted his focus back to Kyra and thought about how to get her into the PD.

"I think the best way to handle this is to wait a couple of days and then have an anonymous source call in and report a sighting of you."

"Can't you just take my statement here? I really don't need to go to the police station."

He knew this stemmed back to her distrust of authority. "And how would I explain suddenly having that information? You're supposed to be on the run, remember? You have to come in."

She opened her mouth to argue, but he spoke over her. "Hey. I'll be with you the entire way. You sit down with us, you tell us what you know, and you're free to go."

"And you honestly think it's going to be that easy? You said yourself I'm still wanted in connection to the killings."

"You are, but I really do. Just explain what's been happening, leaving out all the parts about Noor, of course."

Kyra was silent as she thought through what he'd told her.

"It'll work out, Kyra. I promise. You'll be cleared."

She was quiet for so long, Evan began to fear she wouldn't go along with his plan. He couldn't push her on this; she needed to decide for herself.

Finally, she spoke. "I'll do this, Ace, but there's something I need from you."

He didn't know how else he could reassure her. "What's that?"

"I can't stay here."

"What? Why?" Evan couldn't help but wonder what had prompted this. "It'll only be another day or two."

"I know you said it was safe here, but I don't want to put anyone else in danger."

"And by anyone, you mean 'Big Jake'?" Anna gave Kyra a knowing smile. "We know he snuck up here to see you. He finally told us why he did that. I just hope he didn't bother you."

"Not at all. He was fine."

"Big Jake?" Evidently something big had happened while he'd been away at work.

Anna laughed. "Yeah, Jacob took it upon himself to come see Kyra. Evidently, he'd overheard Joe and I talking and felt the need to offer his protection." Anna returned her attention to Kyra. "I appreciate how you handled that, by the way. Telling him to let us know if he saw anything."

"I figured that's what you would have told him to do already."

"It is. And the request coming from you had an added bonus. He's been giving me a hard time lately about practicing with his shields. But now, in his efforts to protect you, he's actively scanning people to look for Noor, so he's exercising them without even realizing it."

"He said he could see if Noor was inside of someone. How does that work?"

"Jacob's ability is to see a person's true self," Anna explained. "Whatever they are deep down. When Noor possesses someone, he takes over their minds. So instead of seeing that person, Jacob will perceive the head of the beast Noor likes to manifest."

"Big and bear-like, with ram horns and radar antennae ears?"

"Yes, that would be the one." Anna shot a glance at Evan. "You've seen it?"

"Only in my dreams. It chases me sometimes. I swear it's going to devour me, but I can usually wake myself up before that happens."

"That day in the cell," Evan guessed. "That's what had you screaming."

Kyra bobbed her head once. "Not one of my better days. But yeah, he was chomping down on my ass when you pulled me out."

She tilted her head and sent him a thoughtful look. "You seem to be developing a habit of saving me."

"Always." Evan lost himself in the potent depths of her eyes, forgetting anyone else was there until Anna spoke.

"Okay…" The word drug out in a sing-song voice and Anna stood. "I'll just…go…somewhere else." Before leaving she turned back to Kyra. "We'd like it if you stayed. *Big Jake* is more protected here than anywhere else. Between the warding and our family that's in and out all day, he's safe. And so will you be."

"Sorry about the nickname." Kyra winced. "It's just something I do. And he was trying to be big and tough. It just seemed to fit."

"Don't apologize—he loved it. And I know exactly what you mean," Anna laughed. "He was so puffed up and proud when he insisted we call him that. It was so cute. I'm just glad we got him to compromise. It took some doing, but we settled on Jake."

Anna opened the door and glanced at Kyra. "Please consider what I said."

Kyra nodded. "I will."

With a last good-bye, Anna was gone.

Evan turned back to Kyra with a lopsided smirk. "You heard her. You have to stay."

"That's not what she said," Kyra argued, laughing.

"It's what I heard." Evan took her hands in his and brought them to his lips to kiss her knuckles. "You really want to make her mad by leaving?" He watched her pupils expand as need swamped her. "She's small, but she's fierce."

Kyra's breath hitched. "Well, when you put it that way, I guess I'd better not cross her."

Evan released one hand to cup the back of her neck and pull her closer. "Good choice."

When he pressed his lips to hers, she opened up for him. Evan shifted forward and had her underneath him on the couch.

She drew in a breath as he trailed kisses down her throat. "You know, there's a perfectly good bed right over there. Lots more room. Why don't we try it out?"

Evan lifted his head and smiled down at her. "Second best idea you've had in the last few minutes."

15

Hours later, Kyra sat naked on the bed with Evan lounging beside her. They were eating reheated spaghetti that Anna had thought to stock in the fridge.

She couldn't believe the turn her life had taken. It wasn't that long ago that she'd been sitting in that jail cell wondering what the hell she was going to do. Now here she was, having incredible sex with this unbelievably hot guy—in spite of the fact that he was a cop—and eating leftovers.

Kyra would have never dreamed she could be here. Like this.

She didn't expect it to last, but she'd enjoy the ride until then.

Between the sex and the pasta, Kyra was feeling energized. So much so that she felt like working out. Her body was healing, the bruises were fading, and she wanted to see what she could do with some real equipment.

A quick glance at the clock told her it was after ten p.m. "Do you think there's anyone downstairs?"

"Why?" Evan took another bite of noodles and marinara.

"I want to stretch and move my muscles."

Evan gave her a leering grin as he leaned on his elbow next to her. "Didn't we just do that?"

"Ha-ha." She gave his shoulder a bump. "It's *because* of what we just did that I have the extra energy to hit the gym. I'm feeling pumped. I've never gone this long without working out before."

He set his bowl aside and sat up. "Oh yeah? What do you usually do?"

"Some cardio kickboxing, jogging, weights."

Evan gave the injuries he could see a once-over.

"I'm fine. Whatever you guys did really helped. I look worse than I feel at this point. The bruises have healed to a sickly yellow, but there's no pain." Kyra leaned over and kissed him before whispering tauntingly, "Or are you just afraid I'll show you up?"

Evan gripped the back of her head and gave her a smacking kiss. "Bring it, babe." He rolled off the bed and pulled on his sweats.

Kyra stared up at him from where she still sat on the bed. "Unless you want me to kick your ass while naked—which would make your defeat all the more humiliating—I'm going to need some shorts and a tank."

The fact that he actually considered it made her laugh. "You men are just a bunch of pervs, you know that?"

"Guilty." He smirked at her, but he also conjured what she needed.

A few minutes later, they descended the steps into the gym. The security lights that ran all night were plenty enough to see by.

The most prominent feature of the layout was the raised boxing ring. She'd bet that had seen a lot of action over the years. The blue floor was worn where hundreds of feet had danced and dodged while training. The red and blue ropes hung silent now, but how many bodies had been pressed into them while getting pummeled?

Situated next to the ring was an MMA caged octagon. She wondered briefly how many opponents had sweated and bled on that black mat.

On the other side of the room was an open-matted area. On

the far end, heavy bags and speed bags hung from the ceiling. The free weights and benches were set up opposite that.

And that's where Kyra headed first.

"Let's start out slow." Evan must have been anticipating an argument because he went on before she could open her mouth. "You're still healing. We don't want to set you back."

"Relax. I wasn't going to give you a hard time. It's been longer than I want to admit since I worked out. I'm not going to overexert myself."

He seemed to believe her so he let it drop. She moved to the dumbbells and picked up a ten-pound weight in each hand. Kyra got into position and started doing bicep curls. As she switched from one exercise to the next, she lost track of time. It felt so good to feel the burn of worked muscles.

Evan brought her a bottle of water and together they fell to the floor to catch their breath.

"That feels really good." Kyra stretched out one arm and then the other. "I'll be sore tomorrow, but it'll be a good sore."

"I know what you mean. I recently started letting Joe kick my ass." Evan laughed at himself. "I thought I was in pretty decent shape until I came here. That idea faded during my very first workout when I left here thinking I might die before I made it home."

Kyra chuckled. "It couldn't have been *that* bad."

Evan took a drink. "Oh yeah. I crawled into bed that night swearing Joe was a sadistic bastard and vowing I'd never come back. But I did, and now I kind of crave that ache. It lets me know I've gotten stronger. Gotten better. I'll need every advantage I can get in this fight against Noor."

He studied her for a moment. "Speaking of...how's your hand-to-hand? At some point his men are going to come for you. My family and I will try to be there when it happens, but it never hurts to know some self-defense."

"I know." Kyra told herself she was prepared for that. "I

made sure a long time ago that I could take care of myself."

Evan rose to stand over her. "Show me."

"What? Like a test?" Kyra set her water out of the way, leaned back on her hands, and looked up at him. "I don't think so, Ace. Like you once told me, I'm not some trained monkey that performs on command."

"That's too bad. I want to see what you've got." He held his hand out to her as if to help her up.

She'd show him precisely what she had.

Shrugging, she gripped his hand in hers. Before he knew her intent, she jerked him forward and at the same time, planted her feet in his stomach. With one smooth motion, she flipped him over her head. He landed with a thud but quickly rolled to his feet again.

Not bad. Kyra was already crouched and anticipating his next move. When he struck out with a roundhouse kick, she deflected it by pushing his leg up and over her head. While he was still regaining his balance, Kyra swept her foot out trying to catch his and knock him to the ground.

But he was faster than she thought and evaded her take-down move. They went back and forth for several minutes. Kyra landed flat on her back at one point, only to return the favor a short time later.

Punches and kicks flew. They'd pulled them more in the beginning until they learned what the other was capable of. He had some moves, but then again, so did she. And some of them were a little underhanded.

When he swung at her, she ducked and moved in close to him, cupping his package. All movement stopped. Chest to chest, their panting breaths were loud in the empty room.

"You're going to want to be careful there," Evan warned in a husky voice.

"Oh, really," she taunted with a smirk and gave him a sensuous squeeze.

He banded his arms tightly around her and plastered her to his body. The dark arousal glinting in his eyes told of how much he was affected. When his head started towards hers, Kyra wrapped her leg around his, lunged, and took them both down.

They landed hard and Evan swore. "Fuck. Some warning next time?"

Kyra grinned and shifted. She came up sitting on his thighs. "Wouldn't have worked if I'd warned you."

Evan turned the tables and reversed their positions. Suddenly she was under him. He held her hands over her head and fit himself between her legs, pinning her with the weight of his body.

"Kind of like that?"

"Exactly like that." Kyra twined her legs around his waist and thrust her hips up into his. She felt the hard edge of his erection growing against her.

She was waiting for his kiss when he lowered his mouth to hers. Everything was going just the way she'd planned when Evan stopped, dead still.

He separated their mouths a fraction and spoke in a hushed voice. "Someone's here."

Kyra stiffened. "What? Who?" she asked in the same toneless whisper.

"I felt the wards go off. Goons would be my guess."

She didn't ask any more questions; she just got ready. Since he was still staring down into her eyes, she gave him a nod to let him know she was with him.

"There's still some time before they enter the building. I want you to get upstairs and lock the door. My sisters and brother will have gotten the same alert—they'll be on their way."

"And you thought what, to fight them on your own? Well, I'm not going anywhere, Ace. I think I've just shown you I can handle myself."

"You're sore and tired. Let me take care of this."

"Not gonna happen." Kyra pushed on his shoulder, telling him to let her up.

He must have read the resolve in her eyes because he breathed out a sigh and rolled to the side. They both gained their feet.

Kyra swiped at her hair, dislodging where the short brown strands had stuck to her face. "Now tell me where the fuck they are."

"Two in the back, three in the front."

"Is Noor with them?"

Evan shook his head. "Impossible to know."

Kyra nodded. She wasn't looking forward to encountering Noor again, but his stooges were another matter. She had a few scores to settle with those fuckwits. She could almost guarantee that some of them here tonight had allowed Noor to use them as he beat her.

But because she knew Evan was right in that she was sore and tired, she bargained. "If you think you can handle three, I'll take the two."

He gave her a withering glare and then lifted his head as if scenting the enemy. "They're in."

Neither said another word as they split off. Kyra stopped to grab one of the dumbbells she'd used earlier and went to the short hall that led to the back exit. They'd be bottled up coming in this way. If she could take the first one out with a surprise attack, she might get lucky.

She leaned her back against the wall just to the side of the darkened hallway and waited. Kyra shook her head at the noise they made coming in. Granted, they probably thought she was asleep, but seriously? It was enough to wake the dead.

As their elephant-like treads drew closer, Kyra got a good grip on the weight. Just as the first clod emerged, she swung it up and caught him under the chin. She had the pleasure of hearing his teeth snap together hard enough to chip a few before his head flew back and he crumpled to the floor.

His buddy, right behind him, ignored the fallen man and leapt at her. She had a second to react and did it a moment too late. He bowled into her and down they went. Only this time, she was the one on the bottom when they slammed into the floor.

Fuck, that hurt.

As Kyra fought to regain her breath, she looked up into a face she recognized. This was indeed one of Noor's meatsuits. The one that had whipped her bloody.

Rage lent her the strength she needed to push him up and away from her. She came up off the floor like an erupting volcano and rained lava-hot hell all over him.

Kyra didn't know how long she'd been wailing on him when Evan's voice calling her name finally got through to her. As the fury cleared away, she saw Noor's goon was a pile of quivering pulp at her feet.

Evan approached her slowly. "You got him, baby. He's done."

Strong arms wrapped around her and held her tight. In that moment, she was done too. She slumped into Evan's embrace and let him hold her.

"It's okay," he crooned in her ear. "I've got you."

It wasn't long before Kyra became aware of the others. With an effort, she straightened away from Evan. He was reluctant to relinquish his hold, but eventually let her stand on her own. Kyra looked over at his family and smiled weakly.

"A little late to the party, huh?" she chided them.

"How were we to know you'd take care of all five of them before we could get here?" Joe came to her and motioned to her hands. "May I?"

Kyra lifted them and was shocked to see how bruised and swollen they were. Splits in the skin seeped blood.

"Yeah, sure."

While Joe carefully inspected her knuckles, she turned to Evan. "What happened to the three I gave you?"

"They were taken care of." Evan stepped in close to see how bad her hands were and grimaced. *Yup, that pretty much sums up how they feel too.*

"What do we do with them?" Aria asked.

"I say we call it in," Seth suggested. "They broke in here. Joe can press charges and they'll be thrown in jail."

"Sounds good to me." Joe glanced up from working on Kyra's hands. "Five more of Noor's army off the street and out of our hair."

Aria went upstairs with Kyra while the others dealt with the aftermath down below. When she lowered slowly down onto the couch, Aria came to help.

"Are you okay?"

"Yeah, muscles are starting to stiffen up." Kyra breathed out as she leaned back into the softness of the cushion. "Evan and I had already worked out pretty hard before those ass-hats even showed up. The second part of the show was a little more than my body could handle. I'm definitely feeling it now."

"Will you let me help you?"

Kyra smiled softly. "I shouldn't, but I will."

Aria sat next to her and laid one hand on Kyra's arm and the other on her thigh. Kyra floated in a state of relaxed calm for a bit until Aria was finished.

When she heard the door open, she didn't feel quite so wrung out anymore. She was actually able to sit up as Evan, Seth, Joe, and Anna came in.

"What happened?"

"A couple of uniforms hauled them off and will get them booked in." Evan made a beeline for her. "Joe will go down in the morning to make a statement and press charges."

"Well, other than the one you beat the hell out of," Seth chuckled. "He's on his way to the hospital."

Kyra didn't feel at all guilty for what she'd done. "Good. That was the asshole that Noor rode when he whipped me."

Any levity that had found its way into the room vanished and Evan went still next to her. Glancing over at him, she saw his temper flaring behind his dark eyes.

They talked for a little while longer until Anna said they needed to get back home to Jacob. Their parents were there sitting with him as he slept.

As his siblings left, Evan remained silent and brooding. Kyra didn't know what to say to him, and it seemed the others didn't either as they sent her silent shrugs.

Soon they were alone again and Kyra couldn't take it another minute. She rounded on him. "Okay, Ace, spill it. What's got you wadded up? We beat them. They're sitting in jail. Or the hospital."

His face hardened more, if possible. *Ah ha.* So it was the jerk she'd pounded into the ground.

"It should have occurred to me..." He stopped like he couldn't go on.

"What? That at least some of them would have been the ones to hurt me? Well, it did for me, and I was ready for it. Hell, I was hungry for it. I had some payback to dish out."

Evan stalked around the room. "You were hurt so badly. If I'd known he was the one to put those marks..."

"You would have what? Beat him senseless? Pounded him into the ground? I did that. Why do you think it was your job to do? It was *my* back they ripped to shreds."

He winced at that and some of her mad fell away. If she'd come to realize anything about Evan Burke, it was that he was a throwback kind of man. He needed to protect those close to him. She went to him and, standing in front of him, wrapped her arms around his waist.

"Hey. I didn't get a look at the three you fought, but I'm sure any one of them had something to do with my condition when you found me."

Some of the cold anger had left his eyes. "Are you trying to placate me?"

Kyra held back the grin. "Maybe. Is it working?"

"No." A touch of humor made its way in.

"Well," she pressed in closer to him, "what can I do then to make you feel all big and manly?"

"I should be the one trying to comfort *you*." His hands went to her upper arms and massaged the strained muscles there.

Kyra closed her eyes and groaned in pained ecstasy. "Oh, God, that feels good."

"Strip."

She opened her eyes and cocked her head at his order.

"You heard me." He set her away from him with a firm hand. "Get out of those clothes and go lay on the bed. Face down."

When she didn't move, he upped the ante. "Unless you'd rather skip out on a full body massage."

Kyra didn't have to be told again. She was naked and flat on top of the blankets so fast Evan laughed.

He followed a little slower and sat on the edge of the mattress. When his hands found her shoulders, they were exceedingly warm and vanilla-scented. He must have come up with some heated oil to rub her down with.

For the next hour Kyra hummed, and groaned, and purred as Evan's skilled and fantastic fingers dug in and released all the knotted tension in her body. Neck, back, arms, legs, feet. Nothing was missed, nothing was neglected.

At some point she just floated off, and the next time she opened her eyes it was morning. Evan was lying beside her on his back. His face was slightly turned towards her. Those deep dark eyes were still closed in sleep, and his bare chest rose and fell with each breath.

She let her gaze travel over him, taking in every aspect. From the black stubble that covered the lower half of his face, to the strong neck and shoulders. There was a light dusting of black hair on his chest, right in the center. She followed the trail of it down his abdomen and past his navel where it thickened again to point to parts farther south.

Just at his hip bones lay a thin blanket that covered them both. Reaching down, Kyra moved it to reveal the prize beneath. Even in sleep, he was incredible.

She had a sudden urge to taste him.

Moving slowly, she inched down the bed. Taking him into her hand, she began to fondle and stroke him. Too much to resist, she leaned in and wrapped her lips around him.

It wasn't long before his body began to stir. He grew and hardened as she enjoyed bringing them both pleasure.

She felt a hand in her hair and knew his mind had woken too. Kyra tipped her head back to look up the long length of him to his face. His black eyes were on hers and they were heated with arousal. Gazes locked, Kyra swirled her tongue around him and took him deeper.

The first sound in the room was Evan groaning.

But it wasn't the last as they gently and languidly made love.

16

As a way to start the morning, it had a hell of a lot going for it, Evan thought as he parked his car in the lot at the police station. And he was still smiling when he walked past Seth on his way to his own desk.

"I know that look," his partner teased. "Good morning?"

"Dude. Gentleman." Evan smirked and sat down. "And besides, I'm not getting into that with you, as it's my sister you're sharing *your* bed with."

Seth laughed. "Yeah, that would be a little awkward."

"Has Joe been in yet?" Evan glanced over at Seth.

"He's on his way."

A few hours later, Joe had come and gone. The reports had been taken and filed, and the perps were sitting in cells downstairs awaiting arraignment. With that business done, Evan dug in to the never-ending paperwork this job produced.

He didn't know how long he'd been working when the energy in the room changed. The noise level rose and an overall attentiveness took over. Curious, Evan looked up and swore as his good morning went to shit.

Kyra was walking towards him, big as day and calm as glass. She sauntered right up to his desk and stopped.

"Detective Burke. I understand you're looking for me."

He didn't have to feign the shocked look on his face. It was all too real. He couldn't believe what she'd just done. And when he looked over at Seth, he too, was speechless. Evan rose slowly out of his chair. But because every eye was on them, he couldn't ask her what the hell she'd been thinking. This was not the plan.

"Yes, Miss Pride," he said instead. "You're wanted for questioning regarding the murders of five men." If anyone noticed his words were mashed through clenched teeth, no one said anything.

"Burke." His captain's voice rang out behind him and he turned.

"Yes, sir?"

"Take Miss Pride into interview." The *now* may not have been spoken, but the meaning was very clear.

"Yes, sir." Evan gestured for Kyra to follow him. Seth brought up the rear.

Evan fumed but couldn't take the risk of demanding she explain herself. Too much was at stake, and he knew there would be others involved in the case watching. Including his Captain.

He'd have to bide his time and wait until he was sure they were alone and their conversation private.

As he led her into the room, he glared down at her. She gave it right back, except in hers he also saw the nerves underneath it. She was trying to hide it behind attitude, but he knew her now. He understood her.

She hadn't done this to piss him off. She'd come here to prove that she wasn't going to hide from anyone or anything. Her history with police and other authority figures had established a basic distrust and dislike, but she'd done it anyway. She'd put her trust in him to see that it didn't bite her in the ass as it always had.

Evan wanted to take her into his arms and comfort her, but he couldn't do that either. He had to maintain a professional separation. And it nearly killed him.

"Miss Pride, please have a seat." Evan indicated to the table and chairs. "Can we get you anything? Water, Coffee?"

"No, I'm good." She sat on the far side. "I'd just like to get this over with."

Evan and his partner took their seats across from her and set the machine to record. "This interview is being conducted by Detective Evan Burke and Detective Seth Lawson. Please state your name for the record."

"Kyra Pride."

"Miss Pride, as I'm sure you are aware, new evidence has surfaced regarding the recent murders of five men. It indicates another individual was responsible for the killings we thought you had committed."

"You don't say." Kyra slouched back in the chair and crossed her arms over her chest.

Evan had to bite the inside of his cheek to keep from grinning at the sarcasm in her voice.

He nodded. "Yes, ma'am. We need whatever information you might have regarding this situation. We have our own theories, but we need for you to explain how and why you came to be implicated in these crimes."

"So *now* you want to listen to my side of it, Ace? I think I remember telling you I didn't have anything to do with the deaths of those men."

She was busting his balls. And enjoying it.

"Yes, ma'am, you did. But at the time, the evidence overwhelmingly pointed to you," Evan reminded her.

They had to be very careful here and keep any mention of Noor out of it. His questions needed to be geared towards the flesh and blood man who'd done the actual killing.

"Do you know who could have murdered those men?"

Kyra watched him as if judging his sincerity.

"We're trying to help you, Miss Pride," Seth added. "The sooner you cooperate, the sooner we can find this guy and put him in a cage for the rest of his life."

She eyed the both of them for a moment before letting out a breath and dropping her arms into her lap. "I don't know why he's developed this fixation on me. I'd never seen him before in my life."

"Wait. You've seen him?" Evan made sure to add just enough inflection to make the surprise in his voice seem genuine. "You know what he looks like?"

Seth leaned forward and set his elbows on the table. "If we sit you down with a sketch artist, could you describe him?"

"Yeah." Kyra nodded. "Yeah, I can do that."

When they'd gotten every detail they could from her, Evan let Seth escort her to Martinez. While they came up with a drawing, Evan would update the case file.

It was over an hour later that he saw Seth return alone. Kyra was nowhere in sight, and Evan sent his partner a questioning look.

"She insisted on leaving once the sketch was finished. She said to, uh, tell you it's been great. And that she'd see you around."

"What the hell does that mean?" Evan's gut tightened. Had she walked away? She'd been cleared of the charges, so technically she was free to...*Oh shit*. Evan felt sick. He recalled the reasoning he'd used to convince her to agree to his plan. *You come in, you tell us what you know, and you're free to go.*

What the fuck had he done?

Evan pushed his chair back and stood. "I've got to go." He didn't give Seth a chance to ask what was wrong. Though he probably already knew.

He raced to Knight's and was out of his car almost before he'd parked it. He flew through the door and across the room, causing a stir among the men there as he rushed to the stairs at the back of the gym. Once at the top of the steps, he dove into the apartment.

"Kyra?"

Nothing. She wasn't there.

Evan's heart gave an angry thump. She should have beaten him back here. Where the hell was she?

What the hell did he do now? She didn't have a phone. Hers had been lost somewhere, and they hadn't had time to get her a new one. He couldn't just search for her; he had no clue where to start.

Was she on foot? Or had she gotten transportation? He'd had her bike transported back from Dade City, but he couldn't remember if he'd told her that. It was sitting in the impound lot here in Daytona.

On the off-chance he had mentioned it, Evan took out his phone and called the attendant.

"This is Detective Burke. Has anyone inquired about the motorcycle they brought over from Dade City PD?"

"Funny you should call. A woman just came by and picked it up. She proved ownership and there wasn't a hold on it, so I released it to her."

Fuck. Evan wanted to rage but he thanked him calmly and hung up.

Evan wandered around looking for any sign of Kyra. There was none. There was no evidence that she'd ever been in this room. He tried to remember if she'd given any indication that she was planning to leave. He couldn't think of any, but then again, she'd never said she would stay either.

Was it only lust on her part like she'd told him? Had he read too much into her coming to him the other night? Had she only been scratching an itch? Biding her time until she was clear?

If that's the case, I'm not sticking around this empty fucking apartment like some love-struck douche.

She didn't want him, fine. He had a life to get back to. He still had a case to solve, so he'd go back to work and forget about her.

Evan retraced his steps through the gym, ignoring anyone who called to him. He took some satisfaction in slamming his car door before driving back to the station.

He felt Seth's eyes on him, but his partner didn't say anything until Evan had resumed his seat behind his desk.

"Is she gone?"

"It appears that way." Evan grabbed the top case file off the stack and opened it. He stared down at it without really seeing it. "She picked up her bike and left."

Seth didn't say anything else and Evan was grateful. They worked in silence for the rest of the day, and even after Seth had gone home to Aria, Evan remained.

How the hell had this day turned to shit? It had started out so well. Evan couldn't believe it had only been hours since he'd awoken to Kyra's mouth on his body. And now she'd vanished again.

With all avenues of the case covered, Evan shut it down and headed home. He was about halfway there when his phone rang.

He glanced at the number but didn't recognize it.

"Burke."

"Hey, Ace. Where ya at?" Kyra's voice came through the speaker, easy-going and light. "I thought you'd come back to the apartment after you were done at work. I got us some take-out. It's getting cold."

Evan stomped on the brakes, pissing off the people behind him to the sound of horn blasts. "Where the hell have you been?"

She hesitated a beat, clearly hearing the snap in his tone. "Normally, I wouldn't respond to being barked at that way," she bit back. "But I'll give you this one. I picked up my bike first. After that, I ran by the place where I'd stashed some of my gear. I stopped and got a new phone, since I don't know what happened to mine. And lastly, I ordered some fucking

Chinese. Now I'm sitting here waiting for your ass."

He couldn't breathe. She hadn't left. He didn't even care that she was pissed at him.

When he didn't respond, Kyra's tone changed. "Evan, what's wrong? Has something happened?"

The sound of his name on her lips righted his world like nothing else could have. She didn't say it often, so maybe that was why it held such power over him.

He gathered himself. "No, nothing's happened." Checking for traffic, Evan turned around. "I'll be right there."

"See you in a bit then."

Seeing her bike when he pulled into the gym parking lot settled him even more. She'd had the opportunity to resume the free lifestyle she'd led before, and instead she'd decided to stay here. With him.

Evan's entrance was just as rushed but for vastly different reasons. He knew she was up there waiting for him this time. Taking the stairs two at a time, Evan swept into the room. He crossed right to her, wrapped his arms around her waist, and pulled her in close. Burying his face in the crook of her neck, he just breathed her in.

She held him just as tight. "You want to tell me what's going on?"

Slightly embarrassed by his reaction, Evan reluctantly let her go. "I thought you'd left."

Her face registered surprise. "What? Like for good?"

"Yeah." Feeling foolish and a little mad now, he took a couple of paces away. "That message you passed on through Seth sounded pretty final. 'Thanks, it's been great?' What the hell was that?"

"That was me sticking to the plan, Ace." Kyra put her hands on her hips. "You said no one could know we'd been in contact. I was just doing what you told me to and playing my part."

His baseless anger fell away and now Evan felt like a

complete ass. "I know that. Now. At the time, it just hit me in the gut. I thought you were gone. And then you weren't here, and I found out you'd picked up your bike."

"I figured it would be a good time to get some stuff done." She shrugged, unconcerned. "I know how to be careful, Ace. I've been doing it a long time."

Evan swung back around to face her. "Is that why you decided to jump the gun and come in on your own today? I about shit when I saw you there."

"I didn't see any reason to wait. And it all worked out."

Evan shook his head. He should have known he wouldn't get anywhere arguing with her about her trip to the PD. She was headstrong and wasn't going to let anyone tell her what to do.

And he really couldn't blame her.

"I'll agree that it all worked out. Your name is clear, and we know what this bastard looks like, thanks to you."

"Yeah, but how long will it take to find him?"

"We're doing everything we can, including having the house staked out. If anyone shows up there, orders are to follow and see where they go."

"And if no one does?"

"We've got a few other options." Evan didn't want to have to think about those until all...normal possibilities were exhausted.

"And those are?"

"Not something I want to get into right now."

"Look, Ace—"

"Kyra." He took her hands in his. "No one else you know is going to die."

"How can you—"

"Trust me."

The way her whiskey-colored eyes hardened, Evan knew her first instinct had been to disregard the words. The whole concept, really. But slowly the cold warmed again and Evan watched as she battled that learned response back.

"That's not easy for me."

"I understand, and I want you to know how much I appreciate you taking the chance."

Before either could say anything else, Evan's phone alerted to a text. Sliding it from his pocket, he saw it was a group message from his mom calling an impromptu family meeting.

"We'll have to table the rest of this discussion. We need to head over to my parents' house."

"We?"

"Yup."

"I can't imagine she'd want me involved in a discussion that concerns your family."

"There you would be wrong. You're a part of this now, so suck it up, buttercup. It's time to meet the parents."

Kyra looked like she wanted to slap him. Self-preservation had him backing away and heading for the door. Only grinning when she couldn't see it.

17

A few minutes later, he was pulling into the driveway of his childhood home. Knowing she'd not had the same kind of upbringing, Evan tried to see it through Kyra's eyes.

The white, ranch-style home was open and welcoming. His parents had planted the landscaping themselves years ago and had enlisted the help of him and his siblings to keep it weeded and clean.

As he walked her up the sidewalk and into the house, Evan took in the large and airy living room. With four kids and assorted friends in and out all the time, this main gathering place fit them all with no problem.

Branching off the living room to the right was a hall that led to three bedrooms and the extra they'd converted into a library. When he and his quad-mates had been born, Burkes far and wide had sent family journals to Mary. The hope was that something written inside would help them to defeat Noor. They'd needed space for them and for the tools witches required to aid their magic.

Straight back from the great room was the dining area, and through another door was the kitchen. Beyond that was the backyard that butted up against the Intracoastal Waterway. Many a day had been spent out there.

From what he'd read in her files and what she'd let slip, Evan knew she'd missed out on so much of what he'd taken for granted.

The door opening behind them interrupted Evan's thoughts. Ethan stepped in and closed it again.

Just then his mom came in from the kitchen and crossed to where they were standing. "Perfect, you made it."

"Like we had a choice," Ethan jokingly muttered.

Their mom cocked a brow at her youngest son. "You have something better to do, smartass?"

Ethan sobered up. "No, ma'am."

"Good. We're all out back. Dad's got hot dogs on the grill for those of you who haven't eaten yet. It's a nice night; we can talk out there." Mary turned and smiled in greeting at Kyra.

"Hi, I'm Mary Burke. You must be Kyra. So nice to finally meet you."

"Thank you for inviting me, Mrs. Burke." Whatever nerves Kyra had been feeling before didn't show now. And the tone in her voice was one he hadn't heard before. Courteous and polite.

"Please, call me Mary." His mother encompassed them all with her glance. "Grab something to drink and then come on out." She swung around and left the way she'd come.

Evan looked at his twin and grinned. "You never learn. You know she sees and hears everything."

"You bet your ass I do," came the loud reply from the other room.

"Told you," Evan mouthed to his brother.

"I like her," Kyra decided.

"Of course you do," Evan teased. "She busts my chops as often as you do."

"Well, you and Skippy seem to need it."

"How did I get involved in this?" Ethan protested.

"You started it...Skippy," Evan chided.

Ethan sent him what was affectionately known as 'stink-eye.' Evan just smiled happily and took Kyra's hand to escort her out to the backyard.

His sisters and Seth were seated around the table laughing and chatting. Joe and Jacob, Evan saw, were close to the water's edge collecting shells into a canning jar. Evan, Ethan, and Kyra went and sat with the girls and Seth.

It was only a short time later that Paul was carrying a tray of grilled dogs—already wrapped in toasted buns—over to the table. As he set them down amidst the chips, salads, and condiments, he addressed those seated. "Since I already know what your mom wants to talk about, I'll keep Jacob busy." He shook his head and chuckled. "Besides, I need a rematch. He's beaten me the last two times on that dang video game. I don't know how he does it, but I swear I'm going to take him this time."

After snagging two hot dogs, he moved off to collect Jacob. Evan and the others laughed because they knew just how seriously their dad took gaming. He'd never gone easy on any of them. If they beat him, they did it on their own and felt all the better for it.

As Joe approached and sat, Jacob dragged Paul into the house, chattering all the way.

They all tried to keep the worst of this mess away from Jacob. He knew more than he needed, but being targeted by Noor, they realized they couldn't shield him completely. But that sweet child would damned-well have a normal, happy life if they all had to die to make it happen. He'd suffered too much already and was finally coming out from under it.

With the food on the table, they all settled in. Evan was hungry. Kyra had ordered them dinner, but thanks to their miscommunication, neither had had a chance to eat anything. He took a couple of dogs and put two more on Kyra's plate.

She sent him a narrowed look. "I know how to feed myself, Ace."

"Obviously, not well enough." Evan cast a glance down at her skinny frame.

"Leave the girl alone, Evan," Mary admonished from across the table.

"Yeah." Kyra sent him a cheeky grin. "Leave the girl alone."

Evan could see that having these two ganging up on him was going to keep him on his toes. But no matter how much he thought about it, he just couldn't make himself care.

He sent Kyra a sexy smirk at the same time Mary got things started. Evan took a big bite and transferred his attention to his mom. He didn't know what had prompted the late get-together, but it had to be important.

Mary wasted no time.

"As you know, we've been having trouble digging up any information on the trials Noor underwent to gain his supernatural abilities. When we finally admitted to ourselves we were in over our heads, we asked a friend of ours to see what he could find." She paused to take a breath. "He thinks he may have found something."

Aria voiced the question they were all thinking. "You know how he got his power?"

Mary shook her head. "Not yet. But it's another clue to hopefully follow to the source. It was written in an old and archaic language, and it's taken him weeks to piece together and translate as much as he's gotten. He was about ready to set it aside when the mention of five tests caught his notice. He dug a little further and found what he thinks is a name."

"What he *thinks* is a name?" Ethan was leaned forward, arms resting on the table.

"The translation isn't so much a name as it is a...title. The Bringer."

Seth copied Ethan's posture. "The bringer of what?"

"Sin, evil, death, destruction, the end of the world. Take your pick." Joe's voice rang with frustration and Evan could completely understand.

A pall fell over the group. Finding this information was

turning out to be harder than they'd expected. The original idea had been that knowing where the power came from could help to counteract it when the big fight came. But who knew if having that knowledge would even make a difference.

Like his mom had said, though, it gave them and the researcher another jumping-off point.

"On that happy note," Anna broke the silence, "since we're all together, why don't we do something a little more pro-active? I think this might be a good time for Evan and Ethan to try to link up."

Evan knew the last failure had been entirely his fault. He'd been so confused and hiding so much, it hadn't allowed the merge to happen. And if his journey with Kyra so far had taught him anything, it was that matters of the heart were complicated, and he could no longer fault Ethan for falling into Noor's trap when he'd offered Honor up as bait.

He looked over at his twin. "You up for it?"

Ethan took a quick pull on his beer and stood. "Bring it on."

Everyone except Kyra stood and moved out into the yard. Evan bent to her and whispered in her ear, "You're going to want to see this."

She jerked her head back to look him in the eye. A question rode the potent brown depths so Evan wiggled his nose at her.

Kyra quirked a brow at him. "Witchy stuff?"

"Hold on to your hat, baby. The show's about to start."

He and Ethan moved into position with the others circled around them. Kyra moved up next to his mom just over Ethan's shoulder. Evan sent her one last wink and then gave his full focus to his twin.

Facing each other, they grasped hands. Evan felt Ethan slide into his head.

A smile spread over his brother's face.

"What?"

"All this love floating around. First Ari, then Anna, and now

you. Must be something in the air." Evan felt Ethan's chuckle. *"You can bet I'll be holding my breath."*

Evan's gaze tracked to Kyra before returning to his twin. *"Yeah. Good luck with that, bro. The fates work in mysterious ways."*

"Alright, let's show those girls they're not the only ones who can master this." Ethan grinned.

Being inside Ethan's head, Evan knew he wasn't quite as light-hearted as he was pretending. He could feel the love and loss Ethan had suffered. And was still suffering. He was putting a good face on it, but it was still there.

"It can't be too hard if they did it." Evan played along. *"Ready?"*

At Ethan's nod, they called to their magic. Evan first.

"Sand and soil, dirt and stone
Neither you nor I will stand alone
I am Earth and Earth is me
As I will, so mote it be."

Then Ethan.
"Smoke, spark, ember, flame
You and I forever the same
I am Fire and Fire is me
As I will, so mote it be."

Earth and fire answered immediately and formed whirling, swirling manifestations that enveloped them both.

Evan would never tire of feeling his power take him over. The only thing that had ever come close to the exhilaration he felt when he called to his magic was being with Kyra. Each filled him with power and energy and left him all the better for it.

He peered through the twisting mass and saw her. Her eyes

were wide as she saw some of what he could do. Evan laughed to himself. *Just wait, babe, you haven't seen anything yet.*

They let the tempests rage, basking in another essential part of themselves. But soon they took control and gathered the storms into more manageable sizes over their heads.

Powers at the ready, they opened their minds to each other. Ethan's hurt and heartache became Evan's, and Evan's contentment as well as his uncertainty about his situation with Kyra became Ethan's.

Heads, hearts, souls, and magics came to be one. Evan was no longer himself and neither was Ethan. They were one and the same. Two halves that had come back together to form into its original whole.

Identical twins split from one egg. Evan and Ethan were as they hadn't been since that one microscopic being had become two. Above them, the once separate elements were now melded into a single, undulating force.

They knew from their sisters that controlling that force would take both of them, but it was easier than they would have thought. Their minds were already working as one, every thought, every command, was just there.

Evan and Ethan spent some time testing out this new connection. Conjuring and Telekinesis belonged to them both now, each able to tap into the other's power as quickly as if it had always been their own.

Evan had an idea of something to try, and Ethan was already agreeing. In a fight, they couldn't very well stand in one place, holding hands. They had to know if they could put some distance between them and still maintain or establish the link. To test out the first idea, they released one set of hands and then the other.

It held.

Next they backed up a couple of paces. When the link continued despite the distance, they released the bond, becoming themselves again. Once fully detached, they cast out for each other's minds. It was a little more difficult with so much separation between them—they had to push harder, but the merge happened.

Very useful information that the girls could also put into practice.

As one, they turned and met the triumphant smiles of their loved ones. They'd done it. They were one more step closer to mastering the power they would need to defeat Noor for good.

"Should we try combining all?" Evan and Ethan said together, their voices perfectly blending.

"Whoa," Kyra muttered.

Seth laughed. "Yeah, it's pretty trippy. Huge creep factor. It takes a bit to get used to."

Aria and Anna came to stand with them.

"So I guess that means we don't have to touch to form the bond?" Anna asked.

"No," the guys' unified voices answered. "You'll have to reach out more, but it can be done."

The girls nodded and, standing face to face, brought forth their air and water. Soon it was twisting and dancing as one in the night sky as they too joined together.

This is where it would become more difficult. Because even though the four of them had been carried in their mother's womb at the same time, they'd have to find a way to overcome the obstacle of the two sets of twins being in every way the opposite of each other.

That hurdle proved to be the stopping point as they tried to unite four into one this night. No matter how they tried, their connection would go no further than the mental link they'd already established to speak to one another.

"It's no use fighting it," Evan and Ethan advised. *"We'll find it, but not tonight."*

"We don't have much time left," Aria and Anna argued.

"We've enough. We'll get it. We're meant to."

The girls reluctantly agreed and each released the connection they held.

Seated around the table again, the group brainstormed ideas for how to bring all four elements together. They talked for a bit but since it had grown late, everyone decided to leave that discussion for another time.

A short while later, Evan was walking Kyra out to his car. He wondered what she was thinking. She hadn't said anything since that one comment.

She spent the drive to the gym staring out the side window, silent. By the time Evan pulled into the parking lot, he was worried. Had it freaked her out seeing them in their full witch-selves?

He put the car into park and turned in his seat to face her. "I know that was probably more than you bargained for. What we did—"

Evan didn't get a chance to finish. Kyra was across the console and straddling his lap before he could utter another word.

"That was the most erotic fucking thing I have ever seen in my entire life." Kyra was eating at his mouth and then dropped to his neck and blazed a trail of frenzied kisses and bites.

Breathing heavily, she leaned back so she could see him. Her eyes were alight with arousal and fierce need.

"You glowed." She placed her left hand over the earth birthmark on his right bicep and stared down at it. "Here." Her eyes closed and her head fell back as her hips swirled down into his. "God, that was so fucking hot. Watching you wield all that magic. So much power right at your fingertips." Another grind and her hands left his body to glide up her own. "Mmm, I could feel it. It made the hairs all over my body stand straight up."

When they traveled over her rib cage and up, Evan's cock

hardened to a steel spike. He grasped her waist in his fists when she cupped her own breasts and moaned.

Evan shifted under her to get a better position and rapped his knee on the underside of the dash.

"Ow, shit."

Kyra went to work on the button of his jeans. "You have too many clothes on."

"Wait. Hold on." His left hand dropped down next to his seat. "Let me just…" He fumbled to find the button to move the seat. "Come on, come on."

"I'm trying, if you'd cooperate." She gave up and massaged him through his clothes.

He finally found the stupid switch and adjusted it to give them more room. Six foot four wasn't meant to have sex in a car, but he'd give it his best shot as Kyra was quickly killing his brain cells.

She caught his mouth with hers again and successfully wiped everything from his mind. Between kisses and bites, she panted impatiently, "Hurry. Hurry."

Evan fought to open his fly and release his throbbing erection.

"Pants," she ordered. "Get them off."

"I'm getting there." His fingers went to her zipper.

"Twinkle your nose, Ace. Use your fucking magic and get us naked."

"Right. Right." Evan couldn't believe he hadn't thought of that already. He blamed her and the effect she had on him.

With all essential parts finally bared and ready, Kyra lifted up and slammed down on his waiting shaft. Both swore ripely as pleasure swelled.

No matter how many times they did this, he couldn't get over how hard her body squeezed around his. Every time he filled her, it was like pushing into her for the first time. She was so slick, her heat so intense, and so damned tight, he would willingly live out his days buried deep inside of her, letting her milk him dry. The tiny contractions of her inner muscles just about did him in. But he knew if he could hold out and bring her to full orgasm, she would clamp down on him tighter than any fist.

He took hold of her waist again and guided her up and down. As need became demand, she rode him harder and faster. Evan leaned back into his seat and watched this beautiful woman take all he had. And more.

Spent and hollowed out, Evan could only work on getting his breath back as Kyra lay sprawled over his chest. Her head rested on his shoulder and her heart pounded against his.

"I can't move," Kyra mumbled into his neck.

"I've lost feeling in my legs and I think I've gone blind. They'll find us here in the morning."

She actually giggled. He'd never heard her do that before. The sound of it had warmth and contentment spreading through him and settling in his heart.

"You think that's funny. I'll never live it down if Joe has to pull us from this car tomorrow."

That carefree laugh sounded again.

Evan wouldn't have thought it possible, but his body roared back to life. He slowly started to move inside of her again.

Kyra moaned. "You can't be serious."

Evan reached up, grasped her head in his hands, and brought her mouth down to his in a slow and sensual kiss. All humor gone, he showed her what he couldn't say in words just yet.

18

Kyra rolled and stretched as she woke. Remembering last night, she gave a little hum and smiled. She couldn't believe how turned on she'd gotten watching Evan do his witch thing. She'd barely held it together in front of his family. And when they'd been in the car, she'd had to completely block him out or she would have caused them to have an accident.

Smelling him, feeling the heat of him in the confined space of his car had been pure torture. She'd been on fire for him. Her plan had been to wait until they'd gotten up to their room to ravish him, but that had gone out the window as soon as he'd opened his mouth.

Kyra hadn't been able to lock her hormones down for another minute. She'd needed him inside of her before she combusted into flames.

Just the memory of what they'd done had her girly bits tingling. Rolling to her side, she pulled his pillow to her chest and hugged it close. It still smelled of him, which didn't help her current condition.

And he wasn't even there to help her out. He'd left for work a while ago. Kyra had thought about getting up with him but had, instead, gone back to sleep. Now she was twitchy and horny with nothing to do with it.

The clanging of weights outside her door gave her an idea. Maybe she could work some of it off downstairs. Strategy in mind, Kyra threw the covers aside, brushed her teeth, and pulled on her workout gear.

Opening the door, she stepped out onto the landing. Below her were men in various stages of sweating, pumping, and grunting.

She made her way down and over to where Joe was training with some kid in the ring. Kyra stood at the side and watched as they went through different combinations and footwork. The kid wasn't bad, and just the little she saw of Joe told her he had some impressive moves.

With burning off some frustration in mind, Kyra started with a jump rope to get her muscles warmed up and loose. From there, she hit the weight machines.

She was shakily finishing off her last set when Joe walked over.

"Looks like you know your way around a gym." Joe offered her a towel.

Kyra let the stack of weights slap back into place. "I hit 'em where I can." She sat forward and took it from his outstretched hand. "Thanks. You've got a nice place here."

"We like it."

"And thanks for the use of the apartment." She mopped at the sweat on her forehead before catching his eyes again. "I didn't mean to bring my trouble to your door."

Joe slid his hands into the pockets of his shorts. "Don't worry about it. Besides, Noor is everyone's problem right now."

Kyra thought about what Evan had shared with her about what he'd put Anna, Joe, and Jacob through. "I guess. But still…"

Glancing around, she wiped at the sweat dripping down her chest. "I thought Anna and Jacob were usually here in the mornings."

Joe smiled. "They normally are, but with Labor Day done and gone, school has started back up again."

"Oh, I didn't even realize."

Kyra thought about Jake. She'd developed a soft spot for the little guy. "Is he okay there? At the school?"

"Anna's a teacher there too. She's right there if anything happens, and she can put out the call if it's more than she can handle."

"With everything that's gone on, it doesn't worry you to have them away from here?"

"Hell, yeah, it does. If I had my way, they'd be tied to me twenty-four seven. But I know I can't do that. I have to trust in Anna and her ability to protect Jacob, as well as herself. What you've seen from the quads so far only touches the tip of what they can do." He gave a slight laugh. "Let me tell you, there is no way in *hell* I'd go up against those four. Together they're scary as hell, but don't let that take away from the fact that even on their own, they can do some incredible things. Anna pulled a fountain of water right out of the ocean once to take out someone who'd tried to kidnap Jacob. At the same time, she had more of it cradling our son as if he were in her arms."

Joe shook his head. "And your boy, with his earth power." His glance roved around the room. "I've seen him shake this building until I thought it was going to come down around our ears."

A quick memory of her hospital room quaking flashed into her mind. Kyra recalled that Evan had been pissed off and said something about her making him lose control.

That had been him? *Shit.*

Kyra's gaze dropped to the towel in her hand and then returned to Joe. "Do you really think they can end Noor in February?"

There was no hesitation. "Without a doubt."

Did she dare put her full faith and trust in someone like Joe had? As much as she hated to admit it, this situation was way beyond what she could handle. Men with normal human limitations were one thing, but this...this she had no clue how to fight. How could she battle against someone who wasn't really there? Someone who could come into her dreams—where she was her most vulnerable? Or hide behind someone else's face so she wouldn't see them coming until it was too late?

Joe interrupted her thoughts. "They'll have your back, you know. You couldn't have fallen in with more loyal or trustworthy people than the Burkes. You just have to let them help you."

He left her to the rest of her workout after that. Her mind was still reeling a short while later as she mounted the stairs to shower and change.

As the hot water beat down on her, she admitted to herself that though she'd grudgingly allowed Evan and his family into her life, she hadn't completely committed herself to them. She'd held a good portion locked away in hiding for when they all betrayed her. As her past had shown her, it was inevitable that they would.

Was it any wonder Evan had jumped to the conclusion she'd taken off the other night? She'd done nothing to indicate she planned on sticking around.

But that was hard to do when she didn't even know herself. Leaving first had become a way of life for her. Better she make the break than wait for the other person to catch her unaware. Being thrown away by her parents, no matter how neglectful they'd been, had scarred her deeply. And all of life's experiences after that had only reinforced the need to keep herself detached from everyone else.

But then there was Evan Burke. From the first moment she'd plowed into him, he'd been able to slip through her defenses. Even when he'd thought her guilty of murder, he'd come when she'd needed him.

Strapped to that chair, alone and in agony, Kyra had figured she was done for. Until she'd taken a chance. A chance on this man.

As Kyra was dissecting her life and her motives, she made a rather startling discovery. Even though she had her bike and her meager belongings, she had no thoughts of running.

What she had instead was an unfamiliar urge to stay.

Standing there now, Kyra did something she'd never had the nerve to do. Think ahead to the future. She'd never seen the need because no matter how many years passed, she was content in the fact that it would always be just her. And why get your hopes up that something better would come along?

Closing her eyes, she tried to see five years from now. She'd be thirty. Probably still hitting the road on her bike, letting the wind take her where it wanted to go. She was enjoying the sensation of the ride when the sound of another motorcycle caught her attention. Kyra turned her head and saw Evan there, cruising with her.

Her heart thumped in her chest at the sight.

She calmed herself. Five years was longer than she'd ever been with anyone, but it was doable. The real test would be farther out. Like ten years. No way would he still be hanging around then.

As Kyra let her mind wander and take her into her own future, the scene started to open up.

She was in a park. Not her usual hangout, but she went with it. There were kids everywhere, running around laughing and screaming. Having a good time, it seemed like. She turned slowly in a circle looking for something, someone.

Then she saw him, and butterflies in her belly took flight. Evan was walking towards her, huge smile on his face as he carried a little girl with long black hair in his arms. Kyra guessed her to be about four or five.

As they drew near, Kyra felt tears burn her eyes and nose. She stared up at him and saw love shining back at her through his black eyes. Blinking back the moisture, Kyra slid her gaze to the child, supported and secure in his strength.

She caught her breath as she saw a miniature version of herself, but with her father's raven hair. Unable to control the movement, Kyra reached up and touched the side of her daughter's face. Her skin was petal soft and baby smooth.

When she could tear her attention away from the beautiful child they'd made, she peered up into Evan's handsome face again. He grinned at her and leaned down to kiss her—to the delighted laughter of the girl between them.

Kyra moved in closer, needing more of him. More of this dream.

Evan was breathing heavily when he pulled away from her mouth. "You'd better be careful there, babe. That's how we got into this situation."

Kyra felt his hand on her stomach and glanced down to see her belly swollen with another child. Her hands instantly went to the protruding mound and rubbed them over the surface. Answering kicks met her palms and she gasped.

"This one had better be a boy after two girls," Evan scolded jokingly.

"Two?"

Evan's eyes tracked over her shoulder. Kyra spun around and saw a girl of about nine running at them, her mahogany hair flying out behind her as a big happy grin lit her face.

Kyra was abruptly brought out of her daydream by a sudden drop in the water temperature of her shower. She came back to herself as tears mixed in with the now-cool water flowing down her cheeks.

Her hands were pressed to her stomach as they had been in the dream. Only now it was no longer distended. No baby rolled and kicked beneath her palms.

As the water chilled even more, Kyra reached out and turned the knobs off. She ignored the fact that her hands were trembling. Stepping out, she wrapped a towel around her body and caught sight of herself in the vanity mirror. What she saw there was a woman who appeared to be in shock.

What did it mean that she'd seen herself in the future with a family? A family with Evan? Did she really want that? With *him*?

The answer hit her right in the heart. She wanted everything she'd seen more than she wanted her next breath.

She never thought she could have anything like that. She'd been alone for so long, she'd stopped thinking about it. Stopped wanting it.

Until Evan. He made her believe she could have it all.

Kyra thought of that young girl again, and her hands returned to her belly. She could still see and feel the life she'd carried there in the dream.

Did she truly want a baby?

She knew the answer before the question had even formed. If it were Evan's child, then yes she did. Quickly on the heels of that revelation, came another shocking epiphany. She loved him.

She was in love with Evan Burke.

Turning away from the mirror, Kyra walked out of the bathroom and crossed to the bed. That's as far as she made it before she had to sit down. She took a couple of deep breaths, trying to calm her suddenly pounding heart and queasy stomach.

"Okay. Wow. I love him." She was still a little off-balance, but she suddenly felt steadier just for having admitted it out loud.

Another cleansing inhale and exhale. Kyra decided to tuck her secret away for now. When she could think about it and not get light-headed, she'd explore the possibility of telling Evan. Until then, she would hold it in her heart.

~~~
~~~

Evan came in a bit after six that evening with take-out bags. They sat down on the couch with boxes of spicy noodles and sweet and sour chicken.

"So I take it there's no news on Noor's hitman?" Kyra asked around a bite of breaded chicken.

"Unfortunately, no." Evan snagged the container out of her hand. To which she gave a dirty look.

"Why not use me as bait?" Kyra said off-handedly as she picked up the noodles he'd set aside for hers. "I'm sure that would draw him out."

Evan gave an absolute and resounding, "No. That's not happening."

His tone set something off in her. "Why not?" She set the food aside and gave him her full attention. "Let me guess. Because I don't have a penis, I can't possibly know my own mind or how to take care of myself. Well, news flash, Ace. I've been doing just that for most of my life, and I'm still here."

On her way to getting pissed, Kyra got up and stalked a few paces away.

Evan followed. "Look. That's not the issue at all. I know very well you can handle yourself."

"Then what's the issue?" Kyra crossed her arms over her chest. "Are you just going to wait until someone else is dead?" Evan trying to control her actions pissed her off, but the thought of another man dying because of her produced a wrenching physical pain. "You may not have known those men." She patted a hand on her chest, over her heart, which was tearing at the thought of what she'd caused. "But I did. I refuse to let anyone else die because of me."

He tried to take her hand and move her back towards the sofa, but Kyra flung her arm out of his grasp.

Evan held his hands out. "I get it. But can we sit down and talk about this?"

Something snapped inside of her. "Fuck that! I'm done

talking." If he wasn't going to take action, then she would. "That asshole needs to pay!" Riding on her sudden and inexplicable rage, she swung around and headed for the door.

Evan halted her momentum by putting his body between her and the door, blocking her only way out.

Kyra shook she was so infuriated. She balled her hands into fists against the side of her thighs. "Get the fuck out of my way, Ace." She drilled him with a glare that should have dropped him on the spot.

"And where the hell do you think you're going?"

His apparent calmness boiled her temper even more. "I'm going to find that son of a bitch and put a stop to this bullshit once and for all. They want me so bad, they'll fucking get me. On a bright and shiny silver platter. Only it'll be their heads I serve up after I rip them from their shoulders. Now get out of my way!"

Kyra reached around Evan for the doorknob but he shifted to cover it.

"No." With his body still against the door, Evan lifted his hands and tried to grab her upper arms. "You're going to let me and the rest of the PD deal with this."

"The hell I am." She wrenched herself out of his grip, turned, and stomped a few feet away from him. When he pursued her, as she'd known he would, Kyra spun back around, leading with a right cross. Her knuckles connected with his cheek with a loud crack.

As he tried to regain his balance, she darted past him. She'd just gotten the door open when he pulled her back into the apartment and slammed it closed again.

Fire lit his eyes now too. "Damn it, Kyra! I'm not letting you go out there like this. You'll get yourself killed, or worse."

The torment of knowing she'd brought about the deaths of good men and the resentment at having her behavior policed became too much to handle, and Kyra went cold inside. She stood and stared Evan down. "You're not *letting* me? You seem to be under the mistaken impression that you have a say over my life and what I do. I come and go as I please, and I'll do whatever the fuck I want. So unless you're prepared to arrest me, I suggest you open that door."

"I can't do that." He took a breath and visibly tried to get a handle on his own anger. "Look, I know you're upset…"

She tilted her head at him and her eyes glittered. "Upset? You have no fucking clue *what* I am. I gave your way a shot, and it's not working."

"It's been two goddamned days, Kyra. You're not making any sense."

"Oh, I'm not making sense now, am I? Well how about this for a little sense? I'm *done*." She cut her hand through the air. "With you. With all of this. Like everything else in my life, I'll take care of this on my own, my way."

"What do you mean you're done?" His hands fisted at his sides and his tone had gone hard but she didn't care. And why should she? He obviously didn't care if she carried around the pain and guilt of five dead men. Why not make it six? Or seven? Hell, how about ten? If he didn't care about her pain, then she sure as shit didn't care about his.

"I don't recall stuttering, but I'll spell it out so your Neanderthal brain can catch up. I don't need or want your help. I don't need or want *you*. Done means I'm leaving this fucked-up place. For good."

Something flashed in his eyes, but she didn't bother to stay and figure out what it was. She needed to leave. She needed to get out.

Kyra made it out the door and down the stairs. She was halfway across the gym floor when she felt the first rumble. She ignored it and kept walking.

19

The floor rolled beneath her feet nearly pitching her to the ground. Kyra turned back to see Evan standing on the landing at the top of the steps. He was staring down at her with a look of utter fury.

Gaining her balance, she again tried to leave, only to be knocked off-kilter. Fighting against the wave, Kyra braced her feet apart and glared up at him.

Crashing sounded around her as equipment fell like dominos. "Go ahead! Tear it apart! It's not *my* fucking gym!"

"Kyra." Anna spoke calmly beside her. She hadn't seen her approach. "Don't do this. You're hurting and lashing out. And now so is he. It doesn't take an empath to feel how much pain you're both in. This isn't the way to handle it." Anna looked up at her brother. "We sent everyone home when I sensed things were getting out of control, but how do you think he would have felt if he'd injured someone with his gifts? You know he'd never forgive himself. Is that what you want for him?"

When Kyra didn't answer, Anna turned back to her. "Do you know what else I can feel underneath all that pain and anger? Love. How else could you wound each other so intensely if you didn't love equally as deep?"

Now that she wasn't actively trying to leave, the shaking and tremors subsided.

Kyra took a breath and her hand went to her stomach as it

heaved and rolled as the floor had done moments before. She suddenly felt sick. She did love Evan. Hadn't she just come to that realization a short while ago? Why was she doing this? Why was she trying to ruin it? She didn't understand how she could have gone off so completely. And the things she'd said...

Kyra glanced up at Evan. He'd pulled his power back, but he still stood glowering down at her.

Anna laid a hand on Kyra's arm. "This should be between you and Evan. Go. Talk to him."

Kyra could only nod as she took another fortifying breath and started back towards him.

When she reached the top of the steps, she held his heated gaze. "If you're done showing off, there's something I need to say."

He said nothing but turned and went back into the apartment.

Now that her own mood had cooled, she recognized she'd stepped in it good. She'd always had a problem with her temper. In the throes, she almost always said things she didn't mean. It had been another way of hurting people before they could hurt her.

Her heart still bled for the lives taken, but it wasn't Evan's fault. None of this was his fault. And all he'd tried to do was help her and seek justice for those who'd lost their lives.

Bracing herself, Kyra followed him in and closed the door. She knew she had a lot of damage control to do. With her back against the door, Kyra started by trying to make amends.

"I'm sorry. There's no excuse for the things I said to you. I said them to deliberately stab at you, and for that I'm sorry. You weren't the target of my anger, but you were here."

She pushed off the door and walked towards where he stood statue-still in the middle of the room. "I know I'm not a nice person a lot of the time. If I'm too much trouble, if you want me to walk out and not come back, I'll do that. But first I want you to know that I love you. I figured that out just a few hours ago, and your sister helped me to remember that."

He blinked but that was the only outward acknowledgment she got that he'd heard her. She pushed on. "I think I was able to unload on you *because* I love you, and because you've been so strong for me. I knew you could take it and not hate me. But if I was wrong and I've destroyed whatever this is between us, I'll leave."

Kyra felt the burn of tears in her eyes and wrapped her arms around her middle. Protecting herself. "It'll kill me, but if that's what you want, I'll do it."

Evan crossed the space that separated them and took her into his arms. Kyra buried her face in his chest, letting his scent envelop her and fill her.

"You didn't destroy anything." His chin came to rest on the top of her head. "And I'd already figured out you weren't a very nice person. But I love you anyway."

She gave a little laugh and slid her hands around his waist. "I'm sorry."

He held her tighter and they just stood there, letting their souls come back together and making peace with one another.

Kyra leaned back far enough that she could look up into his dark eyes. "As hard as it is to do, we can't take responsibility for other people's actions. But at the same time, we can't let them get away with what they've done. There has to be some way to find him and stop him."

Evan stared down into her face as he was making some decision. His hands came up and he threaded his fingers back through her short hair. He gripped her head tight in his grasp and held her still to kiss her.

It was a chaste one compared to others they'd shared, and it seemed to hold more meaning for some reason.

When he raised his head, Kyra studied him.

"There may be a way." The reluctance in his voice told her it wasn't his first choice of options.

"What is it?"

"A spell. We tried it once with Seth, but his mind was too closed off. He's been working on being more open so it might be worth a shot to try again."

"What kind of spell?" The whole magic thing was still so foreign, Kyra couldn't help but wonder how it worked.

"One that allows us to follow the blood connection back to Noor. Once there, in his mind, we may be able to find the answers we need."

"Who his assassin is and where he's hiding."

Evan nodded. "Among other things."

"Why am I feeling so much reluctance from you? Don't you think it'll work?"

He released her and turned to pace away. "I love being a cop."

"I know." Something was really bothering him. Kyra stayed where she was and waited for him to explain.

"Because of this shit with Noor, my entire life has been pre-programmed. Hell, even my fucking birth was seen centuries before it happened. That kind of weight gets to be a bit much after a while."

Kyra nodded. "I guess it could. That's got to be hard."

Clearly unsettled, Evan wandered into the kitchen and opened the fridge. She followed slowly and stood on the other side of the counter. She wasn't really surprised when he pulled out a beer. Twisting off the cap, he took a quick drink and then continued.

"We've all had our moments of rebellion against what fate has dealt us. Aria ran when she was eighteen. She ended up in Ohio, of all places. But she had a free life for six years. Time where she could live and enjoy life on her own terms. She built and sold magnificent metal wind sculptures until this crap dragged her back in. She still works but can't fully concentrate on it yet.

"Anna secretly started going to Joe to train. It was a year before we found out, and by that time, she and Joe had begun their relationship." He shook his head and gave a half laugh. "That didn't sit well with me and Ethan, let me tell you. We gave Joe a bitch of a time at first until we saw how good he was for our sister."

Lifting the bottle, he took another pull. "Me, I joined the police academy. That was something *I* could control. It had nothing to do with the magical part of my life, and I've kept it that way. Magic and power have had no place in my work. They still don't. Closing a case by my wits and skills means more to me than anything I've done as a witch. So I've made it a point of pride to never use my magical lineage to aid in solving a crime."

He set the bottle on the counter between them. "With all that said," he inhaled and let it out, "I don't think we have any other choice in this instance. This spell may be our only option."

"I'll deny this if anyone asks," Kyra braced her hands on the counter surface, "but you are one hell of a cop, Evan Burke."

He chuckled, as she'd intended.

"And I, more than anyone, understand pride. You asked me once how I'd decided on my name. After all the shit I survived growing up, the sole purpose of my name is to remind me to keep believing in myself. Ace, I'm the only reason I'm still here. No one else can take credit for that. I've worked my ass off to become someone I can be proud of. Whether you use your gifts in your job or not, be proud of who you are and everything that defines you. And if you want to continue this case without the aid of your magic, I'll stick with you. Despite what I said before, I'm convinced you can find the killer without it. But it's not your only option, should you choose to take it."

Evan grinned at her. "Thanks for that. But we can't fumble around anymore. And I can't take the chance of blowing this investigation because I'm too hardheaded to bend. This guy has to be stopped. And this may be the best way."

"Okay then." Kyra grabbed his beer, took a swig, and slammed the bottle back down. "Let's do it."

Evan's cell rang.

"Shit," he muttered. Sliding it free of his pocket, he looked at the face of it. "I gotta get this."

Kyra stood by as he spoke with, she assumed, his partner.

"Yeah. Yeah, okay. Tell them I'm on it. I'll be there in ten."

He came out around the cupboard to where she was standing and cupped the sides of her face with his large hands. "I have to go. But we'll continue this discussion." He kissed her deep and long before turning and heading out the door.

~~~

As life would have it, they weren't able to revisit the topic of the spell for a couple of weeks.

The drug- and gun-running case that had originally brought Seth to town was unexpectedly moved up. Appearing in court took precedence over everything else and consumed Evan and Seth's time and energy.

September moved on as the case dragged into its third week, each side presenting their arguments, questioning and cross-examining each witness. Evan's testimony alone lasted three days. Seth's required more as he'd been the one undercover and had been right in the thick of it.

But that was done now and all parties were headed for steel cages. Some would likely see the light of day again, but the worst offenders most likely wouldn't.

All-in-all, Evan considered it a victory as he sat as his desk and finished off the paperwork. Completing the last form, Evan hit save. Knowing Records would want a hard copy, he printed everything out and slipped them into the file.

Seth was still pecking away at his keyboard when Evan
~~~

stood.

"You're done?" Seth glared up at him.

Evan grinned gleefully. "Yup."

"Man, I sure as hell didn't miss all this paperwork while I was in the field," Seth groused. "I never realized how much there was. Working undercover, this was left to everyone else to do."

Evan chuckled. "Preaching to the choir, bud. I just happen to type faster." He gathered up the file. "Good luck. After I drop this down in the file room, I'm out of here. Got a woman at home waiting for me."

Since there'd really been no need for Kyra to stay at the apartment any longer, Evan had asked her, one night after a grueling day of testifying, if she'd move in with him at his house.

Being as independent and obstinate as she was, he'd almost expected her to say no. But to his surprise, she'd agreed. They'd loaded up what little she had that night and taken it to Evan's place. That had been over a week ago, and things were moving along smoothly. There was something satisfying and comforting in knowing she would be there when he came in from work each night. He could almost see how their lives would be years from now.

She'd surprised him again by actually knowing how to cook. He'd told her she didn't have to, but more often than not, there was a hot meal ready for him when he walked in.

This was a side of her he wouldn't have believed if he hadn't seen it. Almost...domesticated. Though he'd never say that to her.

"Yeah," Seth muttered slowly, hunting out and stabbing at the letters he needed. "I've got one of those too, but I probably won't see her tonight."

Evan laughed at his partner's bitching and headed off down the hall. He pushed through the door to the stairwell and went down one floor.

As his footsteps echoed down the long corridor, all Evan could think about was getting home. When he reached the room he needed, he turned the knob and breezed in. He went right up to the counter and waited.

"Hello?" he called when no one appeared.

No answer. Not a big deal—he'd just leave it in their inbox. When they came back, they'd file it away where it needed to go.

Exiting, Evan pulled the door closed behind him. Turning, he looked up as he started back down the hall.

And saw Edrick Noor standing at the opposite end.

It may only be a projection of the evil son of a bitch, but Evan's steps faltered briefly upon seeing him. He started forward again, his pace confident and determined as he bore down on his opponent.

Noor was dressed in a high-collared white shirt with black pants and boots. He seemed to be stuck in the fashion of the late fifteen hundreds. His dull brown hair was cut short, but his full beard, in the same drab color, hung down to the top of his chest.

Evan could guess why he was here now, confronting him like this.

Kyra.

When Evan was within a few feet, he stopped.

"You've got a lot of fucking nerve."

"*I* have nerve." Noor's hazel eyes widened as if in shock. "It is you who have taken my wife. Again. I demand she be returned to me. This is your last warning."

Evan leaned in and lowered his voice. "She is *not* your wife."

Noor's eyes narrowed. "You do not want to cross me, boy. Give her to me!"

Evan relaxed his stance to show how little he thought of Noor's threat. But at the same time, he was gathering the power of the earth to him should he need it.

"No."

"You Burke witches think you are so self-righteous. Holier than thou. Stepping into others' lives and destroying them. You took my wife and sons from me. I will not let that happen again. Return her to me now."

"So you can do what? Beat the shit out of her again? You think that's a life for anyone? Leaving you was the best thing the real Isabel ever did. Taking those boys and coming to my family saved their lives."

"You destroyed my family!" Noor raged.

"No. You did that the first time you ever raised a hand to them."

He saw something flicker in Noor's eyes. Satisfaction, or a secret knowing. Whatever it was, it told Evan this whole conversation was nothing more than a diversion. Evan pulled his power close and ducked away from the assassin's approach, avoiding the blade by a hair's breadth.

"Kill him!" Noor shouted unnecessarily. Evan could see the deadly intent in the goon's eyes and recognized him immediately. This was the man Kyra had described and detailed for the sketch artist. The one who had murdered five men on Noor's order.

As he made another attempt, Evan brought the earth to bear. The floor pitched and heaved, sending the assassin to his knees. Evan was on him in an instant, grabbing the hand the blade was in to keep it away from his own body.

They grappled, each one fighting for control. Evan lunged and rolled, pinning the other man securely. Evan reached for his cuffs and ended up flying backwards before skidding down the corridor as Noor hit him with an energy blast.

Fuck. He'd been so absorbed in taking the killer down, he'd forgotten about Noor.

While he was still trying to right himself, his suspect jumped up and disappeared from sight. Pissed beyond anything he'd ever felt before, Evan grabbed up the knife the assailant had dropped and hurled it at Noor. He was pleased to see the shocked expression on Noor's face as the blade sliced through his flesh. They couldn't kill him, but at least they could so some damage now.

Noor screamed in shocked rage and pain as he grasped the wound. Just before vanishing, he glared at Evan. "I will have her and you will die. Mark my words."

Evan's voice was cold and deadly. "Do your worst, motherfucker."

Seth came barreling out of the stairwell, gun in hand, as Evan stood seething.

"What the hell happened?" Seeing there was no immediate threat, Seth holstered his weapon. "I felt the building shake and knew there was trouble."

After relaying the events of the last few minutes, Seth just shook his head. "Are you fucking kidding me? The killer had the balls to try for you in a cop shop? *Unbelievable.*"

"With Noor backing him, he's feeling pretty invincible. He's gotten away with five murders. Why wouldn't he think he could get away with this?" Evan paused. "Hey, could you let the family know what went down here? I don't have time to deal with all the questions they'll throw at me—I need to go check on Kyra. The wards on the house haven't signaled anything, but I'd feel better knowing for sure."

"Yeah man, go. I'll take care of it."

Evan headed out, his phone already in hand as he hurried. He tried Kyra's phone but got her voicemail. Hanging up, he tried a second time.

Voicemail again.

More concerned now, he set into a jog. Once in his car, he hit the button again. Still no answer. Pressing hard on the accelerator, Evan sped through the streets of Daytona.

He made it home in record time. Screeching into his drive,

Evan jumped from his car and raced the rest of the way up to the door. When he tore into the house, Kyra was standing there. Obviously startled by his rushed entry.

"Evan? What's going on?"

"I called you three times. Why didn't you answer?"

"Sorry, I guess I left my phone on the charger. I didn't even think about it." Her eyes narrowed as she looked him up and down. "Something happened, didn't it?"

"Let me just check the house and then I'll explain."

He made sure every window and door was still warded before returning to where Kyra waited for him in the living room.

"Noor paid me a visit."

"What did he do?" She came to him. "Is someone else dead?"

Evan knew that was her deepest fear. That another person in her life would die. He took her into his arms.

"No. No one is even hurt. Unfortunately."

She pulled back to see his face, her whiskey eyes drilling into his. "What does that mean?"

"He caught me alone at the precinct." Evan gave her all the details of the encounter.

"And of course, you thought they'd come after me here." Kyra stepped out of his embrace and paced away. "I almost wish they would have."

She swung back around to face him. "The longer this jackass is out there, the better the chances of him taking up his mission again. They can't pin it on me now, but what's to stop him from picking up where he left off, just for the fuck of it? I know you've been busy with the trial, so I've tried to be patient. But it's driven me nuts to sit here and do nothing."

"I know." Evan reached out and brought her into his warmth again. "But now that court is behind me, we can concentrate on finding him." He tightened his arms around her waist and pulled her in closer. "I know this has been hard on you, and thank you for not taking off to handle him on your own." He leaned in and kissed her. "It's difficult for you to put faith in other people—I understand that. I'm just honored that you've put yours in me. I won't let you down."

She settled into him and gave him a sexy smile. "You're lucky I think you're pretty hot when you do your witch thing. Otherwise, I might have just gone vigilante."

Until her, his magic had been a duty. A burden. Something given to him for a sole purpose; an obligation held over his head. If he'd not been born one of the four, it probably would have felt differently. But since he had been, his magical heritage had always felt like a contract—a promise to perform on the date specified, just like a trained monkey would have.

Until Kyra.

She made him see the fun in it. The silly and the sexy. Him being a witch wasn't a topic he'd ever shared with the girls he'd dated. He'd always held that part of himself back.

Evan didn't have to hide anything with Kyra. She'd come in knowing what he was, demanding that he prove it. She'd even had the audacity to twitch her nose at him like the make-believe witches had done on the classic TV show.

It was only because of a flu bug that had kept him out of school that he even knew what she was referring to. He'd fallen asleep to a couple of country boys racing around in an orange car and had awoken to witches twinkling their noses to do magic.

As if, he remembered his eleven-year-old-self thinking.

Coming back to the present, he looked down into Kyra's gorgeous whisky eyes and sent a silent word of thanks out into the ether for the amazing woman in front of him. And just to make sure the cavalry didn't come busting in, he sent a message to his siblings that everything was clear.

Mind back on business, Evan did an exaggerated twitch of his nose. Her clothing vanished.

"Okay, yeah, now you've done it." She boosted herself up,

wrapped her long legs around his waist, and latched her mouth onto his. As she devoured his lips, her hips ground into his. Through the stiff denim of his jeans, he could feel her heat burning him up.

One hand slid across her back and gripped her tight. The other glided over the rounded curve of her ass, along the smooth crease to her wet, scorching entrance. His fingers dipped in and circled the sensitive nub hidden there. She groaned against his mouth as her lower body undulated, trying to follow his hand as he tormented and teased her.

She was killing him. The pants and sighs coming from her beautiful mouth stirred him to the point of madness. He needed her. Now.

Instinct alone guided him to the bedroom. Once there, Evan laid her out on what was now *their* bed. She settled back on her elbows and watched him with a sultry grin, her heated gaze following every move he made to shed his clothes.

"Why don't you ever zap your own clothes away? This would go so much faster if you did."

Evan chuckled. "Two reasons. One, I'm always in a hurry to get you naked. And two, once you are, I usually lose my ability to think."

"Mmm, good to know."

When her pink tongue came out to glide over her lips Evan groaned, remembering how it felt on his skin. On his shaft. He stripped fast and, placing one knee on the bed, came down on top of her.

Kyra spread her legs wider to make room for him, her intoxicating stare holding him in its grasp as her nails scored over his back and ass.

Evan suited up, but what he really wanted was to bury himself deep into her slick heat and feel nothing but her. He mourned the loss of that close contact, remembering vividly how she'd felt surrounding him, branding him with her passion.

If the price of sharing that kind of intimacy was having a child with her, he'd gladly pay it and then some.

As she took him in, all he could think was, *Yes, yes!* This was home. This was where he was meant to be. Every day, for the rest of his life.

20

Sometime later, they fell apart, sweaty and spent. After a quick trip to the bathroom, Evan snuggled back into bed and gathered Kyra close. And with thoughts of her ripe and swollen with his baby, he dreamed.

They walked the beach hand-in-hand. It was the strip near the pier and they had it all to themselves as they strolled and talked of nothing and everything.

Now and again, Evan would stop and just run his hands over her protruding belly.

"Do you think it's a boy or a girl?" He asked.

"I'm pretty sure it's a girl," Kyra answered with a secret light in her eye.

He cocked his head at her. "Do you know something I don't?"

"Just a feeling," she answered coyly. "Mother's intuition, maybe."

Evan leaned in and kissed her perfect lips.

"Whatever it is," a new voice sneered, breaking into their tender moment, "it'll be dead before it's ever born. I'll see to that."

Evan spun around to see Noor lurking a few feet behind them. He shifted to shield Kyra with his body.

Noor looked past him to Kyra. "If you think you will ever have this abomination's child, you and your whelp will suffer that betrayal. You are *mine*, Isabel, and I'll not raise another's bastard. If anyone plants his seed in you, it shall be me. And then I will finally have my rightful heir."

His hand shot out towards Kyra, and she suddenly screamed and buckled to her knees, clutching her stomach. Blood gushed from between her legs, spewing grotesquely and staining the pristine white sands.

Noor faded away, his hysterical laughter echoing all around them. Evan knelt beside her in horror and devastation, helpless to save the innocent child in her womb.

Evan jolted awake with his heart ripped apart. He knew Noor had only been messing with his head, but it had felt so very real. The love, the loss, the heart-shattering grief.

He had to get up. He needed a minute to get a handle on his raw and bleeding emotions. He was torn up inside, but there was no sense in burdening Kyra with it. It was only a fucked-up dream meant to torture him, and in that, Noor had succeeded.

As he made a move to roll from the bed, Kyra woke with a scream.

When he turned back to her, there were tears raining down her cheeks, and she was clutching her midsection just like she had in his dream. A sick feeling swamped him.

Evan wrapped her up in his arms and laid out next to her again. "Shh, it's okay. It's all right. It was only a dream."

"Oh, God, Evan."

"You were there, weren't you? On the beach."

She nodded against his chest and sobbed uncontrollably. Which tore him up that much more because she was usually so strong on the outside.

"I am so sorry," he murmured, stroking her hair and trying to soothe her as she cried.

He held her until the tears washed themselves away. Shifting to a better position, Evan pushed himself up against the headboard. To keep her close, he drew her up so she sat cradled between his legs. His arms wound tightly around her, and they comforted each other until they'd calmed and could talk about what had happened.

"He is such a sick, twisted *fuck*." She was finding her anger in the aftermath of the cutting grief.

"I'm sorry you had to go through that." Evan kissed the crown of her brown hair. "Dreams are his favorite playground. He must have gotten into mine and pulled you in."

Kyra sat up abruptly and turned her body around to face him. "Wait. *Yours*?"

"Yeah." Evan knew for certain it had been his dream, but he found it curious that she could have assumed it was her own.

He watched her now. "Have you dreamt of being pregnant before?"

She sputtered. "That's not the point. Why where *you* thinking about me that way?"

Her evasion confirmed Evan's suspicion, and he couldn't help feeling rather flattered. He decided to come clean and tell her exactly what had prompted the scene Noor had invaded.

"While we were making love," he reached up and traced her lips with his thumb, "I was remembering how it felt to be inside of you with no barrier. I want that again. To feel your burning heat with nothing between us." He ran his hand down the center of her body, stopping at her stomach. "And I thought if the price of that pleasure was that you'd have my baby, I'd willingly pay it. So as I dozed off, I had the image of you pregnant in my mind. I guess it flowed over into my dreams."

Evan returned his gaze to her slightly shocked brown eyes. "Now it's your turn. Do you think about the future and us having babies?"

"Just once," she finally admitted, a little embarrassed.

"And?" he prompted.

She huffed out a breath. "I was playing the five-year game. The one where—"

"I have sisters. I'm familiar."

"Okay. Well, I did the five and saw you and me riding down a road on motorcycles."

"That sounds great, but I don't hear anything about babies."

Kyra sent him a glare. "Then I stretched it out to ten years, just to see if you'd still be there."

He grinned. "And was I?"

"Yes. We were in a park full of people and kids. And I saw you. You were walking towards me, and you had a little girl in your arms. She was about four or five, I think. Black hair like yours. When you were close enough and I really saw her, she looked just like me."

Evan smiled at the picture she'd painted. "She had to be beautiful then."

"She was. She really was." She dropped her gaze to her abdomen. "And I was pregnant too. Pretty far along." She brought a hand up to rest on it. "You put your hand on my belly and said how you hoped this one was a boy since we already had two girls."

That surprised him. "Two? But you said I was only carrying the one child."

"You were." Kyra turned emotion-filled eyes up to him. "The other came running up behind me." Her eyes went dreamy as she saw it again. "She was laughing and happy and free. Her hair was long. Darker brown than mine. It was flying in the breeze as she flew to us over the grass."

Her attention came back to the present. "She had to be around eight, nine maybe. I'm not too good with kids' ages, but it seemed close."

"Eight or nine." Evan did some quick math. "That would mean you'd have to be pregnant right now or become that way very soon."

Was she even now carrying his child? His gaze snapped to hers. "Do you think?"

Kyra shook her head. "No, I'm not pregnant. I'm pretty sure

I'd know. Besides, it was only my imagination. Just a dumb game."

Evan wasn't quite as certain as she was. He knew firsthand how the fates worked. It wasn't much of a stretch to think all these signs didn't mean something. With an overwhelming need to know for sure, he pulled her back into his arms and hugged her close. His hands automatically settled over her mid-section.

"Three kids, huh? What did the girls look like again?"

While she talked, Evan took a centering breath and closed his eyes. The earth and all its components give off differing levels of energy. Being linked to the element the way he was, Evan had felt and been a part of that from the very first moment of his existence. Every living thing on the planet carried within it a life force. And that included humans. He'd never used his connection to the earth in quite this way before, but if he could single out one tiny new life force...

Evan concentrated fully on Kyra. Searching deep, searching for...something. Someone.

It didn't take long. There. Just the smallest of tiny beings. The purest form of energy.

His daughter. Their daughter.

His heart swelled, knowing he was already completely and desperately in love with the child he and Kyra had made.

He came back to himself just as she finished speaking.

"They sound wonderful." Evan hugged her just a little closer.

Noor couldn't find out. If he discovered this secret...he'd make that dream a horrific reality. And that was something Evan could not allow to happen.

Taking precautions, Evan tucked the knowledge of their daughter behind the strongest shields he could construct. And until he could figure out a way to safeguard Kyra's thoughts as well, he couldn't tell her. Not yet. Only when he found a way to protect them both.

As long as she believed there was nothing there, Noor would be none the wiser.

~~~

With Noor's renewed effort to take Kyra, Evan talked her into hanging out at Knight's. He didn't want her left alone, no matter what kind of magical protective barriers he had in place. He also asked Ethan and Aria to check in on her periodically.

Once he and Seth were off shift tonight, they'd all head over to their parents' house. It was time to try following the blood link back to Noor. But before that could get underway, Evan needed to speak with his mother. So as soon as he dropped Kyra off at the gym, he drove straight there.

He found both of his parents in the kitchen seated at the island drinking coffee.

"Hey, baby," Mary greeted in delighted surprise. She slid off the stool and came to give him a hug and kiss his cheek. As she always did, she cupped her hand to his face and looked up into his eyes.

"Something's troubling you."

"Yeah. I wanted to talk to you about it before we all got together tonight."

"Well, come on in. I'll get you some coffee."

Evan sat on the stool she'd vacated next to his dad.

"What is it, son?"

As Mary poured, Evan told them of the dream he and Kyra had shared the previous night.

His mom sat a mug in front of him. "Oh, hon." Sadness filled her voice. "That sounds horrible. How was Kyra after?"

"Upset, as you can imagine. And then pissed off. I asked her again if she thought she could be pregnant, and she told me definitely not. But as we talked, I started to wonder..." Evan pulled the coffee into his hands but didn't pick it up. He slowly
~~~

looked up. "She is, Mom. I saw it. I felt it. There's a little life inside of her."

Mary's hand came up to her chest. "Oh. Well. How do you feel about that? How does she feel?"

Evan relaxed a little and grinned at her. "I feel pretty damned good with it, actually. It was my dream Noor ambushed, and before he got there I was happy. She was happy."

"How does she feel now that it's real, though?" Paul asked.

"She doesn't know," Evan admitted on an exhale.

Mary's eyes narrowed at him. "What do you mean she doesn't know?"

"I don't think it's safe for her to know just yet."

"Evan." She used her mom voice. Never a good sign.

"Noor showed us, in gruesome detail, what he'd do if she ever got pregnant by me. I can't have him finding out until I can protect them. I'm afraid if she knows about it right now, Noor will get into her head and see. As long as she's sure there's nothing there, they're both safe."

"What are you going to do?" Mary braced her hands on the counter. "You can't keep this from her until February. She's a smart woman. She's going to figure it out, son—and a lot sooner than you think."

"I know. That's why I came to you. Is there a spell that could...I don't know...shield or cloak the baby? From Noor?"

His mom glanced at his dad before coming back to Evan. "I don't know. I've never heard of anything like that." She was silent as she thought it through. "But that doesn't mean we can't come up with something. I'll have to do some research. It's going to take some time."

Evan stood and went around the island to draw his mom into a tight hug. "I love you."

She held him just as tight. "I love you too, baby. Don't worry. We're going to keep them safe."

"Thank you." He kissed her. "If anyone can find a way to

make my daughter invisible, it'll be you." He sent her a quick grin.

"Daughter?" Happiness lit Mary's hazel eyes. "Oh, Evan. Are you sure?"

"I'm fairly positive." He explained what Kyra had seen in her fantasy game. "We all know fate has a quirky way of getting what it wants. I think that daydream was shown to her for a reason."

"Three?" His dad looked a little shell-shocked and Evan laughed. Paul then turned to his wife. "I guess we'd better start preparing for all these grandchildren."

Evan couldn't wait to see his parents surrounded by the next generation of Burkes. But in the meantime, they had a war to win. "I'd better get going. We'll see you tonight."

When he walked into the PD a little while later, Seth was there waiting.

"Aria told me everything was good when you got home. No sign of Noor?"

"Not until later." Evan shared the visitation but not what he'd discovered after.

"Dude, that is so fucked up."

"Tell me about it." Evan tried not to think of the complete devastation he'd felt. "Are you ready for tonight? Ari said you guys have been working on the shields in your mind. Do you think you can drop them enough to do this spell?"

"I'm going to try, man. It's time for Noor to get a little something back. If you guys can follow this thread back to him, we might gain the upper hand for a change."

"That would be nice, wouldn't it?"

Evan would still rather find their perp through lawful means, but he knew that may not be enough. Noor's supernatural assist was stacking the deck against them, but if going the magical route gave them the bump they needed to get ahead, they had to try.

There was still a big possibility it wouldn't work, though. And if that happened, Evan didn't want to have all his chickens in the witchy basket. So with that in mind, he worked the case as he normally would.

When everything that needed to be done was, he and Seth got ready to go. With most everyone at the gym, that's where they went first to meet up with them. From there, they headed to the family home.

Mary had food waiting, and as they'd grown to a group of ten, it was served buffet-style. Plates loaded, they spread out around the dining and living rooms.

Conversation was kept light until Jacob could be shuttled off to the playroom. Joe would keep him occupied while the others did their thing.

Just as they had before, Seth sat in the middle of the floor with the four around him. Since he and Aria had been working on getting around his barriers, they would get it started. She sat in front of him and took his hands in hers.

"Be careful now," Mary warned. "If you sense anything off, get out."

"More off than Seth's brain already is?" Evan joked.

"Ha-ha," Seth retorted. "Yours would be wonky too if it had four extra people swimming around in it." He took a deep breath. "All right, let's do this."

"Just like we practiced," Aria reminded him.

Seth nodded and held her gaze.

It wasn't too long before Evan heard Aria in his head.

"We're ready."

Evan reached out for her. He felt the presence of each of his siblings as they too entered their sister's mind. From there, the idea was that they would slip along her connection to Seth. Aided by her established link, they should have no problem getting past his walls.

Except it didn't go that easily. They had no difficulties with the outer reaches of Seth's consciousness, but when they tried to go deeper, where presumably the pathway to Noor was, they were met with resistance.

The group couldn't gain access far enough in to make this work. Seth was still closed off, to all but Aria it appeared. The problem was, she couldn't go in alone. She needed all of them to empower the spell enough to make the trip all the way to Noor's subconscious.

"Shit!" Seth huffed out a dejected breath. "I'm sorry. I really thought it would work this time."

"It's all right," Anna assured him. "It's not something you can control. We'll try another way."

The setback frustrated them all, but there wasn't much else they could do.

Until Kyra cleared her throat. "I've got Noor's blood too," Kyra announced. "Try it with me."

21

Evan's heart stopped. He looked over at his mom and saw that her alarm matched his. He couldn't let her do this. The risk was too high. But he knew if he flat-out told her no, she'd dig in her heels and blast him.

He was frantically trying to find a way to shut it down when Anna's voice whispered into his mind.

"Evan, what is it? Something has you scared."

"Anna, we can't let her do this. Noor cannot get into her head right now." He'd told his mom that Kyra believing she wasn't pregnant would protect the baby, but in truth, there just wasn't any real way to know for sure. And he couldn't take the chance.

"Tell her her walls are too strong. That we can't get in."

"If this could work, Evan—"

"I'll explain everything. Just please do this for me."

He sensed her mind hesitating, but eventually she relented. *"Okay."*

She turned to Kyra. "Would you mind if I tested it out? I can look and see whether or not it'll be possible."

"Yeah, sure." Kyra nodded eagerly. "Have at it."

Anna went silent for a moment and then shook her head. "You're like Seth. The barriers around your mind are just too solid."

"Oh." Her voice was thick with disappointment. "Well, it was worth a shot. So how do we find them now?"

Conversation went on around Evan as he breathed a sigh of relief. He sent thanks to Anna.

"You got lucky. I didn't have to lie after all. Her mind is every bit as impenetrable as Seth's."

"Thank you anyway."

"You want to fill me in now?"

"She's pregnant, but she doesn't know it yet. I found out after that horrific dream. If Noor would have seen…" He left the rest unsaid.

"Oh, Evan." He knew she was thinking of her own child. *"You're right. There's too much at stake. When are you going to tell her?"*

"Mom is trying to construct a spell that will cloak the baby from Noor. I have to shield them, Anna."

"Yes, you do. We all do."

The gathering broke up shortly after that. Upon saying their good-byes, Evan and Kyra walked out to his car.

"Well, that was a big fat bust," Kyra complained as she pulled open the car door.

Evan hated that he was keeping secrets from her, but what other choice did he have? Knowing her mind wouldn't have allowed them in regardless helped to ease some of his guilt, but he still felt awful for knowing something so intimate about her body that she didn't. Especially since he knew how she felt about anyone making decisions for her.

He waited until they were in and buckled before responding. "Seth's been working on lowering his walls, but we still knew this was a likelihood. He'll probably never be able to open himself up to that extent. His survival depended on blocking off a major part of his life and who he was. Living in secrecy for so long was bound to have an effect on him, so it's just his natural state now."

He gave Kyra a sideways glance as he pulled out onto the road. "I imagine the same can be said about you. Given your distrust for most people and how you separate yourself from others, that would make your barriers innate. It's a defense mechanism."

"I suppose." She watched houses and trees pass by out the side window.

They rode in silence for a bit before Kyra spoke again.

"So what's our plan now?"

"We get back to what I'm best at."

And that's just what they did. Evan and Seth hit the investigation hard. They worked long hours and hit up everyone who'd ever owed them a favor. If anyone caught sight of this joker, they were going to know about it.

As the days went on, they inched closer and closer to their suspect.

On the personal front, his mom thought she had what they needed to protect Kyra and the baby. She said she could have it ready in the next day or two.

As far as Evan knew, Kyra was still in the dark about what she carried. He'd worried briefly about her and the baby's health, because weren't they supposed to be on vitamins or something? But his mom had assured him that everything would be fine.

Usually a woman didn't even suspect she was pregnant until the sixth or eighth week in. These few days shouldn't matter. And once they had the cloaking spell, he'd tell her about the baby and get them in to see someone.

He just hoped she was as excited about the baby as he was. She'd seemed okay with the idea of bearing his child when they'd talked about it before, but once it was a reality, he wasn't sure how she would react.

~~~

The more time passed, the more Kyra thought about using
~~~

herself as bait to draw the killer out.

The dilemma she kept running into was whether or not to share her idea with Evan. She'd tried it his way for weeks with nothing to show for it. It was the middle of September now, and still there'd been no sign of him. And no indication that they were getting any closer.

Recalling the fight they'd had the last time she'd suggested it, she evaluated the pros and cons of telling him as she did another rep on the weight machine.

This enforced house arrest was a pain in the ass, but it ended up having a huge bonus. Being confined to an MMA training facility every day, she was in the best shape of her life. She'd put some weight back on and had added muscle.

Joe had even started sparring with her. Cardio kickboxing may have taught her the basic movements, but Joe refined them, showing her how to apply them to practical situations.

When Anna was around, she watched them like a hawk—which was kind of weird—but Kyra didn't think much of it. She was feeling good—strong and empowered. Which only made her want to take action that much more.

Pumping out another ten bicep curls, she let her mind wander. She was sure if she allowed herself to be accessible, Noor's goon would come after her. She had to figure the only reason he hadn't tried recently was because she was surrounded by Burkes and knew breaching their ranks wouldn't be easy.

As far as they could tell, Noor was still MIA after his run-in with Evan in the police station. But Kyra knew that probably wouldn't keep him down for much longer. The man was nuts, and he wanted her. He'd be back; it was only a matter of time.

If Noor were hiding away licking his wounds, could she use that opportunity to lure his dog out and put him down?

She was confident she could handle him when he came. This confrontation would be on her terms; she'd have the advantage.

If she decided to do this, the biggest obstacle she could see would be how to get out of the gym without anyone seeing her. Evan dropped her off every morning and picked her up each evening. People were in and out all day, including members of Evan's family.

Could she somehow slip away? Would she have enough time to entice him into making a move before any of them caught on?

There was still a lot to figure out, so Kyra kept her plans to herself that evening when Evan picked her up. They ate dinner, watched a little TV, and then headed to bed. She noticed she wasn't the only one preoccupied that night. She wondered if Evan had something on his mind too but didn't ask.

She dressed carefully the next morning, just in case she had the chance to make her move. Instead of shorts and a sports tank, she pulled on leggings and slipped a tee on over her tank. Technically still workout gear, but wouldn't seem completely out of place on the street.

After Evan dropped her off, Kyra went about her routine but watched for an opportunity. Since she figured the rear door would be her best bet, she modified her workout with proximity to the exit in mind. She'd only need a few seconds to sneak out.

That time didn't come until late that morning. Anna and Jacob had come in with Joe and stayed. Kyra later found out there was some kind of school holiday that gave them the day off. Getting out unnoticed with them there was going to be next to impossible.

But she'd find a way. She had to do this.

When she saw Anna walk into Joe's office, Kyra glanced around for Jacob. He still thought he needed to act as her protector, so he'd been nearby all morning. He watched everyone who came in to make sure they didn't have anyone hiding inside them.

When she didn't find him, she assumed that maybe he'd taken a bathroom break. Whatever the reason, he wasn't here.

That's all that mattered. Returning the dumbbell to the rack, Kyra wiped her face. Looking to all the world as if she had every right, she headed for the short hall that would lead out the back of the building.

Pushing through the door, she didn't look back. She kept moving until she was around the corner of the structure and out of sight. She hoofed it a couple of blocks before slowing her pace.

Kyra wondered what the best way would be to draw her pursuer out. Wandering aimlessly didn't seem like a good idea. It gave her less control over the situation. So instead she found a small park and picked a bench that would give her a clear view in all directions.

She sat there almost forty-five minutes when she began to feel a tingly type of awareness. Slowly shifting her gaze, Kyra scanned the area. Out of a stand of trees about fifty yards away stepped a man she recognized.

The killer.

And held tightly against his side, with a knife poised at his throat, was Jacob.

Fuck! Kyra's stomach pitched and rolled with nausea as her mind raced.

How could this have happened? She thought she'd gotten away clean. He must have followed her. That's the only thing that made sense. And this motherfucker had snagged him.

She knew exactly what was going through the goon's mind. Use the boy to control her. She knew he wouldn't kill Jake—Noor wanted him too badly—but he could cause him pain. Given the murders he'd already committed, Kyra figured he'd probably like that.

And the thought of it made her sick.

She rose and slowly moved towards them. "Don't hurt him."

"Well, that's entirely up to you. Are you going to come quietly?"

What other choice did she have? She'd make it look as if she was cowed, but at the first opportunity, she'd get Jake out of there. She didn't care what happened to herself—this child would not be put through any more pain.

"I'll do whatever you tell me." She held her hands up in front of her. "Just don't hurt him."

As she drew near, she saw Jacob's lips moving. She wondered briefly what he was doing but returned her attention to the man holding him captive. She was going through her options when suddenly the assassin yelped and jumped away from Jacob.

Deadly intent enveloped his face. "What the fuck did you do, you little shit?" He made a grab for Jacob again and Kyra lunged into the space between them.

"Run, Jake!" She felt a white-hot pain sear across her side but ignored it, concentrating instead on keeping him busy so that Jake could get away.

When she saw him clear the immediate area and run in the direction of the gym, Kyra's mission shifted. This man had snuffed out the lives of five men. Friend or acquaintance, it didn't matter. He needed to pay for that.

She fought now for everyone who'd been lost, knowing this battle was going to come down to her or him. Only one of them would leave there standing.

22

Evan was at his desk when a frantic call from Anna came to him through their telepathic link.

Kyra and Jacob were gone. No one had seen them for at least an hour.

As soon as he heard that, Evan was on the move. He grabbed Seth and, as they raced out of the precinct, quickly conveyed Anna's message. Neither spoke on the harrowing ten-minute drive to the gym.

Heart in his throat, Evan tore into the lot and jumped from the car. He was halfway to the door when he heard his name being shouted.

"Uncle Evan! Uncle Evan!"

He turned to see Jacob running flat out towards him. He was sobbing when Evan caught him up in his arms.

"It's okay, buddy. I've got you." As hard as it was, Evan put aside his own fear for the woman he loved to care for his nephew. He needed to get Jacob inside to his parents; they were already driving themselves crazy with worry. He could find out about Kyra then.

Evan turned towards the building, but Jacob started fighting him.

"No! No! We have to go back! We have to help Kyra! She's hurt!"

Evan's breath stopped in his lungs. His whole world tipped

off its axis. "How is she hurt, Jacob?"

Before Jake could answer, Seth was running towards the building. "I'll go get the others."

He didn't respond. Evan's full focus was on the boy in his arms.

"He had a knife. The bad man. He pointed it at me first, but Kyra jumped in the middle of us. There was so much blood." Jake touched his stomach. "Here."

Oh God.

It took Evan a moment to be able to find his voice again. "Where are they?"

Joe and Anna came thundering out of the building. Joe reached for Jacob first and pulled him in close.

"What were you thinking, leaving like that?" Joe demanded of his son, but there was more fear in his voice than anger.

"I saw Kyra go out the back door. I followed. I had to protect her." His words were said around hitching sobs. "But I couldn't keep up. I didn't see where she went. I looked for her, but he found me. Grabbed me. He had a knife. Then Kyra was there. She jumped on him after I did the spell to make him let me go. She jumped on him and told me to run. I looked back and there was a lot of blood on her."

Anna ran her hand over his head. "You did the right thing by coming to get us."

Evan couldn't hold back any longer. "Jacob. Where are Kyra and the man? Where did this happen?"

"The park." He looked at Anna. "The one you took me to. With the ducks."

The location was no sooner out of Anna's mouth than Evan was headed for his car. Seth jumped in just as he threw it in reverse and spun the car around.

He was so afraid of what he'd find when he got to the park. How badly was she hurt? Was she okay? And what about the baby?

Guilt nearly drowned Evan as he thought about losing Kyra or the baby. Should he have told her about the pregnancy? About the spell?

Could this have been avoided if he had?

Possibly. But he'd thought he'd been doing the right thing by keeping it from her. His mind whirled as he second-guessed his decisions.

But he couldn't let these doubts cloud his mind right now. He needed to put it all aside. If he were twisted up, he wouldn't be able to do his job. And that, right at this minute, was finding the woman he loved.

Gravel flew as he skidded to a stop. Looking out through the windshield, Evan didn't see any sign of them. He and Seth glanced at each other and then jumped out to search for clues. It wasn't a very big park thankfully; a few benches, a small pond, and a large grassy area lined by trees to block it off from neighboring businesses.

So it didn't take them long to find what they were looking for. Dark red stains on the grass could be seen near the tree-line. When Evan could finally tear his eyes away from the evidence of Kyra's injury, he scanned the foliage around him.

"He took her out this way." Evan pointed at the obvious path through the dense greenery. Seth was right behind him as they followed the trail of broken branches, crushed grass, and crimson smears.

But when they stepped out of the overgrowth and into another parking lot, Kyra and her assailant were nowhere in sight.

"Son of a bitch!" It would have been too much to ask that they'd still be here.

"He must have had a car waiting," Seth offered and pointed. "And we'll know what it was, hopefully with a plate number, shortly."

Evan followed Seth's gaze and looked up to see a security

camera mounted high up on the light post. They moved as a unit into the store. He went right to the counter and held up his badge.

"I need to see the manager. *Now*."

The young kid working the cash register stared like a deer caught in headlights for a moment. Suddenly his head jerked up and down before he turned and ran for the back. An older woman came out a few seconds later.

"You gentleman scared the bejeezus out of Adam." She eyed them carefully. "What can I do for you?"

Evan showed her his badge. "We need the footage from that camera out there."

"We haven't had any trouble here. What's this about?"

"A woman was abducted," Seth stepped in, "out of the park on the other side of those trees just a few minutes ago. We believe his vehicle was parked in your lot."

"And the longer you take to get us that footage, the farther away he gets." Evan's words were cold and hard, drawing a short gasp from the manager.

Seth sent him a look that he ignored. He didn't have time for bullshit questions. If anything happened to Kyra or the baby, Evan didn't know what he'd do.

Finally understanding the urgency of the matter, she told them to follow her. She spun and hurried in the direction she'd come from.

"The security equipment is in here." She showed them into a small office.

While Evan was familiarizing himself with the controls, Seth asked the store manager to find them something to copy the feed to. As she rushed off, Evan found the controls he needed. The push of a button had it backing up. He watched everything happen in reverse and when it got to the point he needed, hit play.

On the video he could see a grainy picture of a dull brown

sedan. As they viewed further, a man is seen dragging someone who looked like Kyra out of the wooded area and to the car. He shoved her in through the driver's door and got in next to her.

There was no way to get a number off that plate.

"Why the fuck, with all the technology in this world today, do security cameras still have useless pictures?"

"We're lucky it was a real camera at all," Seth said softly. "Most places won't shell out the money for actual equipment, let alone one with high resolution feeds. Be glad we got what we did."

"For all the good it will do."

The manager came back with a USB flash drive. Seth plugged it in and copied the file to it. "I'll get this back to the tech guys and see if they can clean it up or zoom in on that plate."

Evan knew that wouldn't be enough. They'd played this hide and seek game before and had come up the losers. If it hadn't been for Kyra saving herself the first time, they'd still be hunting for her now. The stakes were too high this time to go blundering around blindly.

"You can do that, but I'm not waiting." Evan stood. He was already walking away when he heard Seth thank the woman.

They were back in the car when Seth asked what Evan was planning.

"We already know we won't find these fuckers this way. If ever there were a time for my heritage to prove its worth, it's now."

Seth didn't ask any more questions. He just nodded.

Evan called to his siblings and told them to meet him at their parents' house. Everything he was going to need was there.

His mom was at the door to meet them, having been called by one of the others. Evan saw the worry clouding her face, but also a fierceness. She held her arms out to him and he walked into them.

"Why would she do this?" he whispered into her ear.

She leaned back from him and grasped his face in her hands. Her hazel eyes locked straight onto his dark ones. "For the very reasons you love her. Because she's strong, independent, and confident. She obviously felt this was something she needed to do. She just didn't factor in a curious little boy."

Mary reached up and kissed his cheek. "Now let's go get her back."

His mother's words calmed some of the fears racking him. Kyra *was* strong. She was everything his mom had said she was. She'd had to be to survive so much. And she would do so again now.

You hold the hell on, Kyra. I'm coming.

Within ten minutes, the house was full of Burke witches. They all gathered around the table in the work room.

Evan glanced around and didn't see the smallest of Burkes. "Where's Jake?"

Anna, fear still lingering in her blue eyes, looked up at him. "He was very upset about what happened. Mom thought it best to give him some tea to help him sleep."

He nodded. "All right. Let's find her."

"Do you have something of hers?" Aria's gaze went from her mother to her brother. "Something to guide the scrying crystal."

Mary glanced at Evan. "We don't have anything of Kyra's here, no. But we won't need it."

"Then how do you plan on finding her?" Ethan's brows came together in confusion.

Evan started rolling up his shirt sleeve. "We'll use a closer link. Blood."

"You have some of Kyra's blood?" Seth was as confused as everyone else. "Did you pick it up from the scene?"

"No. I don't have Kyra's blood. We'll use mine, since the baby she's carrying shares it."

Everyone except his mom and Anna gasped. They'd been the only ones who knew Kyra was pregnant.

"Why would she put herself in this kind of danger, knowing she was pregnant?" Aria was steaming mad. "Why would she risk—"

"She doesn't know," Evan interrupted. "I found out a little while ago, but I didn't tell her." He glanced at his mom, and then at each of the faces watching him. "You all know the dream we shared. We were working on a spell that would shield the baby from Noor. Once I knew they'd be safe, I was going to tell her."

"No one could have known she'd jump the gun," his father said consolingly.

"I knew she was getting frustrated and restless with how long the hunt was taking. I should have guessed she'd try something like this."

"Hindsight is a wonderful thing, son," Mary told him. "But by its very definition, it's not much use when shit is happening. You did what you could with the information you had available to you at the time. Now, let's put that away and find Kyra and my grandbaby."

Mary issued orders and everyone gathered the ingredients and lined back up around the table.

Everything was set up. Mary turned to Evan.

"This is your spell. You need to cast it."

He nodded his understanding and added the specially-mixed herbs and liquids into the bowl at the center of the table. When all that was left was his own contribution, Evan reached down and picked up the knife.

Holding his hand over the vessel, he sliced a cut across the meatiest part of his hand at the base of his thumb. Thick, red, life-giving essence finished the potion that would call to his child.

Next he lifted the milky white crystal. Holding it by the long cord, Evan lowered it down into the mixture. Pulling it out again, he held it aloft over the map. To trigger the magic in the stone, Evan said what was in his heart.

"Blood of my blood I call to thee
Blood of my blood reveal to me
Point the way so that I may see
As I will, so mote it be."

As the last word passed his lips, the pendant began to move. It swayed and arced in wider and wider circles. Evan allowed it to move freely until it suddenly struck the part of the map where they needed to go.

The four, plus Seth and Joe, wasted no time in heading out. Evan was the first to his car, and he barely gave the others time to either jump in or start another and follow. Getting to Kyra was his first priority.

Since scrying wasn't an exact science like GPS, Evan knew once they reached the site, they may have to take some time to search. But when they arrived, they saw only one building in the vicinity. It looked like it used to house an office of some kind in the front with a small warehouse built onto the rear. It had obviously been sitting empty for some time.

He parked some distance from the structure. Joe, in the car behind, did the same. They then gathered to discuss a game plan.

As much as Evan wanted to storm in, he knew that wasn't the way. He had to keep his head. He was a cop, and he needed to distance himself and think with the part of his mind that had been specifically trained for this.

Evan studied the setup. From where they were positioned, he could see that the front section—where the offices were housed—had a double glass and aluminum entry door. On either side of that were large picture windows.

He could see one side of the smaller front area and noted that there were no openings. And of course, the warehouse was windowless. The side may be their best approach.

He turned back to the others. "We have no idea how many are in there," he warned. "This could be Noor's staging area for the army he's building. We may very well be walking into a situation where we're greatly out-numbered."

"Get me close enough. I can try to gauge how many by the number of emotional signatures in the room." Anna watched the target in the distance.

"What if we just flush them out?" Ethan held his hand up and had fire dancing in his palm.

"We could." Evan actually liked the idea. "I know you have wicked control over your element, but until we know where they're holding Kyra, I can't risk her getting hurt. Anna's plan will probably work best."

He looked over at his partner and then to the group. "We'll work our way closer. From what I can see, that side there," he pointed to the solid brick wall, "will get us where we need to be. Hopefully without being seen. Once we're there, Anna should be able to do her thing." He glanced at his sister. "And if you can, try to ascertain where they're keeping Kyra. When we have a better idea of what we're up against, we'll make our move."

Anna acknowledged his order. "Got it."

He and Seth both checked their side arms. Evan saw he had a full mag and one in the chamber. He was ready to go. A quick check with his partner told him he was ready too.

"Let's go." Crouched low and guns at the ready they ran, angling so they stayed on track to gain the vulnerable side.

With every step they took, Evan waited for a cry of alarm to ring out, telling him they'd been spotted. As they closed in on the structure though, all remained quiet.

Reaching their goal, they pressed their backs against the warm stone. He looked to Anna and gave her the go-ahead.

She closed her eyes and concentrated. "I'm only picking up on two here. Satisfaction and seething anger. But neither are near." Anna opened her eyes and looked over at Evan. "My guess would be in the rear somewhere."

"So nothing in the immediate vicinity then?" Evan asked, needing to double-check before they made a move to enter.

"None," Anna confirmed.

"All right. Stay close and stay alert."

Knowing the others would be right behind them, Evan and Seth soundlessly made their way to the right. At the corner, Evan darted his head out for a quick peek. Everything was clear. He slipped around the corner and stopped. The edge of the window frame was a few feet from him. He trusted Anna, but he still wanted a look for himself.

Creeping nearer, Evan dropped to his knees and made himself as small as possible. Moving slowly, he tipped his head forward until he could look through the dirty glass.

He remained still as he took in the room beyond. Directly across from him was a reception area. The wide desk stood empty. No movement.

"All clear."

Cautiously, they moved to the door. Evan let Seth take the lead here, as his partner's lock-picking abilities far exceeded his own. Under a minute, and Evan heard the snick of a lock releasing.

Putting his tools away, Seth repositioned his weapon and grasped the door handle. A short nod and he tugged it open slowly.

They swept the room.

Going on Anna's assertion that their targets were in the warehouse, they moved to the second set of doors straight back. Evan put his finger over his lips, reminding them all to remain silent.

"You girls each take a door. But stay back out of the way. When I give the order, open them fast. Seth and I will go first."

Aria and Anna both nodded and moved into position. Evan

then held up three fingers and began the countdown. When his last finger curled into his fist, the girls wrenched the doors out of the way.

23

The sight that greeted them made the breath clog up in Evan's throat.

Kyra, whose shirt and pants were covered in blood, was standing over the killer. He seemed to be unconscious.

Her head jerked around when they made their grand entrance. The ferocity he saw in her face said she was ready to take on all who dared. When recognition dawned, there was a quick flash of relief before it shifted to a self-satisfied grin.

"What took you so long?" She gave the downed man a swift, hard kick. "I had to take care of this asshole myself."

Evan was about to rail at her for putting herself in danger when her gaze jumped to Anna and sobered. "Jake?"

"He's fine," his sister assured her. "Worried about you. He said you'd been hurt." Anna glanced down to the darkened stain.

Unconcerned, Kyra lifted the ruined shirt to inspect the wound on her side. Evan could finally breathe again when he saw that it wasn't life threatening. Nor was it anywhere near the baby.

"Yeah, fucker got lucky there. Hurts like a bitch, but I don't think he got anything vital. Just the meaty part of my side."

He went to her now. As he drew close, he reached up and cupped her face in his hands. "You and I are going to have a very serious conversation." Not able to stand it another second, he took her into his arms and sealed his mouth to hers for a fast, emotion-laden kiss.

Drawing back, Evan rested his forehead against hers. "You scared the shit out of me."

Before she could reply, Seth interrupted. "We need to figure out how we're going to handle this."

Evan turned his attention to the man on the floor. "We finally got a tip to his whereabouts. Now we haul him in and put his ass behind bars."

Seth smiled. "Works for me."

The next few hours were crazy. Evan hated to do it, but he sent Kyra home with his family as he and Seth took care of the legalities. He knew she would be taken care of. They would see to whatever needs she had and begin the healing of that cut.

He pushed concern for the woman he loved to the back of his mind and turned contempt to the man currently in one of their holding cells. With the evidence they had against him, a conviction would be a slam dunk. And one more of Noor's henchmen would be off the streets.

As he and Seth headed back to his parents' house later that evening, Evan turned his focus to his next dilemma—the best way to tell Kyra she was pregnant. He'd gotten word a short while ago that the spell they needed to cloak the baby was finally ready. Now he just had to explain why he'd kept it all from her. And hope she didn't rip his head off in the process.

Walking in, he found her sitting on the couch chatting with his mom and sisters. She was sipping something from a flowered mug. He'd bet his next paycheck it was his mom's legendary heal-anything tea.

She'd changed into a pair of sweat pants and shirt he knew to be his mother's. She didn't look as if she were in any pain and, judging from the look of her, he'd never have guessed what she'd just been through.

He started to wonder where everyone else was, but the

whoops and cheers coming from the hall told him. His dad, Joe, and Jacob were evidently having a gaming war in the other room.

"How'd it go?" Aria asked when she saw them.

"He's going away for a very long time." Seth crossed to his love and settled in next to her.

Evan felt Kyra's attention on him. He approached and held his hand out to her. "Can we talk?"

"Yeah, sure." She set her cup aside, took his hand, and rose from where she was seated. He saw the wariness in her whiskey-colored eyes and knew she was bracing for his anger. He'd get to that, but first he needed to make sure she knew what was at stake now.

"You might want to take this to the work room," his mom advised.

At her words, Evan nodded. If there were one place he knew *no one* would overhear them talking, it would be in there. Everything magical the family needed and owned was in there. The room was protected better than any other he could think of.

Evan guided her down the hall.

The level of noise coming from the game room was higher here and they could hear Jacob, laughing and carrying on. Evidently, he'd just beaten Joe out of some prize and he was crowing as they passed.

Kyra smiled at the closed door. "I'm glad he's okay."

Evan grinned too. "We all are. He's a pretty great kid."

The next door they reached was the one they needed. Reaching out, Evan turned the knob and showed her into a room not many outside the family had ever seen.

"Okay." Kyra's gaze journeyed around the room, from the floor to ceiling shelves that were loaded with books and vials and pouches and every other tool they could possibly need, to the drying herbs that hung from the ceiling giving the room an incredible scent.

"This is fucking cool," she whispered in awe.

Evan shut the door behind them, sealing out any other sound, and let her take it all in. He was too nervous to do anything but pace. He had no idea how she was going to take this news. He hoped she would be as happy as he was but with her, he just didn't know.

She picked up on his unease. "Look, Ace, I know I shouldn't have—"

He turned to face her. "Kyra, you're pregnant." Out of all the possibilities he'd come up with, straight out seemed best.

Kyra backed away from him, shock now written across her face. "What? No, I'm not."

Evan only nodded.

"How could you know that?"

"I started to wonder after that dream we had, so I looked."

"You looked," she said flatly. "And didn't tell me. You've known *all* this time, and you didn't think I deserved to know? It's my fucking body, Ace. You had no right to keep that from me."

She had a valid reason to be pissed off, but he needed her to understand. "In any other circumstance, I would have shouted it for the whole world to hear. Hell, I'd have rented a plane to pull a banner around Daytona for days. But remember what had just happened."

She was listening. That was good. "Noor had hijacked my dream and killed the baby you were carrying. *Our* baby. And said he would make that a reality if you were to ever get pregnant by anyone but him."

"I've told you over and over that no one makes decisions about my life. If it involves anything to do with me, I'd better fucking know about it."

He'd expected this reaction. But as he saw it, he'd had no other choice. He held her angry glare. "I couldn't take the chance that he'd find out, Kyra. I was afraid if I told you and he got inside your head, you wouldn't be able to hide that knowledge from him. He'd know and he'd retaliate."

Evan took a step closer to her and bared his soul. "My heart was ripped out when I woke up from that damned dream. When I discovered you were indeed carrying our child, I was scared shitless. I couldn't let Noor's threat become a reality. And I'd hoped that your utter belief that you weren't pregnant would protect you both."

"How was that protecting me? I was stabbed, Ace. And had to fight off that psychotic killer without even knowing I was endangering our child." Her words stopped and her hands flew to her stomach. Panic filled her brown eyes. "Oh God. I was stabbed. The baby."

"Everything's fine," Evan assured her quickly. "My mom and sisters checked you over. You and the baby are perfect."

Deep down she must know that he'd never lie to her about something this important. The fear receded from her face. But not the anger.

"This is what happens when you try to play God with people's lives, Evan. Do you think I would have gone off on my own if I'd known I was pregnant? Fuck no, I wouldn't have. If you'd had any faith in me, you would have told me as soon as you found out."

"If it makes any difference, I never planned on keeping this from you for long. And I've kicked myself a hundred times for not telling you sooner, but I thought I was doing the right thing."

She took a breath and let it out. "The point is, you still kept it from me and that can't happen again." She crossed her arms over her chest. "So why are you telling me now? The threat is still out there. What's changed?"

"I just had to wait until we could come up with a way to protect you. I've had my mom working on a spell, one that will cloak the baby and make it invisible to Noor. It's ready."

Kyra was silent for quite a while. Evan just stood back and let her work it all out in her mind.

"This spell will work? It'll keep the baby hidden?"

"Yes," he stated simply.

Her hands returned to her belly. "And you're absolutely sure I'm pregnant?"

With the worst over, Evan approached her and wrapped his arms around her waist, pulling her body in close to his. "Very sure. Our daughter is in there."

"Oh, God." Her voice was shaky now.

"Is that a good 'Oh, God' or a bad one? Because on my end, I couldn't be happier."

"You are? We haven't even known each other that long."

"Long enough to know I want nothing more than to spend the rest of my life with you. And our children. Two girls and a boy, right?"

She gave a nervous laugh. "You can't really think it'll be like my imagination?"

He leaned in and kissed her nose. "I do. The universe has a funny way of getting exactly what it wants. It's not only God that works in mysterious ways."

"I'll probably drive you nuts and piss you off *all* the time. Are you certain you want to take that on?"

"In a heartbeat. And I hope both of our girls are just like you."

"Oh, boy, you've really got it bad."

"I really do. And so do you." He twitched his nose at her and she gave him a real laugh.

"Yeah, I kind of do."

"So what do you say we protect our daughter?"

Kyra nodded. "Whatever it takes."

Evan sent a short message to his family. They'd all gather to cast this spell. The more power they had behind it, the stronger it would be.

"What do you need me to do?"

"Just stay here with me. Everyone's coming."

True to his word, every member of his family—including Jacob—came to help.

Mary wasted no time in getting what they needed set up. Evan noted that she'd already gathered the ingredients and had it all set aside.

Transferring a large tray to the work table, Mary arranged it all neatly and within reach. As she started to drop pinches of this and dashes of that into the bowl, she explained why she'd chosen them.

"Amber for defense from outside influences and psychic attacks. False Unicorn Root to protect mother and baby. Angelica Root creates a barrier against negative energy. And a little Mandrake Root for good measure to boost the overall power of the spell."

Mary picked up the blade and handed it to Evan who stood next to her. "The last two elements are yours and Kyra's blood."

Evan didn't hesitate. He scored the sharp edge over his palm near the one he'd done to find Kyra. Flexing his fist, he held it out over the receptacle and allowed his blood to coat the items already there. Beside him, Kyra did the same without a flinch.

His mom nodded, pleased. "I've written out the spell. I want everyone in this room—magical and not—to recite it. Send every bit of love and conviction you have into your words."

Spell in hand, ten voices rang together.

"A child's innocence, a child's grace
Conceal them now without a trace
Safe in the womb, protected from harm
This family's love is the charm
Evil's ear never to hear, its gaze never to see
As we will, so mote it be."

The contents of the stone bowl in the middle of the table glowed with a soft pink light. Which told Evan the spell had been cast. His child was now protected.

"Did it work?" Kyra glanced to the people around her before settling on Evan.

"It did." Evan leaned in and kissed her softly. "She's safe."

24

Later that night, as Kyra lay in bed listening to Evan's soft breathing, she still didn't know what to think. She was pregnant. Holy shit. What did she know about raising a child?

Could she even do this? How did she know she wouldn't be as fucked-up as her own mother had been? She'd had no one to show her how to be a good mother. But she'd had some stellar examples of what *not* to do.

Maybe that was her answer. Just do the opposite of every other woman who had been in her life.

With the exception of Mary Burke. In the short time she'd known the incredible woman, Kyra had seen the love she held for each of her children. The smiles, the touches, the unconditional support. Even when she was angry, there was no doubt the love was still there.

Kyra ran her hands over her belly. *I promise to do my very best by you, baby girl. When I mess it up—and I will—please know that I love you.*

Maybe sensing her turmoil, Evan rolled toward her and pulled her into the curve of his warm body. She fell asleep knowing that she too was loved.

~~~

Life kind of fell into a rhythm, and for the next few weeks,
~~~

they all went about their lives. Kyra watched all of the Burkes and wondered how they could act like nothing had happened, or was going to happen. She asked Anna about it one day at the gym.

"We don't borrow trouble," Anna told her simply. "It's never good when Noor is dormant for any length of time, but all we can do is prepare and be ready for when he shows up again. And in that downtime, we live. For our own sanity, and to show him he doesn't matter. We're not going to walk around scared or wringing our hands waiting for him to strike again."

"I guess I can understand that."

"We've had a lot longer to process this mess than you have. We've learned to take the good times when we can get them. There's no sense in worrying about the next battle. It'll come and, when it does, we'll do whatever it takes to win it."

Kyra tried to keep that in mind, but it was almost impossible for her not to wonder when and how Noor would strike next. Her nerves were strung tight, she wasn't sleeping well, and her appetite was low.

About a week after her talk with Anna, Evan sat her down one evening after they'd had dinner.

"You can't go on this way. It's not good for you, and it's definitely not good for the baby."

Kyra hadn't allowed herself to think or even talk about the baby with anyone. She was scared to death that Noor would discover her secret.

"We shouldn't be talking about this," she warned Evan in a hushed voice.

"Talk about what? The baby? Hon, she's going to be fine."

"How can you be so sure?" Kyra stood and took a couple of steps before swinging back around to where he sat on the couch. "How can you know that some dried weeds, blood, and a little rhyme is enough to protect our daughter from him?"

He came to her. "Because this is what I do. This is who I am."

"But it's not who *I* am." She spun around to pace away but he grabbed her arm and brought her back.

"I thought you trusted me." His gaze was fierce and she was trapped in it.

She couldn't look away. "I do."

"Then why are you suddenly doubting me? Doubting my abilities?"

She wrenched her arm free and shouted at him, "Because it's not just me anymore, it's her too!"

"She's mine too!" he yelled back. He seemed to gather himself and his voice gentled. "Do you honestly think I'd let her be hurt in any way?"

"No." Kyra rubbed her hands over her face before looking at him again. "But I don't know your world, Evan. How can I put my faith in something I still don't completely understand? It just seemed so little. Herbs and words. How am I supposed to put my faith in that? When I think of protecting my child, my first thought is physical weapons—guns, knives...hell, *explosives*. Something tangible. What you and your family did, that's not tangible to me. It doesn't seem like enough."

Evan held her gaze for a long moment. Then he seemed to deflate. "Fuck. I'm sorry. I should have looked at this from your point of view. Of course you'd have reservations." He reached out and grasped her hands in his. "You've been so accepting of it all that it's hard for me to remember this *isn't* your world."

He guided her back to the sofa. "How can I assure you that... what was it...herbs and words are enough to keep her safe?"

"I don't know. That's the problem." She felt miserable.

He was silent, and Kyra could almost see the wheels turning as he tried to work through something in his head. "I have an idea." Before she knew what he'd planned, he conjured a white rose into his hand.

"What's your favorite color?"

Kyra looked up at his hair and then into his eyes. "Black."

"Not really a color," he laughed. "But we'll go with it. I want to show you the power a spell has when it's done right. This first one doesn't need herbs, just simple words. Ones that rhyme. But look what they can do."

He smirked and held the rose up.

"Never to hurt, never to harm
I seek only a simple charm
A change of color I ask of thee
As I will, so mote it be."

The pristine white turned to the darkest black and Kyra gasped. He handed it to her and she couldn't help but run her fingers over the softness of it.

"That's amazing."

"And there's so much more. Here's a particular favorite of mine. But keep in mind we were sixteen and girl-crazy when we came up with this one."

Kyra didn't know what to expect after that qualifier but was ready for anything.

"Brushed, flossed, and minty fresh
No one wants morning breath
Clean and sparkling for all to see
As I will, so mote it be."

Evan leaned in and kissed her long and deep and, fuck it, his breath was minty fresh. When he pulled back and grinned, she burst out laughing.

"You and your brother, I assume," Kyra said when her mirth finally wound down.

"Hey, we had to come up with something for that first time a date went *really* well." His smile was unrepentant.

Evan showed her several more spells. The last had stars

twinkling on the ceiling of their living room. They reclined against each other and stared up at the night sky he'd created.

"You'll have to do this one for our daughter." Kyra smiled and felt it to her center. "She's going to love it."

The huge weight that had been resting on Kyra's heart dissolved as Evan showed her the scope and power of his magic.

"Will she have gifts too?" She ran her hands over her lower stomach. It was still weird to know someone was growing and living in there.

"Yes." His hand rubbed idly up and down her arm. "We're hereditary witches. We're a long line, and the name Burke holds a lot of respect within the Wiccan community. Because of that, it's a long-standing tradition that every new generation carry the name regardless."

She sat up and turned to look at him. "So when the women marry, they don't take the husbands' names? The children stay Burkes? And the men are okay with that?"

"There are some out there who refuse to follow the custom." He sat up too and shifted so he was facing her. "But most realize the benefit. My father, Joe, Seth—they're all strong, capable men who are willing to sacrifice their own family name to do what's best for their kids."

That was pretty awesome in Kyra's view. She'd never met anyone who'd been willing to sacrifice anything for another person. Until she'd met the Burkes. This family was unlike any she had ever seen.

"You know," Evan reached out and took her hands in his, "we haven't really talked about what we're going to do."

"About what?"

"We're having a baby. We're living here together. Is that all you want?"

Kyra's stomach clenched. "What do *you* want?"

He grinned and shook his head. "I asked you first."

She narrowed her eyes at him for pinning her down but

thought about it. "I've never really considered the future. I guess I assumed I'd just go on as I always had."

"And now?"

Kyra took the biggest leap of faith she'd ever taken. She moved in closer to him. Sliding her hand up his chest, it wound around his neck to the back of his head. Stretching up, Kyra kissed his lips. As she drew back, she held his gaze.

"And now...I can't see my future without you in it. My life changed forever when I plowed into you in that alley. You've shown me what a real family is and what true love feels like. I know that even when I mess up—and that will probably be often—you'll always love me."

Kyra saw that love shining back at her in his dark eyes. That same look she'd been so jealous of between Seth and Aria. Seeing it now made what she was going to say next a little easier. "Will you marry me?"

He grinned down at her. "I thought you'd never ask." He molded his mouth to hers and she reveled in the softness of his lips and the heat of his tongue moving against hers. Until suddenly he pulled back and narrowed his eyes.

"You proposed. Aren't I supposed to get a ring?"

"Shut up, Ace, and kiss me again."

He did that and so much more.

Once they finally made it to bed, Kyra slept as she hadn't in weeks, recouping what her body so desperately needed. So deep was her sleep, she didn't know when the dream started. She just knew it was wrong.

It was dark. Blackness surrounded her. She was alone, yet she wasn't. She could feel him. Noor. He was close. Stalking her. Instead of running, she turned to face him.

"I know you're here," she shouted.

It was as if the curtains parted and out walked the most hideous thing she'd ever seen. The beast. Kyra had gotten glimpses before, but now she glared up at him openly.

Prowling on all fours it was at least eight feet tall. The grotesque creature towered over her, breathing its foul stench down on her, its black body hairless and bulging with muscle. The neck was thick and corded and extended up to support a massive head. The shape and size called to mind a grizzly, and the long muzzle was full of sharp, dagger-like teeth. The fangs were at least ten inches long and as big around as her arm at the widest part. They dripped now with saliva as its beady eyes smirked menacingly at her.

Sprouting out of the top of its skull were horns. Big around and ribbed, they curled back over the head like a bighorn sheep. Shrouded within the curves were tall bat-like ears. They moved and twitched, picking up the slightest of sounds.

"You really are one ugly motherfucker." Kyra held her ground even as her stomach roiled at the sight. She made herself look up into its oily black and hollow eyes. "We both know you're not going to kill me." She was pleased when her voice came out irreverent and flippant. "Why don't you just put that thing away before someone gets hurt? You know…Now that I think about it, I've got to wonder if the size of it is compensating for another area of your life." She wrinkled up her nose. "And dude, have you ever even heard of a breath mint? Yikes."

The beast roared and Kyra smiled to herself. She seemed to have that effect on people.

Suddenly, the creature began to fold in on itself and morph. It was only seconds later that a man stood in front of her.

"I really don't care for this new attitude of yours, Isabel. You've become insolent without my guiding hand."

"Look, Eddie," Kyra shook her head at his persistence, "can you possibly wrap your crazy-as-shit brain around this one tiny," she held her thumb and index finger up until they almost touched, "bit of information?" Kyra leaned forward hoping he'd get it this time. "I. Am. Not. Isabel."

His face actually turned red with rage, and before she knew

what was happening, she was flying back from the magical blow he'd thrown at her. Landing on her ass and tumbling, Kyra swore under her breath. "Yeah, that hurt."

In the bed she shared with Evan, her body jerked but she didn't wake.

Gaining her feet again, Kyra brushed her hands over her ass. "Look, dickhead, I've had just about as much from you as I'm going to take. You fucking touch me again, I'll kill you my-goddamned-self, and then you won't have to wait for the Burkes to do it."

He puffed up in response to her threat. "Do you know who I am? Do you know what I could do to you with just a single thought?"

She stabbed her finger at him. "I know exactly who and what you are, you stupid son of a bitch." Kyra was royally pissed and let all of her anger, frustration, and hate free. "You're a bully who's been having a temper tantrum for five-hundred-fucking-years. So your wife left you. So what!" Kyra threw her hands up. "Get the fuck over it! You treated her like shit. Did you honestly expect her to stick around to take even more?"

Kyra didn't let the fact that his head was about to explode stop her tirade. "Instead of letting it go and getting on with your pathetic, sadistic little life, you swear out revenge like a spoiled child whose toy has been taken away." She cocked her head to the side. "How'd that work out for you, genius? I'll tell you how. *It didn't.* Because you bit off more than you could chew going after the Burkes, and they locked you in a goddamned magical cage!" Each word had gotten louder until she was yelling.

"All that power you gained by going through only God-knows-what-kind of torture has gotten you absolutely *nowhere.* You want to know why?" She didn't give him a chance to reply. "Because evil will *never* win out over good. And the Burkes are as good as anyone gets. They are so much better than you will *ever* be."

Finished, Kyra dismissed him with a wave of her hand. "Now, get the fuck out of my head and don't you ever fucking come back."

He stood silent as her scathing words rained down over him. Suddenly, he screamed out his wrath and the beast returned. Kyra thought for sure she'd pushed him too far and he'd kill her this instant.

The beast took a slow step closer to her. She had to tip her head back to keep his face in sight, but she held her ground. She refused to back down.

"I'll kill you all." His voice in this form was more guttural. The words formed within the growl rolling up his throat. "Every last one of you will suffer and beg for death by the time I am done with you."

He disappeared, and Kyra woke up on a gasp. She lay there for a minute thinking about what had just happened. And it wasn't pleasant. "Well, Pride, you let your mouth override your ass again."

"What?" Evan's sexy sleepy voice muttered beside her.

Kyra turned to look into his handsome face. "Good news. I don't think Noor sees me as his wife anymore...Bad news, he wants to kill me now."

Evan sat up in bed. "Wait. What? Noor? He came into your dream. Did he hurt you?" His gaze and hands checked her over. "What did he do?"

She grasped his hands in hers and looked deep into his eyes. "He didn't hurt me. I'm fine." Kyra recited everything that had happened. Every word she'd said prnd how he'd taken it.

Evan listened to it all and then completely shocked her by throwing his head back and laughing. "You called him *Eddie*?" He laughed so hard there were tears in his eyes when he looked over at her.

Eventually, he caught his breath. "Is it any wonder I love

you so damned much?" He pulled her into his arms and held her.

"You're not mad? I probably shouldn't have antagonized him. He was pretty pissed."

"His threats aren't anything we haven't heard a thousand times. They don't worry us."

"Glad to hear it." Kyra settled into Evan's warmth. Thinking back on the dream, she chuckled. "He almost turned purple he was so mad. I thought his head was going to pop off."

They both laughed at that and Kyra, feeling pretty satisfied with herself, rolled on top of Evan's long, lean body. She tucked her face into the crook of his neck and kissed him. She felt alive. And happy. And free.

Nibbling her way down his chest, she delighted in his hum of pleasure. She followed the trail of dark hair that led lower and lower. Finding him hard and ready, she glanced up and was caught in the emotions shining in those clear, dark eyes.

It struck her then. Both Evan and Noor's beast had black-as-pitch irises. But it was what was in them that was so completely different. In Noor's she saw a yawning nothingness. Devoid of anything good or light.

In Evan's, the man fate had decided would be hers, she saw love and devotion and everything that was right and bright in her world. Kyra sent a silent thanks to whatever force had put them in each other's path.

"I love you, Evan."

He smiled softly down at her. "And I love you. Always."

Still holding his stare, Kyra ran her tongue up the underside of his shaft.

He drew in a sharp breath and his eyes closed in bliss. Wrapping her hand tightly around him, she took him into her mouth.

"Oh, God, that feels fucking amazing."

Kyra played and tormented him until he roughly pulled her

up his body. A quick move had her under him. He stared down at her, holding her locked in his gaze as he slid into her. Now it was her turn to gasp as he filled her.

He set a hard and demanding pace meant to drive her wild. Her short nails scored his back as she fought for something to hold on to. She was lost to sensation. All that existed were him and her and this all-consuming passion they brought to each other.

She panted and moaned as her body tightened and coiled. He knew her now; he knew she was close. Shifting the angle of his penetration, he put delicious pressure on her swollen clit. And that was all it took. Her release burst through her and Kyra's breath caught in her lungs. Everything narrowed down to the contractions he set off deep inside of her.

Her body squeezed and pulled at his, wringing a "Fuck, yeah" from him. Her channel was still milking his as he thrust once, twice more, and then buried deep with a groan.

His orgasm triggered another in her, causing her to swear just as ripely as he had.

Sweaty and spent, they collapsed. He was heavy on her, but she couldn't find the energy to care.

He evidently could as he rolled to the side, taking her with him. Eyes still closed, Kyra felt him shift a little, and then the blanket was covering them. She fell asleep wrapped in his arms and rested undisturbed until morning.

25

Kyra came awake reluctantly. She yawned and stretched, pulling the covers up higher and snuggling back in. Until her suddenly-rebelling stomach had her jumping naked from the bed and running for the bathroom.

After retching, she stood at the sink and brushed her teeth. She did it gently so as not to set off her gag reflex and start the whole ordeal over again. Out of the corner of her eye, she saw Evan enter with a mug and a few crackers on a folded-up paper towel.

"I don't think I can stomach coffee right now."

"It's tea. And saltines." He offered them to her. "It's supposed to help with morning sickness."

"Morning…Oh, right." Kyra hadn't put it together yet. Is this what she had to look forward to in the months to come? *Ugh.*

She took one of the crackers from him. While she nibbled it, he set the rest on the counter and grabbed a robe for her. It was his so she swam in it, but it covered her.

"Come on. Let's sit you back in bed until this passes." He picked up the tea as she took the saltines and led her back into the bedroom.

Kyra settled herself with a pillow behind her. As he handed her the teacup, she asked, "*Will* it pass? I really don't want to do that again."

He sat on the side of the mattress at her feet and chuckled.

"From what I've read, morning sickness varies for everyone. Some women never suffer from it at all, and others have it their entire pregnancy."

"The *whole* time?" Kyra shook her head. "Oh, hell no. Isn't there something you can do, magic man?"

Evan laughed. "I'd have to ask my mom. This is a first for me too."

"Call her," Kyra demanded. "Right now."

"Okay." Evan reached for his cell, still grinning.

Kyra munched and sipped as she watched him dial and place the phone to his ear. She listened to his half of the conversation and tried to figure out what Mary was saying.

By his responses, it didn't sound good for her.

When he hung up, he turned back to her. "She said as much as she'd like to help, this is something you'll just have to go through. It's the body's way of adjusting to what's going on in there. She'll give us the recipe for her heal-anything tea, but it's that and crackers for the duration, baby. I'm sorry."

"What good are you magic people, anyway?" She pouted but he only smiled at her.

Kyra felt the tell-tale signs again and clamped her hand over her mouth. Pushing Evan out of the way, she took off for the bathroom again.

After flushing and cleaning her mouth out again, she moved to stand in the doorway. Evan was seated on the bed, back propped against the headboard.

"What are you doing?"

"Taking care of my girls." He patted the mattress next to him. "Come back to bed."

She started across the room. "Don't you have to go to work?" She crawled in beside him.

He pulled her close and brushed her short hair back away from her face. "Haven't you heard? We just closed a big case. A serial killer. I think I'm entitled to take a day off after that.

Seth can handle whatever comes up."

"I should tell you I can take care of myself and for you to go to work." Kyra closed her eyes and tried to swallow away the tightness in her throat. "But I'd rather have you here with me."

"No place I'd rather be. Puke and all."

She didn't have enough energy to do anything but pinch his side, but she snuggled in against him and hoped that the worst of this was over.

$$\sim\sim\sim$$

Evan left Kyra sleeping as he headed for the kitchen. She'd thrown up a few more times through the morning, but it seemed to have subsided in the last hour. Given that the time was nearing the afternoon hours, he hoped there was a reason they called it *morning* sickness, and that she'd get a reprieve for the rest of the day. For now, he was starving.

Throwing a cold-cut sandwich together, he decided to call Seth and check in. Taking his plate and his phone with him, he went and sat at the table. He took his first bite as he dialed.

"Hey, how's she doing?" Seth said in lieu of a hello.

Evan swallowed. "Better. She's sleeping. It seems to have passed for the time being. Anything going on I need to know about?"

"Not much. Someone tried to bust open an ATM downtown." Evan heard the incredulousness in Seth's tone. "Joker must not have realized, or had been too drunk to care, that all those machines have cameras in them. Got his ugly mug clear as day. Dude's a known dirtbag too. Shouldn't take long to pick him up."

Evan shook his head. "Idiots. At least they make our jobs easier." He took another bite. Around ham, turkey, and cheese he told his partner, "Well, looks like the city is safe in your hands then. I'll leave you to it."

He hung up and set his phone aside to concentrate on the rest of his lunch. He suddenly realized he'd forgotten something to drink. Getting up, he headed for the fridge. Pulling it open, he tried to decide if he wanted a beer, a soda, or water. He reached past the first two and went with the water.

The door swung shut as he twisted off the cap. That's as far as he got, because that's when he saw Kyra sitting in his chair, scarfing down the rest of his sandwich.

She looked up at him and shrugged. "I woke up so hungry," she mumbled around the big bite she'd just taken. "And I could smell this all the way into the bedroom. Weird." She swallowed, looked down, and studied the food in her hands. "Can you get me the mustard? This needs more mustard."

It needed more because Evan hadn't put any on it in the first place. He was more of a mayo man when it came to sandwiches—other than salami, of course. That always called for the tangy condiment.

With a shake of his head, he turned back to the refrigerator and found the yellow squeeze bottle. He returned to the table and set it next to what *had* been his plate. He sat down in the chair adjacent to her and watched in fascination as she took the top piece of bread off, upended the bottle, and splattered a sizeable amount all over the meat.

Evan's jaw twinged just thinking about what that much mustard would taste like. It would most definitely overpower everything else on there. How the hell could she eat that?

He couldn't recall her ever doing this before and wondered if it was a pregnancy thing. Wasn't it too soon for that, though? He was going to have to do some more reading.

"How's the sandwich?" he asked dryly.

"Mmm," she mumbled. "So good. Thanks."

"No problem." Evan laughed and watched her eat with gusto. "No more nausea?"

She made a negative sound in her throat as her mouth was

full again. Once she chewed and swallowed, she went on. "I woke up and felt great. Good as new. Would never know I was chucking up my toenails an hour before."

Kyra enjoyed a few more bites. "Do we have any of those yellow peppers? The ones that come on an antipasto salad?"

"Pepperoncini," Evan supplied. "Not that I know of."

"Shoot. They sounded really good."

Evan watched her with awe and thought she was nuts, but he conjured a jar for her anyway.

Those whiskey eyes sparkled at him. "Aww, that's so sweet. Thank you, Ace." She leaned over and kissed him, and all he could smell and taste was mustard.

Yummy. Or not.

After the spicy sandwich, she ate two of the peppers and finally seemed satisfied. Thank God, because Evan was afraid of what she might ask for next.

"I want to go to the gym," Kyra surprised him by saying after wiping her mouth with the napkin he handed her.

Evan was shocked by her quick turnaround. "Are you sure?"

"I'm pregnant, not terminal." She gave him a disgruntled look that he would even question her. "And besides, I'm fine now."

He held up his hands. "Who am I to argue?" She should know her own body—what she could handle and what she couldn't. He'd still keep an eye on her though. "All right. Let's go."

They walked into Knight's Place half an hour later. Early afternoon meant a lull in activity. The ones who were there were the men who competed on a regular basis and needed to perfect their skills and stay in top form. Evan didn't see Joe anywhere and assumed he was back in his office.

As he and Kyra had dressed in workout clothes before they'd left, they got right into it. He kept a subtle eye on her until he saw that she wasn't going to overdo it. Reassured, Evan settled into his own workout.

Sometime later, he was sweating heavily when he took a break to get a drink. It was just at that moment that about ten guys walked in. He knew right away they weren't here looking for a workout. Not the usual kind, anyway.

Needing to know where Kyra was, he scanned the room. She was doing reps with some dumbbells, but she looked over at him and gave a slight nod. She'd picked up on the vibe of their visitors too.

Evan called to his siblings. *"Kyra and I are with Joe. You all need to get here. Now."*

"Jacob and I were almost there. I'll have to turn back and take him to Mom and Dad's," Anna said. *"What's going on?"*

"Noor's goons, I'm guessing. Ten of them." Evan gave her an abbreviated version of what had happened last night, knowing Aria and Ethan would also hear.

"I called Seth. We're on our way."

"Ten minutes," Ethan promised.

Movement out of the corner of his eye alerted Evan that Joe had finally made an appearance. Evan casually lifted his bottle of water to take a drink and caught Joe's gaze. His future brother-in-law sent the barest chin-notch that he understood what was happening.

Joe moved to intercept the men. "Hey, guys. How can I help you?"

The last man in turned the deadbolt with a resounding snap, locking them all in. They fanned out and he saw Joe bracing.

Evan rose from the bench and made his way closer to where Joe was facing off with the men. He sensed Kyra had also moved forward and his heart stuttered. He wanted so badly for her to separate herself from this, but he knew better than to think she would.

He'd just have to make damned sure no one laid a hand on her.

They were close enough now to hear Joe talking to the men.

"Are you guys really sure you want to do this? I can guarantee your boss didn't give you all the details. Noor couldn't care less if he loses a few soldiers. He can always find more."

"I think we'll take our chances." The designated leader laughed and looked back at his comrades who were all snickering. "Since there are more of us than there are of you."

Joe shrugged. "Have it your way. But don't say I didn't warn you."

Evan didn't know if the thugs hadn't seen the athletes before, or if they just hadn't cared. But they saw them now as the three of them aligned themselves with Joe.

"Got a problem here, Mr. Conrad?"

"Nah, no problem here. Right, gentlemen?" Joe turned to address his client. "I've got this, Tony. Why don't you and the others just call it a day? We'll work on your footwork more tomorrow."

Tony eyed the group critically. Evan thought for sure he'd refuse to do as Joe had asked, but he and the others eventually nodded and left via the rear door.

Evan let out a relieved breath. The last thing they needed was for there to be innocent by-standers if things got out of hand. They'd have a hard time explaining why the building was shaking or why stuff was flying around all by itself.

The gang spread out around the three of them. Evan, Kyra, and Joe shifted so they could keep them all in sight. He cast a quick glance to Kyra.

"Stay safe. Ten minutes, tops." She would know he'd called for backup, and that the cavalry would start showing up soon.

She nodded. "No problem. And just to liven things up, how about a baseball bat, Ace?"

Evan liked her style. He conjured one and passed it to her. Joe, he knew, would prefer his own hands, just as Evan did. But if things got a little dicey, he also had a few tricks up his sleeve.

It was telling that not one of the intruders blinked at what Evan had just done. So they knew he had power, but they obviously didn't care. The commander of Noor's little army gave a hand motion that had his guys splitting off. Four took Joe and three plus the leader zeroed in on Evan. The last two were left with Kyra. *Poor bastards.*

Once everyone was squared off, there was a beat of complete silence. Not even a whisper of breath. Then all hell broke loose.

Evan tried to keep Kyra in sight, but he had his hands full with the four on him. The last sight he'd had of her said she was swinging for the fences.

Noor had chosen his men well this time. They seemed to know what they were doing. Not just street thugs or punks; these guys knew some moves.

Evan took a punch to the jaw that had him seeing stars. Before he could fully recover, two of the goons grabbed him by the arms. As a third approached, Evan used the two for balance and came up off his feet to plant them in his opponent's chest.

He went down, but the fourth man was there to step in. He plowed a fist into Evan's ribs hard enough to force all the air out of his lungs. It took a moment before Evan could suck precious oxygen back in.

While he fought to breathe, he got the call he'd been waiting for from Ethan.

"We're here."

"Dead bolt," he gasped out.

"Not a problem."

Everyone in the room jumped when a loud bang signaled the aluminum framed door being blasted off his hinges. It flew inward and landed a good ten feet from the threshold. The sound of the tempered glass shattering on impact was loud in the startled silence.

Ethan came striding in and the action resumed. Seth and Aria were on his heels. They waded into the fray with no hesitation. Noor's henchmen redistributed themselves to cover the newcomers.

But with the added allies, the battle's dynamics changed. Burke and friends began to take the upper hand. Evan saw that Aria had gone to Kyra and together they were holding off any who came at them. A few of Noor's men, sensing defeat, ran for the exit.

Then Anna called out telepathically.

"It's a trick! Noor's using your attack as a distraction. He sent men to Mom and Dad's to get Jacob. We're holding them off, but I don't know for how much longer."

As the only ones who heard her, Evan and his siblings all felt a quick bite of fear. Even if they could take this whole group down at once, they couldn't get to their parents' house fast enough.

Evan caught the eye of Aria and Ethan and knew they'd figured out the same thing. Was Noor going to win this time? Would they lose Jacob?

No fucking way. He could conjure any goddamned thing he wanted, and right now, he wanted his nephew away from that evil bastard.

"Ethan, keep me clear for a minute."

His brother shifted closer to Evan, no questions asked. Evan backed himself farther out of the fighting.

He'd never tried doing this before. He would have never even thought it possible. But unless he did something now, Jacob would be taken from them. And he would suffer unimaginable torture at Noor's hand.

Taking a steadying breath, Evan closed his eyes. He concentrated on the little boy with everything he had in him.

So as not to freak out his sister, he warned her. *"Anna. I'm going to try and get Jake out of there."*

"Do whatever it takes to save my son, Evan."

"That's the plan."

Evan gathered every bit of Burke power flowing through his veins. He pulled the image of Jake closer and closer to him. Harnessing and focusing that which had been born to him, he took Anna and Joe's son from where he was, and brought him to his side.

26

Evan dropped to his knees once Jacob had arrived safely. He was exhausted mentally and physically, but he reached out and grasped his nephew's hand. Meeting the child's frightened eyes, Evan smiled.

"Anna. I've got him. He's safe."

"Thank God. I'll ask how you did that later."

"Do you want me to try and get you out?"

"No. Now that I know Jacob is safe, Mom and I can get rid of these assholes."

While Evan had been busy, the others had been making progress on Noor's henchmen. Only a few remained, and when those saw there was no hope of winning, they took off in a hurry.

"Jake?" Joe's surprised voice called out when he turned and saw his son. "What are you doing here? Where's Anna?"

"Daddy!" Jacob ran to Joe who lifted the six-year-old into his arms. "One minute I was at Nana and Papa's and the bad men were there, and then I was here."

Evan slowly gained his feet. "Noor tricked us. He used these guys to keep us busy while he made a grab for Jacob. He must have known we'd take him there."

"Anna called to us," Aria added. "But we couldn't have possibly gotten there in time." Her gaze landed on him. "How did you know you could do that?"

"I didn't." Evan shook his head. "But I had to try."

"Are they still under attack?" Seth asked. "Do we need to head over there?"

"Anna just sent word. She and Mom handled them," Evan said. "And with Jacob out of reach again, it wasn't too hard."

Kyra walked into his arms and smiled up at him. "Ace, did you just conjure a kid from across town?"

"Yeah, I guess I did." Evan rested his forehead against hers. He breathed her in for a moment and then raised his head and studied her beautiful face. "Are you okay? No damage?"

"We're good." Her brown eyes shone up at him. "Ball bats have a longer reach than arms. No one got near us."

Joe was still holding his son tight. "I'd feel better knowing my fiancé is unharmed. I'm going over there."

"We'll all go," Ethan added.

They found Anna and their parents seated on the couch in the living room. Evan sent his dad a look and got a nod in return. They were all right.

Joe immediately went to Anna and sat with her. "You okay?"

She took Joe's hand in hers and motioned Jacob to come join them. Once she had her family close, she explained. "We're fine. I'd just rushed Jacob into the house and was telling Mom and Dad what was happening when six of Noor's men showed up. The protection barriers on the house were keeping them out, but there was no telling how long they'd last. Or whether or not Noor would show up."

Anna looked up at her siblings. "That's when I called to you guys." She singled Evan out. "What exactly did you do? How did you get Jacob out?"

"I used my conjuring power to bring him to me."

Anna switched her attention to their mom. "Is that even possible?"

"Apparently, it is." Mary studied Evan for a moment. "In recent months, in times of crisis, each of you has seen an advancement of your powers. Aria, instead of just seeing a vision, was able to connect mentally with the other person to save her life. Anna not only *felt* that something worried Noor, but was able to see an image of our family journals in his mind."

She came back to her oldest son. "And now, Evan was able to expand his conjuring ability when the need was greatest."

Anna set Jacob on Joe's lap and stood. She walked to Evan and put her hands on each side of his face. "Thank you." She pulled his head down and kissed both of his cheeks. "I'll never be able to repay you."

Evan crouched down to wrap his arms around her waist. Standing upright again, he easily lifted her off the floor. He hugged her tight. "I love him too. We all do."

"So, Big Jake," Kyra broke into the quiet, "what's it like getting transported like on Star Trek?"

Anna returned to her son's side while he thought about that. His forehead wrinkled. "I don't know. I don't really remember any of it."

He spun around to Evan with excitement lighting his big brown eyes. "Can we do it again? I'll pay really close attention this time."

Evan laughed. "I don't think so, buddy. I think that's an in-case-of-emergency kind of thing."

Mary rose from the couch. "If no one has to rush off, I'll put some dinner together." She held her hand out to Jacob. "Want to help me? Another set of hands would be nice. This group eats *a lot*."

He jumped up and went off into the kitchen with her, probably expecting to score a snack in the process. Those left in the living room knew help wasn't the only reason. She was taking him out of the room so they could talk freely.

"This was too close," Joe stated. "He was able to split us up, and he almost got his hands on my son."

"Who called you Daddy today, by the way," Evan pointed

out.

Anna's blue eyes darted to Joe's amber ones. There was a sheen of moisture in them. "He what?"

Joe grinned. "He called out to me. He said Daddy. That's the first time he's ever done that."

"Oh, Joe." A tear slid down Anna's face.

Evan let them have the moment before bringing the conversation back around.

"Noor is only going to get more daring and bold in his actions," he warned. "And his army is coming together. Those men today were more skilled and more of a unit than ever before."

"How do we prevent something like today happening again?" Aria glanced at Anna and Joe, worry creasing her brow.

"I don't think we can." And Evan hated that. "I think we just stay prepared."

"That's not enough," Kyra interrupted. "It's not enough to just be ready. You need a plan for when it happens again. Because it *will*."

"What kind of plan do you suggest?" Joe pinned her with a questioning look.

Kyra smiled at Evan. That didn't bode well for him.

"Maybe something along the lines of the old shell game," she offered. "If Noor gets close, Ace here can just blip Jake right out."

"I've done that exactly once, Kyra," Evan argued. "How do you even know I can do it again? Over and over, if it comes to that?"

She gave him a smirk. "Because you're Evan Fucking Burke, that's how."

His dad, who had been silently listening up to that point, snorted out a laugh. "She's got you there, son."

"Dad—" Doubts filled Evan.

"For as long as you kids have been alive, you have amazed me every day. There's nothing you can't do when you put your minds to it. And just like Aria and Anna have had to practice their extended abilities, so now do you."

Evan looked around at the faces of his family. Not one of them showed any reservations about what he'd have to do. Joe and Anna both wore expressions of complete trust. His gaze then tracked to Kyra.

The woman he loved beyond all reason.

And in her he saw everything. Who he was, and everything he could one day be. Cop, witch, father, husband. And realized he wanted it all. In that one moment, he understood—each of those pieces was just as important, just as vital, as the next.

Like a lightbulb going off in his head, Evan shed his uncertainties and fears and finally embraced every part of who he was. And for the first time, took pride in all of it.

"Okay. Let's set this up. Anna, can you call Jacob in here for me, please?"

They left a few hours later with a plan in place. Evan would continue to practice and perfect the skill needed to keep Jacob safe. And when the time came to enact it, there'd be no worries and no hesitation.

"You know," Kyra mentioned when they crawled into bed, "I was thinking. You get pretty good at popping Jake around, and when the time comes, you could just zap this baby right out of me. No labor, no pushing. No muss, no fuss."

Evan chuckled. "I don't think that's a good idea."

"Why not?"

"I'd rather have your doctor take care of helping her out of there. That's his job."

"Chicken."

"You betcha," Evan laughed. "When it comes to delivering babies, I don't want any part."

"How long have you been a cop? And you've never had to?"

"Nope. And I'd like to keep that record going, if you don't mind."

"Well, don't think I'm doing this all on my own. You're going to be there every step, Ace. Right through delivery."

She was silent for a moment, and by the sinister look in her eye, Evan knew he was in for trouble. "As a matter of fact, I think I'll ask my doctor about you catching the baby and cutting the cord."

The thought of watching his child slide free of her mother and being the first to take that tiny girl into his arms…It filled him to bursting with love.

Evan pulled her close and nuzzled against her neck before pulling back to look her in the eyes. "I know you only said that to scare me. But I honestly can't think of anything that would make me happier."

~~~

It became evident in the ensuing weeks that Noor, already fucking crazy, was going farther and farther off the deep end. After his failed attempt at Jacob, his attacks came fast and hard. Between the mind games and the trouble his men were causing, Evan and his siblings were doing everything they could just to stay a step ahead.

Then one day, about a week before Halloween, it all stopped. Noor's end went completely silent. And that fact scared them more than the relentless battles ever had.

Because it could only mean that he was gearing up for a major showdown.

Not knowing when it would hit, they took measures to ensure they'd be ready for whatever Noor tried. Every chance they had, they worked on their linking and tested its limits. They'd also attempted to join Aria and Anna's force with Evan and Ethan's again, but were as yet unsuccessful.

They only had three months left to get it right. Time was swiftly closing in on their twenty-fifth birthdays. Would they
~~~

be ready?

Evan had to believe they would be. They *had* to be. There was no other option. Noor needed to be put down, forever. Evan didn't want his daughter coming into a world where she would be hunted simply for being who she was.

As Halloween approached, they tried to keep things as normal as possible for Jacob. Noor had taken so much from him already, Joe and Anna refused to allow the evil bastard to deprive him of even one more childhood experience. Jacob would have a traditional Halloween and he would go trick-or-treating, just like all the other kids.

But he would also have the biggest escort any child ever had. Every member of the Burke family planned on accompanying him around the neighborhood just as a precaution. None of them liked that Noor had gone underground, but they wouldn't let that stop them from living or showing Jacob how fun life could really be.

October thirty-first started just as all their other mornings. With Kyra jumping up out of bed and rushing to the bathroom. Evan followed his usual routine by going to the kitchen to get her a cup of tea and some crackers.

He met her coming out of the bathroom after the first round. Normally she would rest while he got ready for work. Then they'd head to Joe's gym, where Evan would drop her off for the day. But today was not only a holiday, it was Sunday. And he had the luxury of settling them back into bed for a few more hours.

While she sipped at her tea and nibbled at the crackers, Evan thought about the future.

"Just think," Evan smiled down at Kyra, "next year, we'll have our own little witch to take door to door."

"Won't she be too little?"

"She won't remember it, but we'll have the pictures to embarrass her with when she gets older."

"I take it you speak from experience?" Kyra laughed lightly.

"Oh, yeah." Evan smiled in remembrance. "My mom documented every event in our lives with hundreds of pictures. Some are so cringe-worthy I threatened to burn them. To which she countered by saying she'd put a protection spell on them to make them indestructible."

"I am so going to ask her to see those," she teased before suddenly sobering. "Crap. Here we go again."

Evan watched as she leapt out of bed. He was waiting when she returned and bundled her back into his arms.

"The great thing about having an identical twin," he went on as if there hadn't been an interruption, "is that I can blame some of the more embarrassing ones on Ethan."

"Nice try." She snuggled into him. "I don't think that's going to work for you, Ace. I'm sure your mom took detailed notes of who was who. And I'm pretty sure I can tell you apart, even back then."

Evan huffed out a breath. "Unfortunately, you're probably right."

They took it easy for the rest of the morning, and within a few hours, she was back to herself. The morning sickness never seemed to last beyond eleven.

And true to her new custom, she was starving. Her food cravings had taken a turn for the bizarre. Spicy seemed to be the taste of choice, so they'd stocked up on a variety of things that appealed to her now.

After lunch, they shared a shower. As the water tumbled down upon them, Evan held her against him. With her back to his front, his hands palmed her still-flat belly. He couldn't wait until he could feel their baby resting in there. He wanted to enjoy every part of this pregnancy with her.

Evan laid his lips against Kyra's shoulder. Placing leisurely kisses up her neck, he found the spot right behind her ear that drove her wild. His hands traveled up to cup her breasts, his thumb and forefinger gently rolling and pinching her sensitive nipples.

Kyra's breath caught and her head dropped back onto his chest. Her short, cropped hair gave Evan complete access to the long, elegant column of her neck. He took his time and feasted his fill.

Leaving one hand to massage her breast, the other slid down her water-slicked body to find the juncture of her thighs. He skimmed his fingers lightly over her mound, stroking her.

Her hips followed, wanting the intimate touch she knew was coming.

Using two fingers, Evan parted her delicate folds. Separating them just enough, he glided the rough-skinned digits down either side of the little nub. Back and forth he rubbed her until her knees threatened to buckle.

Tucked against her backside, his engorged shaft jerked and pulsed. He was so hard it hurt. All he wanted to do was grind it against her soft cheeks. Find solace in her body.

But he held himself under control. He loved to watch her come apart in his arms. He planned on wringing as much pleasure out of her as he could before finding his own release.

As he worked her, Kyra's hands found purchase on his thighs and held tight, her short nails digging into skin and muscle. He was her only anchor in the world of sensuality he wove around them.

She peaked in his arms, riding his hand as her core throbbed and spasmed. Her breathing came in pants and her legs shook as he relentlessly took her up again. When she fell the second time, he turned her and pressed her back against the tiled wall of the shower.

Pinning her body with his, Evan ran his hands down her legs and lifted them to rest around his waist. She locked her arms and ankles behind his back and held on to him.

Evan stared into the rich brown depths of her eyes as he

positioned himself to fill her heated, tight channel. As he thrust, he took care to keep the pace languid and dreamy. Such was their focus on each other, they could have been the only ones on the entire planet.

Within the cocoon of steam and water, Evan was lost. The way her inner muscles gripped and pulled at him as he withdrew nearly cost him everything. The return trip deep inside of her was no less mind-shattering. She was made for him. She was perfect.

Evan started to feel the tension gather in his groin. It spread out and through his center in the most pleasurable way. He knew he was reaching that point of no return. That point where the world could crash down around their ears and nothing would stop the explosion that was imminent.

One stroke, two. His muscles tightened and his heart beat faster. Still held in Kyra's gaze, Evan withdrew again and drove back into her. Buried deep, he felt an orgasm take her over a third time.

The additional spasms and contractions were more than he could take. Evan slammed home one more time. Unable to stop it, his eyes closed and his mind went blank as he throbbed and convulsed inside of her. There wasn't a single part of him that wasn't involved in the release. His entire system felt like he'd grabbed onto a live electrical wire. And surrounded by that, the warm glow of love.

27

As the sensations gradually faded, Evan settled his weight into Kyra a little more heavily. His heart was still pounding in his chest and his breath was rasping in and out of his lungs. He knew he needed to move but he couldn't find the energy.

Kyra seemed to be in the same condition. Her legs had slid down his and she hung limply in his arms.

Evan mustered enough strength to reach down and turn off the faucet. "We can't stay in here."

"Okay," Kyra mumbled against his shoulder but didn't move.

"You're going to make me carry you out of here, aren't you?"

"Uh-huh." A small nod went with it.

He braced an arm around her shoulders and bent to scoop the other under her knees. Holding her high against his chest, he carried her out of the shower. Grabbing a towel on the way, he took her back into the bedroom.

Next to the bed, he stood her upright and wiped down every inch of her. Once they were both dry, he tucked them into bed where they slept until two.

When Evan came awake, Kyra was pressed into his side. What a way to spend a lazy Sunday. In bed with the woman he adored.

They'd have to meet up with everyone later, but right now they still had hours. And Evan would use them in the best way he knew how. Slowly kissing Kyra awake before taking her again.

When they finally made it to Anna and Joe's later that afternoon, they were both relaxed and happy. Everyone would be gathered in the backyard for a cookout, and they'd enjoy a great meal together before taking Jacob out at dusk to hit up the neighbors for candy.

As Evan and Kyra rounded the house, Jacob galloped by, his war-cry echoing. Already dressed as a knight of old, he rode his faithful steed—a stuffed horse head on a stick. With one hand holding his mount steady and the other brandishing a foil-covered cardboard sword high, Sir Burke guided his destrier into battle.

It didn't surprise Evan that Jacob had chosen to be a knight. He'd had a fixation on the men-at-arms ever since meeting Joe. And Joe had only reinforced that connection since by protecting Jacob from the evil hunting him.

"Hey, Sir Knight," Evan called, "where did you find such a cool ride?"

"Nana brought it," Jacob yelled back as he trotted in circles. "She said it's old but I can borrow it for today."

Evan's mom grinned when he glanced down to where she sat watching the littlest Burke.

"It was mine. I've had it stashed away in the attic for years. I tried to give it to you kids when you were little, but you didn't have any interest in it." Her loving gaze followed Jake's progress around the yard. "It's a good thing I held on to it."

"He really seems to enjoy it." Evan laughed and motioned for Kyra to have a seat at the picnic table. He leaned down to her as soon as she was settled. "Do you want anything to drink?"

"Water would be good."

Evan kissed her gently and grinned. "Coming right up." He straightened to his full height and headed for the sliding door on the back of the house that led to the kitchen.

As he neared the grill—manned by his dad, Joe, Ethan,

and Seth—he heard a good-natured argument going on. As he glanced over the hamburgers and hot dogs cooking there, he spied the problem. One half of the grill was blackening the meat into charred bits, while the other looked to be cold.

Only a portion of the briquettes had caught and heated.

Evan eyed Joe critically. "You know, you have a pyro-head standing right next to you. He could have those lit and cooking at the perfect temperature with just a thought."

"Yes," Joe cocked a brow at him, "I do know that. But as we're trying to teach Jacob that he can't rely on magic for everything, it wouldn't be right to fall back on it now." His tone was only slightly patronizing. "They'll take off and the heat will even out; it's just a matter of time."

"I applaud your teaching methods, son," Paul told Joe. "And under normal circumstances, I'd totally agree. But you've got a hungry hoard here. And those aren't going to be fit to eat the way they're going." Paul shook his head. "I think you need to concede defeat here, Joe."

Joe cast another glance at the coals and then to Ethan. He nodded.

And as luck would have it, Jacob ran by just as Ethan made a move with his hand and took control of the cooking fire.

"Heeeyyy," Jacob scolded. "You're not supposed to use your magic for that kind of stuff." He turned accusing eyes to Joe. "Dad, you and Mom said I couldn't do that, so why can Uncle Ethan?"

Just before Evan turned and retreated to the safety of the house, he saw Joe blast his dad and Ethan a scathing glare. At the same time, Seth choked off a laugh. Evan was still grinning as he entered the kitchen and crossed to the fridge for Kyra's water and a beer for himself.

When he exited a few moments later, the men were still trying to explain to a peeved six-year-old why one rule applied to him and not to another.

Kyra motioned with her head to the discussion going on. "What's that all about?"

"A glimpse into our future." He relayed the story as he straddled the bench facing her.

"Oh, man. I've been trying not to think about what it was going to be like to raise a child who can wield magic." She turned anxious eyes to Evan. "Just how much power is this little one going to have?"

"No more than we can handle." Evan wrapped his arms around her waist and pulled her close. But he couldn't resist teasing her. "Anna only flooded the living room once." He pretended to think about it more. "Oh, and Ethan did scorch the couch. But only that one…or maybe it was two times." Evan bit the inside of his cheek. "Anyway, I'm sure we'll be fine."

Kyra's rounded eyes flew to meet his. And they quickly narrowed as he couldn't hold back his mirth any longer. She gave him a jab to the ribs. "That is so not funny, Ace."

He held her elbow to stave off any further retaliation and leaned in to kiss her. "If she's anything like you, she'll be amazing. And…we'll have a very large extended family to help with whatever magical snag we run into."

She settled into him as talk and laughter went on around them. It took some doing, but an excited Jacob was finally corralled long enough to actually eat something. And soon after that, with the dinner mess cleaned up, the group assembled and started their tour of the neighborhood.

Mary and Anna both carried cameras, so they dogged Jake's steps documenting every moment. The large entourage moved with ease as they kept a careful eye on what was happening around them.

As the sun set, the streets teemed with more and more kids. Some parents trailed behind, some remained in the cars and slowly followed the progress of their child.

Evan could remember the four of them running from house

to house, not a care in the world, as their mom and dad watched and laughed and snapped photos. He couldn't wait to do this with his own children.

He glanced down at Kyra and saw her smiling softly at Jacob as he tugged on Joe's hand, trying to make him move faster. Knowing what he did of Kyra's childhood, he began to wonder if she'd ever taken part in things like this.

Had her parents ever showed her any fun? Had any of the foster homes she'd been in? Evan thought to ask her but didn't want to drag down her mood by bringing up potentially bad memories. Whether or not she'd had the same experiences he'd had, he would make sure that she had them now. She could make those moments together with him and their daughter.

They strolled up one side of the street and down the other until eight p.m.—the cut-off time the city had put in place. And that was apparently late enough, as Evan saw that Jacob was starting to lag some. Between the excitement of the day and the constant walking, running, jumping, and skipping the kid did, he was clearly exhausted.

And he wasn't the only one, Evan noted. Kyra was dragging ass too. He'd observed over the last few days that this pregnancy seemed to drain her energy. Taking her hand in his, he brought it up and laid his lips against the supple skin just past her knuckles.

She turned her head to look up at him but stared at something she saw over his shoulder. Her eyes cleared of fatigue and went razor sharp. "We've got company," she murmured softly.

Evan nodded but didn't make a move to look. If there were one, there were certain to be others.

"Just keep walking."

Silently, he sent a message to his siblings. *Party time. We need to get Jacob under cover.*

The ones who had heard carefully passed the word to those who hadn't. The tone of the outing changed very subtly. To anyone watching, they seemed just as carefree as before. But behind that façade, they were all hyper-aware now.

Thankfully, the closer they got to Joe and Anna's place, the thinner the trick-or-treaters became. A lot had already been taken home to gorge on the sweets they'd received. Hopefully, the few remaining would be far enough away to miss any of the action that was likely to ensue.

As they neared the house with neither side making a move, Evan thought they might get lucky. Maybe they were just there to observe. But mere steps from their destination, Noor proved that thought wrong.

His massive beast appeared in the yard and completely blocked their path to the house. Before they could skid to a stop, he sent a wave of energy that took them all off their feet.

The ten of them went tumbling. As Evan finally caught himself, he saw that Joe had somehow kept a tight hold on his son. As Joe quickly gained his feet again, he pushed the boy behind him.

Evan searched out Kyra and found she was unhurt—pissed off but otherwise good. He took a swift inventory of his family and was relieved that all seemed to be in the same condition.

Those with abilities struck back, hitting Noor with everything they had. Evan was about to join in when he saw the contingent of goons advancing on them from behind.

"Watch your backs!" Evan called out as he sent the earth beneath the men's feet trembling and shifting. It slowed them down some, but Evan knew they would keep coming.

When he caught Joe's eye, he saw a father's desperate need to protect his son. Anna was trying to make her way to their sides, but even with the magical onslaught she was sending out, so far she'd been unable.

A lot of discussion had gone into how to safeguard Jacob if a situation like this had ever presented itself. How would they ensure his safety when they were all needed to fight? Where could they secret him away that he'd be okay alone for a while?

In the end, Joe and Anna had decided to open a section of wall in their master closet. They made sure to make the area big enough for Jacob to fit inside comfortably. The doorway into the space was then reattached in such a way that it was indistinguishable from the rest of the closet.

Strong wards and spells lined the cubby, making it as secure as possible for him. Supplies had been stocked for him so no matter how long he had to stay hidden, he wouldn't be left without.

The plan had been that someone would physically lock him in without Noor ever knowing he was there. That wasn't an option here. If Noor, or one of his men, saw them dart into the house and then come out without Jacob, they'd know he was still in there somewhere and rip the place apart until they found him.

Maybe Evan could *send* him into the crawlspace. Up until now, he'd only ever pulled Jacob to him from varying distances away. But if this worked, Jacob would simply disappear. Noor would have no idea where he went.

On the off-chance Noor also had it in his head to try for Kyra, Evan thought briefly about sending her with his nephew. Not only were those thoughts futile, but she'd kick his ass for attempting it. Resigned, he concentrated on what he had to do. He motioned for Joe to release his hold on Jacob. Joe reluctantly let go, and Evan gathered his magic and sent the boy away.

When he blinked out of sight, the beast roared out his rage at being denied his prize once again. But this time, instead of slinking off when his plan had failed, he showed his discontent by raining hell down upon them.

The world around Evan went crazy. Everything turned to shadow while fire and thunder swelled. Horrifying screams rent the air and stabbed into his brain like heated blades. He didn't know from which direction they came, or even from whom they'd erupted. They just seemed to echo all around him in every direction.

Did they belong to the ones he loved? Were they all being tortured, or was this a trick of the mind? He couldn't be sure.

Evan squinted through the red-tinged night but there was no sign of anyone. Were the others here somewhere with him? They'd only been a few feet away before it all had changed. Why couldn't he see them? He tried to call out to his siblings, but no one responded.

Noor had gotten into his head before—made him and Seth believe they were trapped and burning alive. They'd felt the heat, smelled the smoke and scorching flesh. They'd truly thought they were going to die.

Was this the same? Had Noor manifested this nightmare as he had the fire that had consumed them? Was this all just a hallucination?

As he tried to figure it out, suddenly something slammed into him. The force of it spun him around. That was followed closely by a burning hot pain across his ribs. Before he could recover from that, another hit and more pain, this time down his left arm.

Evan swung out at his invisible assailant but his fist met only air. He looked quickly in every direction, trying to see what or who was attacking him. But still he saw nothing.

He felt something wet on his hand and glanced down to see blood dripping off his fingers from the massive gash on his bicep.

"What the hell?" Becoming aware of the pain in his side, he made a quick inspection and confirmed that it too was flowing freely.

He had to get the hell out of here. If he were experiencing this, the others had to be also. His sisters and brother. And what of Seth and Kyra? Had Noor included them also? His heart kicked in his chest knowing she may be trapped in a similar place. And he was helpless to guard against something attacking her.

Evan couldn't just stand here and wait for whoever it was to pick them off, one by one. If he were unable to break out of this on his own, there were three others out there somewhere he could connect with to even up all their chances.

And if he could reach anyone, it would be Ethan. The other half of himself. Evan closed his eyes and concentrated on finding his twin.

A sound like a melon being split open sounded in his ears milliseconds before his head exploded in blinding agony. Evan fell forward, landing hard on the unforgiving ground. He groaned, fighting off unconsciousness. Not sure what had happened, he slowly raised his hand to where the pain centered.

His fingers met a gaping wound on the back of his head. Big enough that three of his fingertips fit into the opening. His mind was floundering in a riptide of torment and confusion. How could he fight an attacker he couldn't see? He had no idea when the blows were coming or from where.

He could figure out who; that wasn't difficult. Noor's men were toying with him while Noor held him defenseless.

Evan forced his foggy brain to work. He thought of Kyra and the baby and knew he had too much to live for to succumb to Noor's treachery here. Still lying prone, Evan sent a probing link out to Ethan. He just hoped his brother was out there to feel it.

He ignored what must have been a kick to the ribs, focusing all of his magic and energy on finding his brother.

Many minutes and many blows later, Evan finally sensed another mind. He grabbed onto it and was relieved to discover it was his twin. Their minds, souls, and magic merged in an instant.

Once joined, each suffered the other's trauma. With abrupt and painful knowledge, Evan learned that Ethan bore the wounds of several knife cuts, his kidney had taken some damage, and his right knee was wrenched, badly. He also knew that Ethan was experiencing Evan's injuries. But they locked all of that out and bore down on confronting the one responsible for all of this.

The combined force of their power ended up being stronger than Noor's will and ejected him completely from their minds. With a sudden pop, the hell he had created to hold them vanished, and the real world came back into focus.

As Evan and Ethan gained their feet, the beast roared, clearly displeased at having lost two of its targets. To protect themselves from any further attacks, and to give them a moment to analyze the situation, they built a protective force around themselves.

Looking around, the boys discovered that their sisters had also united and were battling the throng of attackers alongside Seth, Kyra, Joe, and their parents and were still greatly outnumbered.

"I've had enough of this bullshit."

"I say we just take him out. Period."

Their conversation went back and forth, their merged voices speaking each idea and response simultaneously. It was very strange and took talking to yourself to a whole new level.

Before Noor knew their intent, they gathered their elemental magic and built a whirling tempest of earth and fire, fed by the need to keep their family safe. Its size grew to be as large as Noor's beast, Evan and Ethan controlling it almost without thought. It writhed and churned just behind them.

When they'd infused it with enough power, they let loose their magic. It flowed through and over them to meet the monster head-on with a resounding crash.

The force of the collision threw the creature back to land with a heavy thud. But it was quickly on its feet and swiping out with its massive claws.

It fought to rend their magic to pieces. It slashed and tore at what they'd made. Though he only struck their whirling power, they felt the blows as if it had struck their bodies, adding levels of agony on top of what they already suffered.

Why was he able to hurt them like this? Was it because he'd grown that much stronger? Or was it because as Noor grew more corporeal over time, so too did their power? Evan and Ethan didn't know.

Right now, they needed to deal with this rabid fiend.

"And the best way to do that is put it down."

An idea began to form. Could they separate Noor from his beast? Make it so that he couldn't manifest into this visage any longer?

If possible, it could hurt him. Set him back, and give them a reprieve to heal and garner their strength again. The energy he'd already expended building this hell world, added to losing a part of himself, could give them the time they needed.

It would take massive power on their end to make this work. But if it did, it would be worth it.

The entity that was Evan and Ethan quickly began to construct a spell. When it was ready, they spoke the words.

"Burke witches grant us your grace
We call to thee in this time and place
Lend us your aid to end this beast's reign
Never to be used as evil's puppet again
Rend beast from man this we decree
As we will, so mote it be."

Huge paw, raised to strike, stopped mid-swipe before the beast settled back onto all fours. Black, soulless eyes stared at them for a beat, then two. Fear gathered in the bottomless depths as the magic swelled and washed over its large muscled body.

Gaping mouth opened to roar but instead reverted to the feeble screams of a man. The hulking physique of the beast jerked and heaved. It rose up onto its hind legs and towered over them for a moment before crumpling to the earth. It lay panting, fighting the decomposition of its own form as he watched.

Suddenly its head thrust back and released a shriek that split the air. Evan and Ethan looked on as black hairless skin melted and contorted and became pasty white flesh.

Noor, prone and defeated for now, braced his upper body on trembling arms. He glared up at them with disgust and loathing.

"What have you done to me?"

They answered in unison. "We stripped the beast away from you. You'll never again use that monster to terrorize and torture."

With Noor's power drained, he faded away.

Evan searched out Kyra and found her, a little battered, but still standing. She smiled over at him and didn't see the punk coming at her from behind. Evan and Ethan rapidly conjured a shield around her. The man rammed into it just before being thrown backward and landing with a crunch. Looking around himself in confusion, he turned and ran when he realized the tide had shifted in the prey's favor.

Seeing that their advantage was no more, the rest of Noor's henchmen abandoned the field.

When all that remained were the bloody and bruised Burkes, they gathered together. Evan and Ethan released their bonds and became wholly themselves again.

Joe and Anna took off for the house and Jacob.

Evan understood their fear. He immediately took Kyra into his arms. "Are you all right? The baby?"

"We're okay." But before she could say any more, Mary spoke up.

"Let's take this inside."

The group hobbled and limped into Joe and Anna's house. As they settled in the living room, the couple came back with their son between them.

He had a ring of chocolate around his grinning mouth.

The entire room, knowing what had happened, erupted into laughter. Seeing that pleased expression on his dirty little face took the edge off the seriousness and severity of the evening.

"You just *had* to send his Halloween bucket with him, Evan?" Anna narrowed her eyes at him.

Evan tried to wipe the smile off his face, but it refused to budge. "I'm really sorry."

"You just wait." She pointed a finger at him. "One of these days, I'll return the favor and overdose your kid with sugar too."

He looked down at Kyra sitting next to him. "Oh, I have no doubt about that."

They took a little time to clean up and dress wounds if needed. Healing energy was passed around like...well, candy.

Joe and Anna took care of their son and got him ready for bed. Which wasn't an easy feat as he was so hyped up on sweets. They ended up leaving him to play a hand-held game in his bed until he wound down enough to sleep.

Once everyone's needs were seen to, they assembled again to talk about what had happened.

"Noor looked pretty beat down," Seth started. "Who did what to him?"

"Ethan and I took the beast from him." Evan filled them in on what had taken place in that other world. "We knew we needed to get everyone out of that hallucination so we could fight back. We were sitting ducks to be picked off at will."

"We tried to keep them off of you." His dad was rubbing sore knuckles. "We didn't understand what was going on at first. We didn't realize you weren't aware. One of Noor's guys hit Ethan, but he just stood there. It wasn't until the attack was done that he finally reacted. But then he was striking out at nothing as the guy moved out of range. He'd never seen what hit him. I told Joe and Mary, and we tried to act as a barrier between you and them. But there were so many, some got by us."

"Everyone was just gone." Anna turned her gaze to Joe where he sat beside her on the couch. "I tried reaching out with my mind, but no one was there."

"They seemed to concentrate most of their assaults on the guys," Joe added softly.

"Lucky us." Ethan massaged his knee.

"Well," Mary studied each of her children, "at least he should be out of commission for a while."

"He was expending a lot of energy by keeping us all in that illusion," Evan said in agreement. "Even if we hadn't leached the rest of it by destroying his beast, I don't think he would have been able to maintain it much longer."

"I don't like that he was able to physically hurt you through your magic this time." She eyed each of her boys. "He's gained so much strength. And will only gain more the closer we get to February."

"But so will we," Evan reminded her.

They talked a little longer, but they were all wiped out. With kisses and hugs, everyone left to return to their own homes. By the time Evan got Kyra home, she was all but asleep on her feet. He helped her in and guided her to the bedroom. They assisted each other with their clothes and crawled into bed.

Exhausted and wrapped in each other's arms, they dropped instantly into sleep.

28

A couple of weeks had passed since Halloween and life was settling back into its normal patterns. Noor was down—for God only knew how long. And his men were MIA with him out of commission. Kyra still had to be careful, but the absolute lockdown she'd been under had lifted.

With more freedom than she'd had in months, Kyra was on a mission today. There'd been something she'd been meaning to do for a while, and now was finally her chance. Evan was at work and would be there until late afternoon. That gave her plenty of time to accomplish everything on her list.

With her new condition, she wouldn't be riding her motorcycle for a while, so she'd reluctantly put it in storage. She and Evan had gone car shopping with something sensible in mind.

But Kyra just couldn't do sensible. She needed something that still had a little flair. After looking at what was out there, she'd decided on a Dodge Charger. It had four doors, but it was still sporty enough to suit her.

She jumped behind the wheel now and hit the start button. The roar of the Hemi engine made her grin. Putting it into gear, she backed out of the driveway and headed off down the road.

Returning home several hours later, she hauled everything in. Plan in mind, she began to set her stage. Once it was just how she wanted it, she looked at the time and saw she had about an hour before Evan got back from the office. Her schedule was moving along perfectly.

Walking into the bathroom, she turned on the taps in the tub and poured in her favorite bubble-bath. For the next half hour, she soaked in the fragrant water.

Stepping out, she dried off and applied a scented lotion that matched what she'd used in the bath.

From there, she dressed carefully, smoothing the soft material over her breasts and down the curve of her hips. She wished for the time when she'd see and feel the evidence of her pregnancy. Right now it didn't seem real yet.

Other than the morning sickness, of course. That reminded her every day.

Ready, she went back to the kitchen and did some last-minute checks there. She'd just tasted dinner one last time when she heard the front door open. Kyra, nerves jangling, walked out of the kitchen and into the dining area to meet him.

When he saw her standing there in a deep blue figure-hugging knee-length dress and heels, he stopped and could only stare. Her brown hair was fluffed and styled, and she'd taken the time to do her makeup in a sultry smoky shade.

"Holy..." His voice came out in a strangled whisper and his eyes tracked over every inch of her.

That was the best compliment she could have gotten.

"I made dinner." She sauntered forward and ran her hand down his shirt front. "And after, I have a surprise for you."

His pupils expanded and he drew in a deep breath. She knew he was pulling the lavender and rose scent of her skin into his lungs.

He finally snapped out of his muddled state and wrapped his arms around her waist. He grinned down at her. "Can we skip dinner and move right on to the surprise portion of the night? I'm dying to know what you have on under this dress." He ran his palms up and down over her ass as if searching for clues there.

"All good things, Ace. All good things." Kyra patted his chest, turned, and walked away, running her hand along her hip and calling attention to the uninterrupted lines which implied there was nothing underneath.

"Go wash up. I'll serve." Once in the kitchen, she took a deep breath of her own. She should have known playing with him would affect her as well. He tended to bring that out in her. One look, one touch, and she was burning up.

Settled, Kyra plated up her mushroom asiago chicken with rice. She garnished with a sprinkle of grated parmesan cheese and carried the plates to the table. She set each down on the black placemats in between the silver cutlery. A lit candle and a bouquet of flowers finished the intimate dinner for two.

When Evan returned, she was pouring sparkling grape juice into tall champagne flutes. Ones she'd had to buy since a search of the house had only yielded basic glasses that would just not do for the night she had in store.

Evan sat and looked over all she'd done. "This looks and smells amazing." He leaned over and kissed her. "But not better than you."

Kyra grinned. "Flattery, though appreciated, will not get you your surprise early, Ace."

His smile spread and he nuzzled her neck. "You do smell incredible."

She had to fight off the shiver of longing his lips wrought from her. "Let's enjoy this meal before we move on to the rest of the evening."

Evan slowly released her. His gaze stayed locked on hers as he picked up his juice to sip. The heat in those dark shining eyes nearly had her throwing his present at him. But she kept her wits as she thought about what his reaction would be to her gift.

A secret smile touched her lips and had his brows dipping.

"What was that grin for?"

"You'll find out." Kyra laid her napkin over her lap and lifted her knife and fork. Still smirking, she cut into the perfectly cooked chicken thigh. Stabbing into it with her fork, she brought it up to her mouth. Wrapping her lips around it, she slid the utensil out and slowly chewed.

"Your goal is to kill me, isn't it?" Evan shifted in his seat.

"Not yet. Eat up."

She purposely kept the conversation light, talking of a recent lunch she and his sisters had shared and some trouble Jake had gotten into. Some new moves that Joe had taught her the last time she'd been to the gym. He'd modified her workout to accommodate her pregnancy, but they'd continued.

They enjoyed being together and discussing a little bit of everything over good food and sparkling fruit juice.

When they were finished, Kyra cleared away the dishes. Evan insisted on helping and soon the kitchen was clean and shining.

"Why don't you go have a seat on the couch." She shooed him out. "I'll bring dessert and a little something extra."

"Kyra, all kidding aside. You and this wonderful dinner you made is more than enough. I don't need anything more than what I have—the woman I love and the daughter we've made from that love."

"Aww, Ace, I love you too." She gave him a quick kiss. "Now go sit down."

As he begrudgingly left, Kyra turned and went to the cupboard where she had it hidden. Pulling it down, she opened the box to take one more look at it. She thought it was perfect and had enlisted his mom's help to make it that way. She just hoped that he would like it.

She'd found a tray earlier and placed the box plus two small bowls of Dulce de Leche ice cream on it.

When he saw the bowls he grinned, but as she set the tray

down, he saw the box and his smile slipped.

"What is that?" He eyed the box again before looking over at her as she sat beside him.

Kyra picked it up and with it facing her, opened it. She examined the sterling silver band with decorative etching that was also an old-world protection rune.

She'd wanted something that would safeguard Evan in his daily life as well as his magical one. So she'd asked her future mother-in-law if such a thing existed. She'd been excited when Mary had found this one and had worked with the jeweler to make it just right.

Taking a breath, Kyra turned it around so Evan could see it.

"I asked you to marry me, but as you so blatantly pointed out at the time, I didn't have a ring." She held it out to him. "I'm hoping this one will do."

His focus dropped to the box in her hand, and his eyes widened at what he saw. He reached out and slid it free of its velvet bed. Turning it in his fingers, he studied all the sides.

Did he recognize the etching?

Still holding it tight, Evan glanced up at her with mischief twinkling in his gaze. "It's about damned time too. I didn't think you'd ever make an honest man out of me."

Breath she'd been holding gushed out of her. "Hey. Been a little busy here, Ace."

He leaned in and softly laid his lips to hers. "I love it. Thank you."

"Your mom helped me with the scrollwork. It's actually an old rune meant for protection."

"Is it?" Evan looked it over again. "Maybe we'll just repeat the process when we get you one. Can't be too careful."

"I thought you could wear it on a different finger until the day, you know?" Men didn't get an engagement ring and a wedding ring like women. So Kyra thought that might solve any confusion until they set the date and finally tied the knot.

And he'd still be wearing it in the meantime.

Evan fit it onto the ring finger of his right hand. "Perfect. I love it. And I love you."

Kyra settled into his embrace and thought life couldn't get any better. "I love you too, Ace. And I can't wait to spend the rest of my life showing you just how much."

EPILOGUE

Ethan sat on the soft green lawn—his long legs folded in front of him. As he thought about what to say, he idly picked at the freshly mowed grass. Taking a deep breath, he got on with what he'd come here to do.

Open his heart and own up to the mistakes he'd made.

"I'm sorry it's been so long since I was here last." His dark eyes slowly lifted to settle on the granite headstone before him. His gaze landed on the name etched there, *Honor Andrews*. "I haven't been as strong as I should have been," he admitted, "and I couldn't face you."

Reaching out, Ethan pulled at the longer blades the groundskeeper had missed around the base. "I tried to move on like you would have wanted…and I think I was actually doing it." His attention switched to the debris in his hands. "Until…" he laughed derisively. "Yeah, until. Until I fucked up. Until Edrick Noor used my love for you to manipulate me. Until I almost cost my family everything. Until I hated myself and knew you'd hate me too if you knew what I'd done.

"God, it's been unbearable without you." Ethan dropped the clippings and scrubbed his hands over his face. Feeling the scruffiness of his short beard, he remembered how Honor had always run her hands over it, loving how it tickled her palms.

"Four years. It feels like a lifetime since I last saw you. Last touched you. Last kissed you." Ethan's heart gave a painful thump. "Everywhere I go reminds me of you. I think I see you or hear you, but when I turn, you're not there. You'll never be there again."

His eyes burned but he blinked the tears away. "When this is all over, when Noor is defeated, maybe I'll take off for a while. Get out of here. Away from all the memories. Away from all the new love floating around."

Movement caught Ethan's attention. He turned his head to see a young couple getting out of their car. Probably going to visit a loved one too. He watched them for a moment then continued.

"All my siblings have someone now. They're building committed and happy lives together. Making families. Aria and Seth. Anna and Joe with little Jacob." He laughed again, but this time he meant it. "He's a great kid, Honor. You'd love him. Such a little character. He had a pretty rough start, but he's doing really well now. And he's going to have company soon. Evan and Kyra are having a baby. Probably next summer. They're sure it's going to be a girl. That's going to be so crazy. Seeing the next generation of Burke witches running around. Causing trouble like we did."

Ethan took a deep breath. Let it out. "They're all so happy, baby. So in love. You can see it, feel it. I remember what that's like. And it hurts to know I'll never have that again."

He lifted a hand as if to stop her from arguing. "Even if I do eventually find someone, it won't be the same. It won't come close to what I felt for you. What I *still* feel for you. You were my one, Honor. The person I was supposed to spend the rest of my life with. But I can't. Because you were ripped away from me in the worst possible way." Ethan shook his head and took a breath to ease some of the tightness in his chest.

He repeated the same words he'd said so many times. "I'm so sorry I wasn't able to get to you that night. I tried. I just hope you didn't feel anything. I hope the smoke took you before the rest ever touched you. I hope wherever you are, you and your parents are happy. And at peace."

Ethan looked around and noticed that the sun had started to set and the light was fading. "I guess I'd better go. I promise I won't stay away so long next time." He gained his feet, kissed his fingers, and laid them over her name. "I miss you. I love you, sweetheart."

He turned and walked away from the only woman he'd ever loved. Once in his car, he sat a few minutes to piece himself back together. It was always hard coming here, but after he'd been, he always felt better for having come.

Starting the engine, Ethan pulled out and drove towards home. Not the home he and Honor had been thinking of buying. But the apartment he'd found near downtown Daytona. It was small and cheap and worked great since it was just him. And he could cover the rent with the odd jobs he took.

He liked to work with his hands and had learned how to do just about anything. If he didn't know, he'd just look it up online. There were videos out there for everything—home improvement, auto repair, whatever the need was.

Most of the projects he took were by word-of-mouth. And most of his clients were single women and the elderly.

Ethan guessed that over time, he'd become one of those rent-a-husbands, doing for others what couldn't be done themselves. It usually kept him pretty busy, but with all this Noor crap going on over the last few months, he'd kind of taken a hiatus. He really needed to get back to it. Between that and the workout regime Joe had designed for him, he shouldn't have a lot of time to think about how much he missed Honor.

As he turned onto his street, he glanced up and thought he saw a quick flash of fiery auburn hair. It always caught him off guard to see that particular color. Honor's hair had been that exact shade. He'd kidded her that while he may wield fire, she was the one who'd tamed it. Her hair had been amazing and he'd loved it. Long and thick and soft as silk.

As he maneuvered through traffic, Ethan kept on eye on the woman. Her back was to him as she walked along the sidewalk in the same direction he was driving. The nearer he drew to her, the harder his heart beat.

Everything about her made him think of Honor. Her shape. Her walk. The way her hair lifted on the breeze with each step. As the pain of losing her swelled all over again, he almost wished he'd never caught sight of her. But now that he had, he couldn't take his eyes off her. He knew in his head it wasn't her. It wasn't the girl he loved.

But in his heart, he needed to see her face—just to be sure. One quick glance would put it all to rest again.

As he passed her, Ethan craned his neck around.

And the breath stopped in his lungs. That face. It was hers. It was Honor.

Misha McKenzie has been an avid reader since learning how at four years old. Countless books later, she still loves to immerse herself into the lives of the people within those pages. After graduating high school, she went on to earn a degree in Business Administration, married her high school sweetheart, and had two beautiful boys. At thirty years old, while working as an office manager for a construction company, a family of witches began to brew, and The Magic of the Heart Series was born.